CRIMSON CLOVER

ISBN: 0984561633
ISBN-13: 9780984561636

Disclaimer: This is a work of fiction. While, as in fiction, the literary perceptions and insights are based on experience, all names, characters, places, and incidents are either products of the author's imagination or are used fictitiously. No reference to any real person is intended or should be inferred.

Cover: Lee Nielsen

CRIMSON CLOVER

CHAPTER ONE

For a moment Lisa Billingsley Armstrong glimpsed flashing lights ahead, but the driving rain mixed with mud thrown up from the road obstructed her view. The scrape of Pacific Northwest huckleberry bushes against the van's door cautioned her to slow down. She punched the washer lever. The windshield cleared as she took the last curve of the gravel drive. Relief swept over her. His friends were here, celebrating the new house, surprising him with a policeman's welcome, doing it up as only small town folks knew how. She shook her head and spoke softly to herself. "You fool, Lisa. He was caught up here without the phone. He wasn't off somewhere avoiding you."

The rotating lights of a police car and a fire truck warned her away from the front of the house where the windows burned warmly with a fireplace blaze. She stopped, momentarily nonplussed. There was nowhere to park.

A uniformed figure stepped out of the night.

She lowered her window and peered up at him. Cold October rain pelted her perfectly trimmed blonde hair. "I should have known you guys would do this," she called. "You could have at least phoned me to join you."

Jim's partner seemed not to know her. "Lisa? Lisa, you shouldn't be here."

"Why not? Did you bring dancing girls? I can handle that."

He wiped one hand over his face brushing droplets from his forehead and cheeks.

Sweat. He was sweating on a cold, wet night like this. She looked again to her dream house. Cold fear sent blood pulsing wildly through her temples. She held her breath until one anguished gasp escaped her constricted chest. It was not the fireplace inside that burned so brightly, but the house itself that lighted the starless night through ghostly shattered windows.

"Oh, Christ!" She pushed open the door and felt her feet sink into the cold muck raised by heavy vehicles that had come in before her. "Oh, Jesus! Oh, Jim! Where is he?"

Wet stinking wool arms held her.

She slipped in the new baby grass, lost her shoe, and felt cold gelatinous mud squish between her stockinged toes.

"Lisa, stop!"

"Jim!" She fell against her captor.

He held her with both arms as her van, still in gear, moved away.

She watched woodenly as it collided with the ancient cedar tree that Jim had so lovingly spared when they cleared the area for the house.

The collision brought another officer running. "What the hell? Who's there?"

"His wife."

"Oh, shit!"

She pulled free and ran toward the house.

The second man caught her. "Take care of the van and get the sheriff." He pulled her sideways from the waist and forced her to stumble along until she felt the rough bark of a tree against her back. She could no longer see the house. She slumped to one side and again caught sight of the mesmerizing lights. For a brief instant a draped stretcher being loaded into an ambulance came into view. "Jim. Oh, my God, what's happened?"

"You have to wait, Ma'am."

"I need to help him."

"You can't, Ma'am."

"I can. I really can. You've got to let me in there."

The headlights of a larger vehicle blinded her. She heard its window power open and recognized the face of Owen Swenson.

"Sheriff, please. You've got to help me. They won't let me go into my own house. Please."

He climbed from the truck and stood before her. "Lisa, girl, something's happened here."

She pounded her clenched fists against his chest. "No. I won't listen! I want Jim! I need to help Jim!"

"Lisa, honey. He can't be helped. Do you hear me?"

"No. No, I don't hear you! Jim!" Her voice echoed hollowly through rooms of falling rain.

"You need someone here."

"Don't lie to me!"

"I wish it was a lie. Let's call someone. Your dad. Shall I call your dad?"

"It's not Jim. You're lying! It's not my Jim!"

"Call her dad," he said to someone in the truck. "It's Doctor Billingsley. There's an emergency number in my book."

But it was not her father who she needed now. He was a man of healing, not someone who could insert himself into the middle of a mess like this. She needed someone who could get to Jim, someone who could get past the firemen and policemen and who could help her husband.

"Clover. You call my sister Clover! She's the one I need."

Clover Winters soothed the cloth over her freshly shaved leg and let it fall slowly into the scented bathwater. She reached back, straightened her plastic pillow until the inflatable red lips comfortably cradled her damp head.

Junk. Surrounded totally by lovely, unpretentious junk, and no one to fault her for it. From the half-read romance novel to the crimson bath accessories, this dream was hers and hers alone.

She raised both legs from the water and studied them critically. The lean, lithe lines of a model and the bone structure of a fragile child were both genetic gifts from her birth mother.

Her breathing stuttered. Poor mother. Was she alive somewhere? She leaned back, dropped her book to the tile floor, and closed her eyes.

The crimson glow of a redeemed brothel lamp filtered through her eyelids as she slowly breathed in the scent of cinnamon rising from red candy hearts in a crystal bowl.

She would not go into another mother crisis – her mother's or her own.

The ring of the bathroom wall phone jarred her upright. She allowed the machine in the living room to answer.

A stranger's voice. What was he saying? An accident? Long Lake?

She reached up and pulled the receiver to her. "Hello?"

"Clover?"

"Yes."

"I'm sorry. The machine."

"Yes. Wait. It will turn off in a second." She waited for the machine to stop. "Okay."

"About the incident . . . "

"Who is this?"

"Oh, sorry. This is Sheriff Swenson. I must have said that before."

"There's been an accident?"

"An incident."

"A car accident?"

"No, something else. A problem. Lisa asked me to call."

"What kind of problem?"

"A house fire. Lisa's house."

"The old house or the new house?"

"The new one at Long Lake."

"Is Lisa okay? The children?"

"Lisa is pretty upset."

"Can I talk to her?"

"She's not near a phone right now. She asked me to call. Could you come?"

"Yes, of course. Where did you say you were?"

"We're here at the new house near Long Lake."

"Sheriff?"

"Yes?"

"Is Jim there?"

"Yes."

"Has anyone been hurt?"

His silence stretched out toward eternity.

She riveted her eyes on her slender hands as they grasped the crimson phone, on her newly manicured nails in matching red, on the large diamond ring she had not returned to her senator husband after their divorce.

"Yes. I'm afraid so." Swenson's voice revealed hesitancy unusual for a man of his stature. "It's Jim. He's fatally injured. Can you come?"

"Fatally? Fatally? Did you say fatally?"

"Yes. Your sister could use your help."

"I'll be there. I'll be right there."

She stood and reached for a towel. She didn't realize the strength of the tremors that wracked her body until she tried to replace the receiver and knocked the dish of candy onto the tile floor. She also didn't notice that, as she walked through shards of crystal glass and into the living room, the blood from the soles of her feet exactly matched her luxurious crimson carpets.

∽

Sheriff Owen Swenson stared at the touchtone phone and scratched his balding head. The line was open and yet Jim Armstrong hadn't called for help. A man in severe pain, bleeding, should've reached for the phone, knocked it over, pushed it with a toe. Man in his condition, desperate. Yet there were no prints on its new plastic shine.

He shifted the bulk of his weight from one foot to the other, picked up the receiver, and tapped out Roger Parrish's number. Roger had been following a trail of animal mutilations in the area for a decade. Until now they had both discounted the crimes as a bunch of kids playing with the devil. Now they'd have to change their tune.

A brusque voice answered. "Yeah?"

"Roger. It's Owen."

"Yeah?"

"I got another one for you."

"Aw, shit! Where this time?"

"Long Lake Road. South fork. The new house below Old Maggie's."

"Show horse?"

"No. Not a horse."

"What? Another dog?"

"A man."

"Do I know him?"

"Jim Armstrong."

"Bullshit!"

"Truth, Rog."

"Jesus! Any witnesses?"

"None that I can tell."

"Suspects?"

"One."

"Who?"

"A plumber. Must've worked here today. Left a box of his tools behind."

"Plumber huh? That might fit."

"Might. You want to come out here, have a look?"

"Yeah. I'll grab Duke and be right there."

❦

Plumber K.C. Casey slammed both doors of his old van hard enough to knock a rusty piece of hardware off the back bumper. It tinkled against the bricks that lined his in-law's driveway. The small box. He'd left it at the Long Lake place. All his cutting tools and small fittings were in the darned thing. He couldn't start work in the morning without them and he had to get in as many jobs as he could or he and Jenny would be living with her folks for another six months. God, what a thought.

He peered toward the house. Its lawns and walkways were lit up like a Christmas tree. Guests expected. He shouldn't be late again, but the cop at the Long Lake place had said he'd be in and out all night. Maybe he could still catch him.

He climbed behind the wheel, turned the key with weary determination, and swung the top-heavy van onto the main road. The die had been cast, might as well go for broke.

❦

Clover counted six vehicles pulled in at odd angles in the muddy square that had been a green lawn hours earlier: two sheriff's cars, one fire truck, Lisa's van, another old gray van with a half-naked lady painted on the side, and an equally old Chevy pickup with a regal German Shepherd at the wheel.

The dog eyed her curiously as she ducked through the rain.

A uniformed deputy stopped her at the porch stairs. "Can I help you, lady?"

"I'm Lisa Armstrong's sister."

"Too late. Mrs. Armstrong left already."

"Her van is here. Where'd she go?"

"The Morton's happened by and took her home. Good thing, too. She really fell apart."

"Where's the sheriff?"

"Inside. Not sure he'd want you in there."

"He called for me."

"Well, then, go on in through the side door. Watch the yellow tapes and don't touch nothing."

She moved cautiously along the taped walkway through the home office and into the lighted dining area.

Three men sat hunched over the Eastlake table Mom Billingsley had given Lisa and Jim on their tenth anniversary. The tabletop was blistered and uneven. On the wall, behind the scorched sideboard and on the hardwood floor, someone had splashed a wild design of crimson and dark red, intermixed with black ash. Acrid air burned her nostrils.

"Sheriff?"

Three pale faces came sharply into focus. Two of the men stood. The third, a brawny guy in denim coveralls, was restrained by the sheriff's hand on his shoulder.

"Clover," Owen Swenson took her cold hand in his, "I appreciate your coming all the way out here, but I'm afraid you just missed Lisa. The Morton's have taken her to your mother's."

"And Jim?"

He held tightly to her hand as he placed a fatherly arm across her shoulder. "I'm sorry. The coroner has already been here and left." He steered her away from the men toward a side table and the phone. "You can call your family if you'd like."

A cardboard box, water soaked and blackened with soot, rubbed against her leg. Its cold damp caused her to shiver.

"What happened, Sheriff?"

"The fire inspector will be here any minute."

It was all a big mistake. It had to be. "And Jim?" she persisted.

"They'll be doing an autopsy tomorrow."

"He's like a brother to me. Please. Tell me what happened."

"We're not sure, Clover. First we knew of trouble was from Old Maggie. She called 911 and said the house was on fire. When the fire department got here they made quick work of the blaze. That's when they found Jim."

"Please, Sheriff. I'll need to tell my family something."

"We'll have to wait for the coroner's ruling. With your background, you understand how that works."

She had graduated from Harvard Law and worked as an aide to her senator husband, but none of that had prepared her for this. 'Get more flies with honey than vinegar', she could hear Mom Billingsley say. Even though she had never agreed with the proverb, it was worth a try. She softened her voice and lowered her gaze. "I guess I don't quite understand. I can't go to Lisa without some explanation."

"It'll be clearer in the morning." The sheriff gave up on the phone and pressed her toward the side entrance.

She reached out and touched one finger to a red-black pearl on the wall. It was wet and sticky. "Is this blood?"

"Don't touch anything, Clover." His tone lost its warmth. "Better go and see to your sister. We'll get answers to you as soon as we know something definite."

Vinegar it was to be. She shrugged his arm from her shoulder and moved to the table. "I don't believe I've met either of you gentlemen." She offered her hand. "Clover Winters. Jim Armstrong's sister-in-law."

Neither of the men accepted her hand.

She pulled out a chair and sat.

"This is police business, Clover," the sheriff warned.

"I'm aware of that, Sheriff. It's also Billingsley business. Will you introduce me to these men?"

"Police business," he repeated.

"Billingsley business. I'm sorry, Sheriff. You know how my father can be. I won't leave until I have some answers for him."

As a council member and a powerful political force, Doc Billingsley's support was vital to Owen Swenson's elected position.

She folded her hands together on the battered tabletop and hoped the men would not see how badly she was shaking.

༄

Dick Morton waited in the car while Lisa and his wife Elizabeth collected the children from their sleeping bags in the nearly empty house and herded them, yawning and grumbling, into the backseat of his new yellow Mercedes. He eyed them warily as they settled themselves on his rich leather upholstery and silently thanked God that he had none of the messy critters. He never had understood why a young couple like the Armstrongs would choose to have five expensive additions. Jim's policeman's salary was barely enough to cover even one such financial drain.

The Billingsley's big bucks and doting ways surely made up for any financial deficits their darling daughter might encounter. However, young Lisa and her sleepy, pajama-clad crew were about to get a sudden jolt of reality. That thought cheered him, as did the fact that in the presence of her brood, Lisa had stopped the horrific sniveling that had annoyed him on the long ride to their neighborhood.

And the children, sensing that something both sinister and exciting had occurred, were awed into silence as they entered his expensive vehicle.

With new owner's pride he maneuvered the grand car along the rain slicked road, fighting the urge to sing, "Over the river and through the woods to grandmother's house we go", while Elizabeth kept up a soothing banter with Lisa, who now stared coldly into the black night. God, he hated these anticlimactic endings. If he weren't driving the new car, he might take a curve too wide and manufacture a little mayhem to energize the quiet scene.

He pressed his perfectly shined black shoe onto the accelerator and smiled as the finely engineered vehicle took the turn smoothly. Best get this done and Elizabeth home before she got herself all wrapped up with the Billingsley family again. He was quite sick of the pull they had on his sweet-tempered wife.

❦

Roger Parrish pushed forward to the edge of his chair and straightened his back as he tried to decide whether to stand and leave or to stay in the hope that Owen could dislodge the pushy woman.

The plumber's story, although almost believable, had been weakening under their continuous barrage of questions. With the arrival of the woman, the man had clammed up like a colt sensing the bit. Now this Clover dame was acting as if she were the fat guy's lawyer even though Swenson said she was just a damned teaching assistant at the Tacoma Law School.

"I've read him his rights, Clover," the sheriff tried.

"Don't say another word," she repeated to the Casey guy who slouched in his chair with his head bowed.

Roger flattened his palms on the table. Asshole had been caught red-handed. Arrogant bastard had come walking in all innocent and flustered and pretending he knew nothing about the murder or the fire. He certainly wasn't the smartest guy in the world, but he was big enough to overpower Jim Armstrong and his behavior fit the profile of an arsonist. From what he'd seen of Jim's body, this guy was the sicko he'd been tracking for years. The creep had probably come back to get some perverse sexual pleasure out of watching his handiwork warm the night. They would have had him blabbing the whole story if this pushy woman hadn't shown up.

He studied her as she hung up the phone.

"Lawyer's on his way." Getting no response from either him or the plumber, she turned to Swenson. "I can't stand by and watch this man's rights violated, nor do I want to see a case fall apart in court if he's guilty."

Roger pushed his chair away from the table and slowly straightened his six-foot frame. "Be seeing you, Owen. Got livestock to feed."

Swenson leaned back in his chair, but didn't speak. His eyes said everything Roger needed to know. He couldn't stand up to Doc Billingsley and remain sheriff. His hands were tied as tightly as Jim Armstrong's had been.

∽

Maggie Bamford absent-mindedly pulled one hand from beneath the cozy afghan to pat the head of her whining dog. "Good girl," she crooned. "Good dog." As she rocked slowly forward in her chair, she kept her eyes on the window and the scene down the ridge at her new neighbors' home.

If she had better boots and the new rain slicker that she had mail-ordered, but was slower in coming than the U.S. Government, she would have walked down there hours ago. As it stood now, what with the rain pelting down and the darkness deepening, she would be soaked to the skin before she picked her way to the cut-off. Her old body couldn't take that kind of abuse anymore. Best to sit here with the dogs, stay warm by the wood fire, and let Owen Swenson worry about the events at the Armstrong house.

Nice boy, Jim Armstrong. Smart. Picked the best of the lot for a girl while still in high school. Staked his claim on Lisa Billingsley and never once relinquished it. Nice, nice boy. Never thought of him as a police type. Too smart for that. But not too smart to get in trouble now.

Her eyes held to the string of lights along the edge of the lake. Trouble over there for sure. She pulled the afghan closer and tried to shrug off the memories of a similar scene seven years before when a hiker found her granddaughter's body along the lake. Best not to dwell on that. She patted the dog once more and leaned back into the sturdy rocker.

Dogs had tried to tell her there was trouble on the wind. They had been restless and growling all afternoon. Dogs were always quick to sense trouble, but today she too had felt a tightly strung edge accompanied by a vague sense of unrest at the very center of her soul. She had kept a close watch on the new house, as an endless string of vehicles moved the family into her vast and largely uninhabited neighborhood.

She had seen Jim Armstrong come roaring back long after the moving vans and service trucks had left for the day. All alone, he was, carrying nothing, and in an awful big hurry. Yet once he reached the wide porch, he had paced the cedar decking like a man waiting for a new young one to be born, and, Lord knows, he should have been an expert at that kind of wait. She could tell that he suddenly reached some kind of decision, for he had slammed into the house and never even turned on a light.

Not long after, the dogs had begun to whine and scratch at the door. When she let them out, they had milled around the small yard, anointing bush after bush, as if to ward off evil spirits and howling so eerily that she had been sure an earthquake was about to shake her and her small house into Long Lake itself.

When that hadn't happened she'd put supper on the stove, settled into the rocker, and placed the thirty-aught-six across her lap. She knew that whatever was coming would show itself soon enough.

Then, just when the dogs had settled at her feet again, here came the Armstrong boy, tall as an oak and quick on his feet, ducking from his double front doors, down the wide stairs, and into his red truck. Off he went, hell bent toward town, as if the devil himself was on his back.

That's when she'd seen flames begin to shoot up in the front window of the big house. That's when she'd called 911 to report a fire on Long Lake Road. That's when she'd begun to feel real sorry for Jim Armstrong and his need to meet the social standings of his wife's family. Poor boy had given into the evil of status and had allowed the friction in his wallet to rub against his brain until the heat had started up a fire that would forever change his life. Now he would never be able to live up to society's expectations. He had doomed himself.

She had lost her appetite for dinner. The dogs' whimpers were now more about an opportunity missed than an adventure about to begin. She, too, was disappointed by the speed of the events that had unfolded to such a tragic end. They, like her life's major markers, had happened too fast and unpredictably with lots of waiting time interspersed within the unfolding of events, so that now, with the glowing lights of the last-to-leaves still in focus, she felt as if nothing occurred. Most likely nothing new would be discovered tomorrow that would change the events of tonight. It had happened and was done.

The dull glow from the windows of the new house, the vehicles lined up across the ruined lawn, and the weakening storm that drizzled rain down in such weary rivulets that even it had lost its punch, were all that remained of a life-changing event.

Maggie pulled the woven wood shade over her window. "Come on, dogs," she called. "I think you'll like my supper better than I would have." As she bent to fill their bowls with the hot stew, her shoulders drooped with sadness for Jim Armstrong and his young family.

CHAPTER TWO

Dad Billingsley's white hair and graying beard intensified his haggard appearance. He opened the door wider and gathered Clover into his arms. "I'm so glad you're here. We've been waiting."

"Where is she?"

"Sleeping. We all agreed a sedative would be most humane. She's in her old room. The children are settled in the guest rooms. We haven't told them yet. Mom can't bear the thought. We'll wait until morning."

"What will you say?"

"I don't know. We need some time to prepare. Were you able to learn anything?"

She nodded as she turned to hang her wet raincoat on the mudroom wall. She was still in shock. She had to slow down, think clearly, and prepare to reveal to her innocent family the awful things she had seen and heard. She sat on an antique bench and slowly removed her mud-caked shoes. She took a deep breath, stood and leaned her forehead against his strong chest. "It's so horrible, Dad, I don't know where to begin."

"Come on." He led her toward the spacious dining room. "Mom's waiting. We'll have some tea and take our time with this."

Mom Billingsley's hug was perfumed with the familiar scents of her bedtime lavender lotion and vitamin-A cream.

Tears stung Clover's eyes. "I'm sorry." She stumbled toward a chair.

"Sit down, Dear. Maybe you need something stronger than tea?"

Clover shook her head. She wrapped her shaking hands around the Spode cup, sipped the hot sweetened liquid and met her mother's eyes. "It is horrible," she whispered. "I'll try to tell you. Are you sure the children won't hear?"

Dad pulled the double doors together and latched them. "They're all tucked into beds upstairs."

"I made rounds on them," Mom said. "So far they've been pretty calm, but they know something is wrong. It's a lucky thing the Morton's happened along. Elizabeth was wonderful with them."

Clover took another sip of tea. "I'll start from what I saw and then tell you what little the sheriff had to offer. You'd better sit down."

∾

Roger Parrish poured himself a full glass of rum and sank into his worn recliner. The security lamps in the yard bathed the small room in harsh white light. He patted the dog that had settled on the rug at his side before he took a long pull of the liquor. "Never seen anything like that in a man before, Duke. Never."

He laid his head back into the coolness of the leather and closed his eyes. "Was bad enough when it was poor old Blacky down there by the road. Old horse could hardly make it to his food, wouldn't have resisted much. And the two pups, barely weaned, left there in the kennel yard so we could see. But, this… this is too much. Who could do that to a man? How does someone develop the stomach for such a thing? Gotta have an awful strong will, much stronger than I'll ever have."

He finished his drink in two long swallows and laid the glass on the carpet next to the dog. The other shepherds in the kennels howled for their dinner. The sound brought a strong feeling of melancholy into the warm room. "Who could do such a thing, Duke? Who?"

The dog raised his eyes to his master and creased his brows.

"Sometimes, Duke, old boy, I think you understand every word I say."

He stood, pulled on his jacket and, with the dog close at his heels, started for the kennels.

∽

Swenson scanned the vehicles in the parking lot of the restaurant. It was long past the dinner hour, but it looked like there were enough hangers-on to keep Tiny solvent. He pushed through the employee entrance, mumbled a greeting to the cook and made his way to the front.

The restaurant owner smiled as she placed a cup on the counter in front of him. "Ya look a little peaked, Sheriff."

"Bad night." He took a sip of the flavored brew and winked over the rim of his cup. "Good coffee."

"Only the best for you, Owen."

A little whiskey in his coffee had been their secret for all the years and late nights he'd been about. He'd had a yen for it in his younger days, but tonight he felt his stomach knot up as the liquor hit. Would ask for a new cup but she might not understand. Like his wife, she'd been in the habit of serving him far too long for sudden change. She would have served him in other ways, too, if his bed at home hadn't always been so warm. He half-turned and studied the scattered tables in the steamy room.

"You know, Owen, you really don't look so good. You want me to get you some grub? Cup of soup? Homemade chicken noodle tonight. Something to pick you up?"

He shook his head. "Tired, Tiny. That's all."

The second shift from the plywood mill was beginning to trickle in. The workers spoke quietly, but their voices held an urgency that caused Owen to pause and study each face. He recognized two high school friends of Jim Armstrong who belonged to the card-playing club at the Ram. Might be interesting to talk to.

He picked up his cup and made his way toward their table.

A hand came up and grabbed his arm. "Going to pass right by and not say a word?"

He laughed, shook the offered hand. "Sorry, Al. In another world. How ya been? How's the wife?"

"Fine. Daughter's staying with her tonight. Thought I'd have a little break. Come on. Sit down. Cheer up a lonely old soul."

Swenson stole another look at the plywood crew before he took the offered chair.

"Place has been quiet all night," the old man said. "Ya woulda thought somebody had died."

"Yeah."

"Out at Long Lake, eh? At the new Armstrong house."

"Hell, Al, how'd you know that?"

"Son works on the ambulance crew. Jackie. Remember him? First job he's held in years. Doin good. Doin real good."

"Didn't recognize Jackie out there."

"Wouldn't. Cleaned up. Cut his hair. Looks like a man now. Finally let go of all that hippie stuff."

"Jackie, huh?"

"Yeah. Big kid. Always wears that fatigue jacket. Last piece of the war he has. Can't let it go. Still wears the damned thing like a badge."

"Yeah, I did see him out there. That was Jackie, huh?"

"Oldest boy."

"God, time has flown."

"Ain't it so? How about that Armstrong kid though? Awful thing to happen. Is it true what Jackie said? Had his balls cut off?"

"Told you that, did he?"

"What's the world coming to, Swen? Where's it gonna end? It's the drugs, you know. Kids get all hopped up, do gruesome things."

"Had you seen Jimmy Armstrong lately? Heard anything about him? Rumors? Gossip?"

"Nah. Clean kid. Nice wife. Nice kids. Straight. Couldn't be bought. Woulda made Chief one day."

"You think so?"

"Course he woulda. With Doc Billingsley behind him and the kind of guy he was, he'd a been a shoe-in."

"You don't think he could have been fooling around? Little girl on the side? Somebody else's girl, maybe?"

"What? With that little blonde dish waiting for him at home? Get real, Swen. No Way."

"Never heard anything?"

"Nothin. Like I said, the guy is squeaky clean. But I get your thinkin. Would have been a reason for someone to cut off his balls. About the only reason I woulda thought of. Imagine doing that to a man?"

Tiny wrote orders from the plywood gang and after handing the sheets through the window, brought coffee and refilled their cups. "Just heard about Jimmy Armstrong. It ain't true, is it?"

"Jesus! Word travels damned fast around here. Where did you hear about it?"

She pointed one shoulder towards the mill crowd. "Guy's brother is a fireman. Called at the plant and told him. Whole plant is upset. Half the evening shift went to school with Jimmy."

"What are they saying?"

"Say he had his balls cut off. Say somebody tied his hands together and let him run all over that new house while he bled to death. That true, Owen?"

Sheriff Owen Swenson slowly nodded.

"Jesus! I didn't believe them! I'd better call Aunt Maggie. She's out there, all alone, except for her dogs. She's gotta lock up tight, can't trust nothing nowadays." Tiny hurried toward the kitchen.

"Can't imagine anyone safer than Maggie Bamford," Al chuckled. "Be a fool indeed who'd come up against her on a dark night."

"Word gets out, the whole town will be locked up tight."

"Small town, Owen. Ain't nothing like this ever happened before."

"And it's my job to be sure it never happens again. How can I find the guy if everything about this is front page news?"

"Doesn't seem like any of em get caught anyway. Look at all the detectives they got on those prostitute killings in the city. Keep the case locked up like a tomb. Got all those people working on it and still the killings keep happening. Ten years they've been going on. Shame is what it is."

"This is different, Al. Those are prostitutes who live on the streets and set themselves up for the perverts. This is an isolated case. This is a small town job, where the murderer knew the murderee. This is an upstanding young cop. This isn't some Goddamned serial killer thing. This is a local job and somebody local did it."

"How can you be so sure, Owen?"

"I can feel it in my bones. I can just feel it. Jim Armstrong knew the person who killed him. Jim Armstrong let him into that house tonight."

K.C. Casey pounded both fists against the van steering wheel, but the pain generated didn't stop his arms from shaking. Why had he gone in there? He knew in his heart that he shouldn't, especially after he'd seen the fire trucks and police cars. Yet there he'd gone, right into another mess. How would he explain this one to the Linds? They would jump all over him, sure of his guilt, sure he could do such a horrible thing. Heaven knew if he could seduce their innocent daughter, he was capable of almost anything.

The porch light announced Jenny's arrival. He watched her swollen form come carefully down the stairs until she stood outside the van, hands on her hips.

He opened the door slowly. "Hi, Jen. Jeez. Sorry. Late again, huh?"

"Late? Late? It's not even the same day you were supposed to be here. Where have you been, K.C.? What is going on with you?"

"Hon, please. Give me a minute. I've had a terrible night."

"You've had a terrible night? What about me? I'm the one who had to sit at dinner with my parents and their best friends and make stupid excuses for you. Couldn't you have called? What is wrong with you?" She trailed him as he locked the van, walked across the drive, and sat heavily on the porch stair. "Answer me, K.C.! Answer me! What is wrong with you?"

He stared off into the night. "Everything," he mumbled. "Everything."

"Damn it, K.C., you're acting like a moron."

To his shame he placed both his callused hands over his face and began to sob. He couldn't take anymore. He couldn't sit here before his young wife, waiting to face her gracious parents, in their gracious home with their gracious good manners. No, he couldn't face any of that. He stood up, took one last look at Jenny and, sobbing loudly, ran off into the night.

∾

Clover looked in on sleeping Lisa and the children before she opened the door to her old room and flipped on the light.

Posters of The Diva still covered the walls and ceiling. Something in the entertainers poses, hairstyles, costumes, and blatant sexuality reminded her of the long absent woman who had abruptly abandoned her in a tiny rented room twenty years before. As a teenager she had tried to find her mother in the posters. It hadn't worked. She remembered very little of the first eight years of her life.

The Billingsley's had taken her to counselors who discussed how unlikely that a mother would abandon her only offspring without good reason. After many sessions over many years, it had begun to make sense. Her mother had loved her, had provided for her, and had left far too abruptly to have planned her departure. She had not taken clothing, make up, or personal items and had left behind a beautiful sable coat, its pockets full of trinkets that had been the basis of their memory games.

Clover could still name every small object tucked into those pockets: lucky green rabbit's foot on a chain; set of metal keys; three hair barrettes – pink, red, and orange; lady's silk handkerchief – white with a monogrammed L in one corner; beaded baby bracelet, white with C-L-O-V-E-R spelled out in pink; cheap crimson cigarette lighter; tiny gold baby ring and a man's gold wedding band tied together with a pink ribbon; four silk hair ribbons – white, teal, orange, and crimson; plastic Barbie heels; ballpoint pen from the Clearwater Hotel, Seattle; a miniature set of playing cards; miniature sewing kit – unopened; two buttons, one red, one orange; a gold plastic comb; a small folding knife; and a Lilliputian kaleidoscope with a bubbled end.

She vaguely remembered sitting on a train next to her mother, reciting the trinkets, and laughing each time she was correct. Although the coat now hung in her townhouse apartment, each small token in its original pocket, she could no longer see her mother's face.

Once she accepted that something terrible had happened, that her mother had no choice, she had been able to quell the explosive anger that often erupted during her first years in the Billingsley household.

With that acceptance and her new family's love, the need for her mother had slowly faded into a vague and untouchable ache in the pit of her stomach – an ache very much like the hunger that had plagued her during her first weeks alone. Most mornings of those weeks, she had gratefully made her way to the warm third grade classroom and to Lisa, her first and constant friend, who had gently pried out the reason for her easily shed tears.

When Mom and Dad Billingsley showed up at the shabby rented room, Clover had again collapsed in tears. They brought her here, to this home, to this family and into a new miraculous life.

The Billingsley family had saved her. They had understood her hunger for a real blood relative, for her fears that they, too, might suddenly disappear without warning, and for her obsessive need of close personal connections. They had taught her the nuances of grace, charm and the ability to say no without offending, while accepting her need for the vibrant colors and passionate expression of rhythm that flooded her soul.

Now, with a familiar but intensified pain tugging at her belly, Clover Winters lay down on her childhood bed, pulled her knees to her chest, and tried to sleep.

CHAPTER THREE

Sheriff Swenson didn't try to hide his irritation. He rapped his phone against his knee and began again. "Jenny, now don't you go giving me any more runaround here. I told your young husband to stay by the phone and he damned well had better be there. I need to speak with him."

Jenny Lind Casey held the phone in her trembling hand and gazed with red-rimmed eyes out through the picture window where her father, perched on the kitchen stepstool, was frantically manipulating a coat hanger through the van's side window. "Why, Sheriff? Tell me why!"

"Because I have some questions he needs to answer."

"What questions?"

"Jenny, please. Your husband was at the Armstrong place on Long Lake yesterday. Have you seen the morning paper?"

"No. Wait! It's right here." She picked up the Tribune and stared at the headlines. "Oh, my God!"

Jenny Casey dropped the phone, stepped into her boots and pulled her husband's huge raincoat over her bathrobe. Wobbling precariously side to side, she ran out the back door past her angry father and the locked van that blocked his garage, past her mother's meticulous rose garden, and into the darkness of the forest.

K.C. was in trouble, real trouble, and she had shouted at him, as a mother would shout at a child and, like a child, he had run away. She hurried up the sodden trail that led through the old growth towards Long Lake. She knew where K.C. would be. She would go to the cabin where he played his weekend survival games and she would apologize to her hapless husband.

ᘜ

Clover twisted on the ruffled pink stool in front of the matching dressing table and took her sister's hand. "Lisa, it's too soon to talk about this. You have the children to think of. This whole thing is going to be catastrophic for them."

"I am thinking about the kids. Can you imagine what they're facing? The entire school will be asking questions. They have to know some kind of truth. I have to know who did this and why. Oh, Clover, I don't know if I will survive this."

"You have to. You have no choice. Oh, cripes, I want it to be yesterday. I want us to be able to go on a cookie binge and have everything turn out okay. I don't want this to be real."

Surrounded by plump pillows and ruffled chintz Lisa appeared, for one brief instant, to be the perky hazel-eyed teenager who had long ago occupied this room.

"Clover, I need you to help me."

"I will. I'll do anything I can."

"I want you to find out what happened to Jim. I want you to find the people who did this to him and my family."

"God, Lisa, I wouldn't even know where to begin."

"You're smart and you know how to cut through the red tape. I need you to promise me you'll do it. I need you to promise now."

"Lisa…"

"I'm not listening. I can't hear you. Promise me."

What could she do? This was Lisa, her one and only perfect sister. Lisa had never let her down. Now it was time to repay her for years of kindness. "I promise."

They sat in silence, each with their individual fears and anxieties playing through their heads, but each confident in their sisterhood.

Clover spoke first. "Tell me about last night. Tell me everything you can remember."

⌒〇

From the wall of windows that overlooked the lake and allowed her to see miles of surrounding forest, Maggie watched a figure moving through the trees on the southerly ridge. It wasn't until the hiker cleared the big trees that she was able to hone in with the birding scope and identify Jenny Lind. Jenny, with a new last name and a swollen belly that told everyone exactly why she'd married in such haste. What was her new last name? Something as nondescript as Lind. Something with a railroad ring.

Now, like the-little-engine-that-could, she was lumbering up the west side trail, spewing forth cold mouthfuls of steam and completely ignoring the fragility of her condition. Oh, if only these young things would follow the old traditions and stay at home. Seemed like they had nothing to guide them. Here she came, in a state of precarious life giving, exerting herself foolishly as if someone's life depended on her.

Now, after all the horrible goings-on at the Armstrong place having been clarified by her girl, Tiny, and after having seen smoke arising suspiciously from the survivalist's cabin situated midway between the pregnant girl and her own warm cottage, she would have to venture out on her old arthritic legs and see that no harm came to the child.

She hefted a forty-five pistol into her overalls, pulled her wool coat over her sloping shoulders and clicked at the dogs. "Wup, boys! Let's go."

The dogs jumped to their feet with excited yips and gathered at the door.

"Hush, now. Quiet down. No need to tell the world that we're on the way. Heel!"

As if leading a parade, she walked spryly toward a worn path. One by one, the dogs filed in behind her and disappeared into the steaming forest.

❧

Roger Parrish sat in his truck sipping coffee from a tall cup and watching the dayshift canine officers file into their patrol cars. "There goes one of your sons, Duke. Don't that make you proud?"

Duke licked his master's ear and rapped a staccato rhythm against the pickup window with his tail.

"I think they saw you, boy. But they're good officers and never batted an eye. Good dogs, those sons of yours."

Duke watched with interest as the cars drove off.

"You stay here now. Down. Good dog." He bounded into the Tacoma Police Department and weaved his way to the Chief's desk.

"Morning, Sir."

"What the hell are you doing here?"

"Truffling."

"Better get your nose fixed, no truffles here."

"Smell a rat then."

"Yeah?"

"Armstrong boy."

The Chief exhaled and sank deeper into his vinyl chair. "Yeah. You have one there."

"Tell me."

"Rog, you know it's against the regs. Get out of here. You have no official position."

"Yeah, but this is personal."

"Worse yet."

"Look. The way it happened. What they did. Revenge? A hit? A warning? What?"

The Chief shrugged his slumping shoulders. "Don't know. Not a clue. Armstrong was my best. Damned good. Died without a clue."

"You have to help me."

"Can't. Don't have anything."

"What was he working on? Who were his contacts? What did he do yesterday? The day before?'

"He was moving, Roger. He was a family man moving into a new home. He hasn't worked for a week."

"What kind of caseload did he have?"

"That's restricted information."

"I'll find out anyway. You know I'll get it sooner or later. Make it sooner. Help me out here."

The man turned away and stared out the window.

"You owe me one, man. I was once your best."

When the chief turned back, his face was florid with rage. "You still would be, you butt hole! It was you who screwed the pooch! Not me! And this case has nothing to do with me! The sheriff's department has it. County problem. You know Swenson. Go ask."

"He doesn't know who would want Armstrong anymore than you know what the kid did yesterday. Tell me, Chief. Who had a grudge against him? Who'd he piss off enough to trigger mutilation? Just give me that. His most important case. Just one."

"And we're even up?"

"Even up."

"Official info. No leaks. Understand?"

Roger could feel his adrenalin pumping. He focused his eyes until the chief appeared as one big clear picture framed in bright light. He nodded.

"Serial murder cases. The prostitutes. Was working with good old pimp Sammie and Sammie's girls. He was becoming friends with the hustlers, looking for a thread."

"And he found one?"

"Presumably."

"And he died with the info?"

"Far as I know. Maybe because of it."

"That's it?"

The chief turned away, gazed out the window at the industrial tide flats that smothered under a pall of smoke. "The girls are being mutilated too," he muttered.

"Like Armstrong? Cut up?"

"That's all. I won't say more. Have a good day." He waved one hand in the air, dismissed Roger without facing him again.

Roger hurried back through the familiar room and across the back lot, head down, looking neither right nor left.

"Got it, Duke," he said as he flung himself onto the truck seat.

The dog didn't rise up, but lay his head on both front paws and whimpered.

"Tell you what. We'll go home, saddle up one of the horses and take a good ride up to Old Maggie's place. Could be she saw something last night. What do you think?"

The dog yipped his approval.

Having been left hanging on the phone by Jenny Casey, Owen Swenson took a legal pad to the kitchen table and began to write. As his hovering wife fried bacon and toasted bread, he began to list the possible motives for Jim Armstrong's bloody death.

By the time he finished breakfast, he had concocted a list of Biblical sins that have been preached from church pulpits from time immemorial: sins of omission and commission, sins of the body and sins of the soul, all the sins of the world that might cause one man to emasculate another. And yet, he had not one good shred of a clue as to why someone would do that to young Jimmy. Unless, of course, that man was an absolutely, positively, raving maniac.

He shook his head. His small town didn't contain any of those creatures. At least not as far as he knew and he knew everyone in town, except for one. And that one, curiously enough, was K.C. Casey, plumber and new husband to Jenny Lind.

He would have another talk with Casey soon enough. In the meantime he was going to prowl around and look for Jimmy's missing truck. Whoever took the life of the boy, took his truck as well, and therein was another mystery. How did the person get all the way out to Long Lake without a vehicle, and if he did drive a vehicle, how did he drive two vehicles out of there? That brought up the prospect of having two maniacs on his hands.

He donned his uniform and set out for Tiny's and another token cup of coffee.

K.C. Casey also awakened early. He pulled on full camouflage gear, cleaned his paint-ball rifle, and consumed a huge breakfast. Spending time in the great outdoors always gave him an appetite. No matter what else happened, he had this one day in the woods to clear his head. He packed some energy bars and a flask of water into his web belt and set off into the big woods away from the damned lake and the Armstrong house that lay over the ridge at his back. From the cabin he took the downstream path on the edge of Clear Creek.

At regular intervals, he dodged, crouched low, and took aim at startled Chickadees and tiny Pine Siskins. He didn't waste pellets on such minute prey, but liked catching them in his sight. The heavy rains of the evening before had washed the creek-side clean. It was a perfect tracking day. His head began to clear and he became hungry again. He would make himself go four or five miles before he would allow himself a snack.

Three miles downstream he picked up the prints of a fox, followed by two tiny sets of kit prints. Imagining the mother fox with her babies caused Jenny to pop into his thoughts. He sank onto a fallen log and buried his face in his hands. Poor Jenny. She didn't deserve any of this. Neither did he. He had done nothing to deserve the Sheriff's suspicions. If not for that Clover woman, he would be sitting in county jail this very morning facing a murder rap. Jenny had no idea what he was up against.

He stood, paced a tight circle for a few minutes, and set off with a determined stride towards the east. He would hike out to the highway, flag down the first car that came along and turn himself into the sheriff even though the lawyer guy had said not to. Jenny deserved that much.

He didn't see the blackened vehicle until he was almost touching it. Funny, he couldn't remember seeing it on Saturday when he'd practiced last. New model. Trashed. All burned out. Dumb thing for someone to do, drive a new truck down an old logging road and burn it up.

He circled the vehicle and scanned the surrounding woods.

When convinced he was not being watched, he bent over and studied the license tags. A nearly melted bumper sticker caught his eye. Tacoma Police Department. Holy Cow! The cop's truck. The one the sheriff kept asking him about. Now how would he explain this one? He couldn't. He wouldn't. He had to get away from here.

K.C. Casey dashed back into the woods and thrashed his way through the underbrush towards Clear Creek.

෴

Clover strode to the counter, ignoring the overt stares of the elderly early risers.

Tiny smiled as she offered coffee. "Ain't seen you around for awhile."

Clover settled onto a stool. "I've been back east. Married. Divorced. Home again."

"Any kids?"

She poured sugar into her cup. "No kids. Some bad choices. You know how that goes."

"Yep. Throw in a few kids and a few more husbands and you'll paint my picture."

Clover sipped the hot drink. "You and Lisa caught the kid thing. I've been immune." She felt no need to reveal her sterility, or the painful reality that she may never know another human who shared her genes.

"How's she doing?" Tiny folded her arms and leaned one hip against the counter.

"Not great. She's a bit barmy. Sedated."

"Shots?"

"Yeah."

"Worse thing they can do."

"Oh?"

"When my daughter was killed, I lost a week with the shots. The whole thing is a blur. Had to wake up and start bawling all over again. Better to get it all out while the rest of the folks are still grieving. Not much good comes of crying alone."

Clover tried to recall the details of the murder of Tiny's daughter. They had found her body out by Long Lake. Had never found the murderer or the cause of death. Consoling words would mean nothing to Tiny. "Dad believes in medicines," she said instead.

"Yeah, makes folks feel better, like they got everything under control. But doesn't do a thing to help the pain. In the long run, it might even make it worse." She shook her head and turned away. "I don't know."

Clover caught the glint of tears in the older woman's eyes. "I'm so sorry, Tiny."

"It's okay, Hon, I get like this sometimes. It's been seven years. Let's just skip it okay?" She picked up the coffee pot. "Want a Danish to go with that?"

"Yes. Oh, yes. One with cream cheese frosting and extra butter melted on top."

"I swear, Clover, you never change. Skinny as ever and with that sweet tooth to beat all heck. Don't think you'll ever get filled out." She pulled a plated Danish from the glass case and placed it in the microwave.

"Pure luck or good genes, I don't know which. You seen Swenson today?"

"Yep. Was in early, then headed up to Aunt Maggie's place." Tiny placed the pastry on the counter and moved across the room to seat some customers.

Clover cut into the sweet dough, placed it into her mouth, and rolled her eyes in appreciation. She smiled as she remembered neat-as-a-pin Maggie; square-shouldered, short in stature, but with a powerful presence that filled the grade school classrooms whenever she visited. The old woman had the warmest golden brown eyes Clover had ever seen and a mop of silver curls that she kept neatly away from an angelic face.

When speaking to the school children, Maggie's voice was sweet and mellow, but Clover had also seen her address local politicians, including Dad Billingsley, in the booming voice of a logger, complete with expletives that shrank the most powerful down to size. An advocate and protector of the few remaining old growth forests, Maggie was a force to be reckoned with in the environmental wars that plagued the former logging town.

Tiny placed an order up for the cook and came back to the counter. Clover pushed her empty plate and cup aside. "How is Maggie?" she asked.

"Same as ever. Driving around with a truckload of dogs, stirring up the government, taking potshots at trespassers."

"When I was in grade school, I loved those cookies she brought in for holidays; orange and green pumpkins, turkeys with rainbow tails, Santa Claus with raisin eyes, big red hearts that said 'I love you' in big white loops."

"Doesn't do the school thing anymore. Still loves kids. How she can be so bad to grown-ups and so sweet to kids is beyond me."

"I was there when she let her dogs loose on the mayor during the Fourth of July parade. I cheered with the rest of the crowd. What a firecracker!"

"You're lucky you didn't have to go bail her out of jail. She was still cussing and cutting up the mayor. He hasn't ever suggested raising land taxes again. Learned his lesson that year."

"The first week after my mom left, Maggie was the one person to offer me hope."

"Yeah? What'd she do?"

"She came to the school with cookies. When she bent down and looked into my eyes it was like she had seen a real person. She wiped my nose on her apron, straightened my collar and said, 'Beautiful child. Beautiful.' Then she slipped me two more cookies."

Tiny laughed. "That's Maggie. We both got something to be grateful for with her. When my mother went to jail, she took me in. Ended up raising me and helped me raise my own kids. I never can get around to calling her mom. She won't put up with none of that sentimental stuff. Couldn't have kids. Something wrong with her innards. Outlived three husbands, though, and raised a whole lot of step kids."

"She's a good old gal. The very best." Clover felt a twinge of remorse. Would she too outlive the men in her life and end up alone? She placed a fiver on the counter.

"You going out to her place?"

"Yeah. Thought I'd track down the sheriff."

"How about taking some sweets out with you? Maggie's got an appetite like yours. She'll love you forever. Guaranteed."

～

Jenny Lind burst into the survivalist's cabin full of forgiveness and misgivings, but when she found the remains of breakfast and the recently abandoned sleeping bag carelessly unrolled on a lower bunk, she stamped her feet and muttered, "Idiot! Crazy, useless, half-witted idiot!"

However, being a sensible woman with two to feed and nearly starving after not being able to eat dinner last evening and accomplishing an enormous hike, she set about collecting the remainder of her husband's scrambled eggs and ham. She scraped what was left onto a plate, pulled some pilot bread from a tin and filled a cup with coffee from the still warm stove.

When she had eaten her fill and cleaned the mess away, she stood at a small window that faced the trail. She reached back with both hands and began to knead a nagging pain at the base of her spine.

A noise behind her caused her to turn. One strong push slammed her against the rough wall. The blow knocked the wind out of her, caused her to slip down along the wall.

She stared into the horror-stricken face of K.C. His skin was slick with sweat. The distended veins in his neck pulsed with the rage of a madman.

Before Jenny could speak, another voice snarled, "Move an inch and I'll blow your kidneys out." A hand reached over and tore the rifle from Casey. "Now just move away."

Like a small boy, K.C. stepped backwards.

Jenny's quivering legs folded. She slipped to the floor.

"Get up against the wall!" Maggie Bamford ordered.

"She's my wife," K.C. whispered. His splayed hands wavered at chest level.

"Sure she is. And I'm Father Christmas."

"She is. Jenny, tell her. Tell her!"

Jenny's eyes fluttered. Her face flushed. "How dare you, K.C.? How dare you hit me like that?"

"I didn't mean it, Hon! Ah, shit! Everything's all mixed up! I didn't know it was you."

"Of course it was me!"

"Well, yeah. Now you are. But how was I to know? There's a killer loose, you know! What the hell are you doing out here? And with our baby to think of?"

"With our baby to think of? Were you thinking of our baby when you hit me? You could have killed her!"

"Ah, Jenny." He forgot the gun at his back and the old woman's warnings. He fell to his knees and tried to cradle his wife.

She wasn't to be babied. "You idiot, K.C.! You Goddamned idiot! What are you doing out here dressed in that outfit when half the county's looking for you? How can you play cowboys and Indians now? When are you going to grow up?"

"Jenny. Honey. I saw the truck. I found the cop's truck!"

"What truck? What Goddamned truck? What's a truck got to do with almost killing your unborn baby?"

Maggie, who was standing above the two with her forty-five still pointed at the place where K.C. had stood, but was now pointing at his head, came to life. "What truck? What truck did you see?"

"The guy's truck." He turned and faced directly into the gun. "I saw the cop's truck. All burned out, just like his house."

"Where?"

He jerked his thumb towards the cabin door. "Out near Clear Creek."

Maggie contemplated the information, distrusted it, then decided that this new lump of a husband of Jennifer Lind might indeed have made an important discovery and that she, being the kind of person she was, would have to see this discovery for herself. She locked the safety and replaced the gun in her overalls before she clucked for her dogs.

Growling and long-tongued, the dogs surrounded the young couple on the floor.

‰

Owen backed into the shadows of the porch as Clover stepped from her sporty convertible. Despite her jeans and mannish jacket, there was something very seductive about the high-breasted, small-waisted line of her body. Not just the looks, he decided as she stepped forward, but the way she moved, the hip action that, though natural and smooth, made a man think of individual body parts that she seemed to offer up, one small morsel at a time; body parts that made it difficult to take in the whole woman at once.

She stood near her car, studied the towering forest, the pad-locked garage, and the cabin before she bent and lifted a bakery box.

Nice ass, too. He could almost feel the firm softness of it through the blue jeans.

She turned and listened for a moment to the sound of the wind whispering through the old growth.

Mentally sharp. Calculating. Careful. Sunlight raised golden highlights in her long chestnut hair.

Her full red lips broke into an easy smile. "Good Morning, Sheriff."

He stepped into the sunlight. "Morning, Clover. What brings you out here so early?"

"Brought some sweet rolls for Maggie."

"Just happened to be coming out this way, eh?"

"No. I was actually looking for you, Sheriff. Tiny told me you would be here." She placed the box on the porch table and turned to study the view.

He could smell the womanly scent of her, the hint of perfume emanating from her hair. He was surprised by his physical reaction. He shifted his weight from one foot to the other.

"Fantastic!" she breathed softly. "Look at the lake. My God, you can see half the county from here."

"Makes you understand why Maggie stays."

She moved past him. "Is she home?"

"Probably out for a walk. Dog's are gone." It was difficult to keep his eyes from her.

"Door's not locked."

"Tiny said she talked to her about that. Woman too stubborn to change her ways."

She turned and leaned forward over the porch rail. Her eyes focused on the Armstrong house far below. "Really sad about the house. Lisa will never live in it now."

"Wouldn't expect she could." Swenson moved to stand beside her.

"Do you think Maggie saw anything?"

"Tiny tell you that?"

She shook her head. "Have you talked to Maggie?"

He turned his gaze to the forest. The soft whinny of a horse and the deep command of a male voice came from the head of the trail where it entered the yard.

Roger Parrish broke through the cover of dense maples. His horse was lathered, but still running strong. His big dog, Duke, didn't slow as he neared the house. Roger reined in and walked the Arabian closer. "Morning, Owen." He tipped his hat toward Clover. "Maggie here?"

"Doesn't seem to be."

He turned the horse, walked it to the garage and peered into a dusty side window. "Truck's here." He dismounted and tethered the horse to the garage door. "Hoped she'd have some coffee on." With three long strides he took the stairs. "Are we all here for the same reason?"

"Coffee?" Clover asked sweetly. "Or purely a social visit?"

"Maybe a little of both." Roger joined them at the rail.

"I'm here on official business," the sheriff said. "I'd rather it was kept private."

Clover laughed. "Don't mind me, Sheriff. You two boys want to discuss the case, I'll not interfere."

"When Maggie returns, I'll speak to her alone."

She shrugged. "Will you exclude the cowboy, too?"

Roger smacked his riding crop against the porch rail.

Swenson stared into Clover's eyes. She didn't seem very sexy now. "Roger's working on a special angle of this case."

"Special angle? Ok-aa-aay." She sang the words. "Is he paid by your office to work this 'angle'?"

He shook his head. "It's police work."

"I see. I'm working on a special angle too. It's family work. The victim's family. Does that give me special privileges, Sheriff?"

Roger didn't hide his anger. "It's none of your God-damned business."

Swenson reached out a restraining hand. "Let's say he has a special police interest in the case."

"But it's private?"

"Yes."

"You've heard of victim's rights, Sheriff?"

He was quickly loosing patience. "Victim's rights have nothing to do with my interviewing old Maggie. This is strictly police business."

"And what business do you have with the police, Cowboy?"

Roger didn't answer.

"I understand you train canine patrol officers and sell them to the various departments for a profit. Are you actually employed by the department? Are you on a payroll somewhere?"

Roger's eyes met hers, but he remained silent.

"I gather that is a negative. In which case, I have as much right to be here as you." She moved to the inside, leaned her back against the table, and addressed the sheriff. "If he stays, I stay."

Duke growled, raised his ears and eyes to the steep trail behind the house.

Maggie and her dogs broke into the clearing.

Sheriff Swenson bolted toward the stairs.

"Looks like she's conducting some kind of tour," Clover said. "Who's with her?"

"The plumber and his wife."

Clover's smile faded. Jenny Lind was the last person she wanted to see. Jenny's crowd of preps and jocks had filled her high school days with teenage angst. And now, despite the huge raincoat that did nothing to hide her advanced stage of pregnancy, she still appeared as young, fresh, and polished as the day they graduated.

"Morning, Owen," Maggie sang. "Got a real prize for you."

"You sure do." Swenson stepped forward and placed a hand on K.C.'s arm.

Maggie pushed between them. "No need for that, Owen. No need. Come on now, kids. Come on. We'll all have a cup of coffee and tell the sheriff what we know. Morning, Roger." She climbed the stairs one at a time, taking a breath on each step. "Not getting any younger. How are you, Roger? And who is this?" She turned her full attention to Clover. "You get married on me, Roger?"

Roger snorted.

Swenson answered. "This is Jimmy Armstrong's sister-in-law, Maggie. Clover Winters." There was a warning in his tone.

"That so?" She soothed a lock of Clover's hair away from her face.

"Clover's a lawyer."

"Too pretty to be a lawyer."

"I'm a teaching assistant at the law school," Clover corrected. "I'm not practicing law."

Roger snorted again.

"And what's this?" The old woman touched the box on the table. "Tiny's sweet rolls? Now who brought these?"

"Tiny sent them." Clover lifted the box.

Jenny followed Maggie and K.C. up the stairs. Her eyes took in Clover with a cool, sweeping stare. "Clover? Clover Winters! What are you doing here? And what did I hear? A lawyer? Why the last time I saw you, you were still receiving charity at the Billingsleys. Don't tell me they sent you to college too?"

"Scholarship, actually. Harvard." She turned away and slipped through the door behind Maggie.

Maggie turned. "You're the Billingsley's Clover?"

Clover nodded.

"My goodness. Always were a pretty little thing. And you're smart too? Harvard? Isn't that something? Come on then. There's people to feed. Cut up those rolls and put them on the table. Here, Jenny, you put out the cups. I'll see to the coffee." She stopped on her way to the polished wood stove and gazed through the birding scope. "Down dogs! Treats!" Without taking her eyes from the scope, she used one hand to fish biscuits out of a box and hand them one by one to the dogs. With her other hand she slowly moved the scope across the valley before her. "Good dogs." Each dog took its treat and settled near the stove.

Seeing nothing of particular interest through the scope, Maggie moved away from the window, hefted the full graniteware coffeepot and began filling cups. "Made plenty of good hot coffee this morning. Knew I'd have company before the morning was over."

Once Maggie pushed aside her rocker and footstool, the table easily accommodated six. "Bet you thought I'd have breakfast, didn't you, Roger? Fooled you, didn't I? Went for a walk and found these two. Here, have a roll."

Swenson studied the camouflage clothing of the Casey boy. Survivalist. Probably knows every tree and creek in the big woods. Could have been watching the Armstrong place for weeks. Could have hiked into the place, then driven back out.

"Now don't you go giving him the evil eye, Owen. I've had a long talk with this boy. He ain't no killer and he's got some things to say that might be of great interest to you."

"I'll talk to you alone, Maggie."

"Hah!" She preened her hair and patted her cheeks. "Little old for you, ain't I boy?"

Clover laughed.

Swenson scowled. "I need to have some matters kept quiet, Maggie."

"I know exactly what you need, Owen. Oh, I know all right. Just like you needed everything kept quiet when Tiny's little girl disappeared. Keeping quiet didn't much help then, Mr. Owen Swenson, and it sure as hell won't do much good this time either."

"Well then, Maggie," he pushed back his chair and stood. "If we can't talk in private, we won't talk at all." He stood and started around the table toward K.C. "I'll not sit here and sip coffee with you and talk about the weather like a couple of old biddies." He glared at Maggie. "Come on, Casey, we'll drive into my office and get this business done right."

"You're not going anywhere, Owen." Maggie met him face to face before he could lay a hand on Casey. "You just sit yourself down and stop acting like the asshole that you are and when I've had my coffee and my sweet roll, we'll all get in my truck and we'll all go and investigate Mr. Jim Armstrong's vehicle. Just might be something of real interest waiting there for you."

"Armstrong's truck?"

"Yes, we found it. Now sit down and we'll get to it in our own time, won't we children?"

⁓

The three women sat in front of Maggie's truck. K.C. and the dogs rode in the open back. The sheriff and Roger followed in the patrol car.

Maggie drove slowly with both hands on, and both eyes peering through, the wheel. She knew exactly where she should turn and which hastily pushed in Forest Service road she should take and which unmarked fork she should veer to the right or the left on, so that, within fifteen minutes, they were all piling out of the pickup and carefully approaching the burned out hull of Jim Armstrong's small red truck.

"I thought it was Jim who drove out of there," Maggie murmured. "I thought it was him who was so hell bent to get going from that brand new house, and, here, all the time, it was someone else." She shook her head slowly.

The dogs sniffed and whined and tried to pick up a trail, but no matter how many times and in how many directions, Maggie tried them, they kept returning again and again to K.C. Now they milled around the young couple who snuggled and whispered behind Maggie's truck.

Prohibited by the sheriff from nearing Jim's vehicle, Clover lounged on a dry bed of needles at the base of an old growth fir. Roger Parrish leaned against the other side of the trunk. Maggie jabbed at debris with the knarred walking stick she had pulled from behind her truck seat. The sheriff busied himself stringing yellow plastic ribbon in a wide circle around the clearing.

"There's nothing to cordon off," Roger murmured more to himself than to Clover. "What the hell's the use?"

"Makes him feel like he's doing something," Clover answered.

"Yeah." He lit a cigarette and inhaled deeply.

"We could work together on this, you know."

He coughed, blew smoke through his nose and mouth. "Work together! What the hell is there to work at?"

"You want this guy and so do I. It would be more efficient if we pooled our efforts."

"Honey, I don't work with anybody. Especially not with a woman."

She shrugged. "That's your problem."

He threw his cigarette into the dirt and sauntered over to Maggie.

Clover studied him openly. Afraid. Probably afraid of all women. Except maybe old Maggie. She chuckled to herself. Some men really weren't too bright. Out of all the women on earth, the one who Roger Parrish should truly fear was Maggie. Well, she could certainly take advantage of that. No man was easier to manipulate than one who was fearful of the female gender. She stood, brushed off the back of her jeans and, lifting the newly strung yellow ribbon, strolled to the scorched pickup that had been Jim's.

Maggie Bamford pushed her stick deeper into the debris at the edge of the clearing. Too soft. Should be hardpan in this area, shouldn't give at all. She placed both hands on the stick and pulled it towards her. Bits of fur and a few small bones cut the surface and lay like glistening treasures on the soil's surface. She dipped the stick again and pulled. More and larger bones this time, maybe a dog or possibly a sheep. She probed again and fished out an elongated skull. Dog. Definitely a dog. "Roger, look here."

He bent and with his bare hand lifted the skull. "Big dog," he said.

"But look at these others."

He retrieved some of the smaller bones and laid them in a line on the dirt. "Looks like a dog, but too small for the skull."

"I got a claming shovel under my truck seat," she said.

By the time Maggie returned with the shovel, Roger had unearthed two more skulls and caught the attention of Sheriff Swenson. "Don't touch a thing, Maggie. Didn't you hear me say that?"

"I heard you loud and clear, Owen. But this here's outside your little yellow ribbon. I thought this was free game."

"Not a thing. Jesus, why can't I make anyone understand that this is a crime scene. Clover! Get out of that truck. I need to have it dusted for prints."

"There isn't a piece that hasn't been burned, Sheriff," Clover said. "You're not going to find any prints here."

"Get out of there!"

She shrugged, walked over to him and handed him a small piece of metal.

"What is it?"

"Looks like a scalpel blade. The kind Dad Billingsley uses in his operating room. Found it near the driver's side door."

"You should have left it there."

"You had already walked on it, Sheriff. I didn't want it to get tamped deeper into the dirt."

Owen Swenson was losing his cool. "Roger, stop digging, do you hear me?"

"Too many bones for one small spot, Owen. You'd better get a team of people out here. I think we may have found a murderer's midden."

Maggie held aloft a leather dog collar studded with colorful stones. She waved it like a piece of bait below the Sheriff's nose. "Remember that gal that disappeared about nine or ten years ago, Owen? Didn't they say she was into some weird sexual stuff? Didn't they say she liked to wear a studded leather collar? Don't this look like it could fit a small woman?"

"Put it down, Maggie. Right where you found it. And none of you, not one of you, touch another thing."

CHAPTER FOUR

Clover churned her satin bed sheets into a luxurious downy mound that tangled about her legs and torso as her mind's eye followed Jim Armstrong through the shadows of his final day. She watched as he loaded the last bits and pieces into his pickup. She hovered among the shadows on the wet pavement as he steered around the steep curves of Long Lake Road on his final drive. She gasped as he skidded sideways in the muddy rivulets of his newly graveled drive and she breathed in the cedar perfume of his recently finished deck. She followed him into the open-beamed, new-carpet-fresh-paint-scented house where furniture and stacks of neatly labeled boxes lay strewn about. She watched as he shifted cartons to the children's rooms and hung clothes on closet rods. She peeked out of freshly washed windows and smiled as the wind bent tall trees toward the canvas of Long Lake. There she lost him. That was the end.

She beat her silken pillow as she tried to recall, word for word, the revelations that Lisa had lined out. "I couldn't see. It was raining hard and the road kept throwing up mud. When I reached the top of the drive, I saw lots of colored lights. I thought the guys from the station house had ambushed him – that they were throwing him a new-house party. That made me happy. I said to myself, 'See. He'd never lie to you'."

Lisa had shaken her head as she mouthed the words; her movements sluggish, as if she were speaking in a film that was running on slow. "I thought, 'you fool, Lisa. He was caught up here without the phone. He wasn't off somewhere avoiding you.' The lights of all the trucks and cars blinded me and I couldn't see where to park."

While Clover had waited for her sister to continue she made a decision. She decided to ask Dad to stop the medications. Tiny had been right. Once the initial shock was past, Lisa would do better with the family to support her, not drugs.

"A cop stepped out in front of my headlights. I rolled down the window. The rain was horrible. It ruined my hair. He smelled like wet wool." She laughed like a drunk who felt they'd told a humorous joke. "Can you imagine? I was worried about my hair and his wet uniform."

Clover had patted her sister's hand. "You didn't know, Lisa. You had no idea. Who was the officer?"

"Max. It was Max, Jim's detective partner. But he was so strange. He didn't seem to know me."

"What did he say?"

"He said, 'you can't go in there, Lisa. I said, 'why not?' He was sweating. That's when I saw it. It wasn't our fireplace that was making the smoke. It was the whole house burning. Oh, Christ, Clover, it's all gone. The house, my life, my family… my husband! We'll never be able to live in that place. I can't bear it."

Clover had moved to the bed and cradled her sister while she sobbed, had rocked her gently until she quieted. "We can do this another time," she said.

"No. I want to do it now. I want you to know everything." She pulled away and wiped her tears with fisted hands. "I remember pushing open the car door and fighting to get past."

"What did he say?"

"He kept repeating, 'Lisa, you can't go in there. You can't go in there.' The van was still in gear. It moved away and hit that big old cedar tree that Jim saved from the contractors."

"You're lucky the van didn't hit you."

"But I feel like it did. I feel like I was hit with something ten times bigger. Maybe a hundred times bigger. I feel like I would be better off dead." Her shoulders had begun to shake again as she held back sobs.

Clover struggled to keep her voice low and even. "Then what happened?"

"That's it. The sheriff came out and asked me who he should call. I said, 'call Clover'. Then the Mortons drove up and they brought me home."

Now Clover was wide-awake. She untangled her legs from the sheets and sat up on the side of the bed. Who? Who lurked in the shadows of those rooms? Who ran pell-mell down the front porch stairs, head down? Who climbed into the red truck? Who drove like the devil, round the curves of Long Lake Road as furious wiper blades pushed the rain rudely aside?

She imagined a sickening lurch as Jim's murderer momentarily lost control and skidded sideways into the rutted muddy road. He had to have been familiar enough with that clearing to know that flames from the burning truck couldn't be seen from town or Maggie's cabin.

Light began to show between the crimson drapes. She roused herself, went to the balcony door, stared out at the dying geraniums on her deck. Her body shuddered with a coldness that exceeded the October chill.

While the gas heater hissed to life in the fireplace, she pulled her mother's coat from the closet and wrapped it closely around her shivering body. With mystical grace she settled into an ancient brooding posture before the fingers of flame. Meditation might take her closer to her objective. However, as she warmed and chanted, she found that could go no farther down that rutted, bone-strewn road. She could follow him no more.

She would have to bring the man to her. If she could entice him into the light, perhaps she could identify him before he became aware of her silken trapping strands. Perhaps. Perhaps, though, he might be smarter and better at trapping than she.

❦

A sea of umbrellas undulated in the relentless wind. Mourners huddled together as the long service droned on. To her extreme embarrassment, Clover sobbed and keened shrilly, while, Lisa, supported by her father, swayed gently, but remained controlled and dignified. Five somber, wide-eyed children, as impressive as their mom, pressed between family members like so many baby chicks seeking refuge under outstretched wings.

Clover wished that she could find some softness in the picture, but the threat of her own hysteria would not allow her tenderness.

She forced her gaze away from her family. She had stood apart to study the crowd. He was here again. She could feel him. Did he relish this result of his handiwork?

"Amen."

The crowd slowly came to life and broke into small cliques. Dad Billingsley reached out, pulled Clover into the family fold, and guided her to the proper limousine for the drive to the post funeral dinner.

⟢

The hall, a few blocks from her townhouse, was warm and brightly lit. A wedding party celebrated in an adjoining room.

Clover and Lisa shuffled along in silence holding hands until a joyful bride, her white gown flowing out behind her, pushed past. Lisa collapsed against Clover and broke into heartrending sobs.

Dad Billingsley stepped in and took her to one side, as Clover continued on with the children.

The somber party gratefully bowed their heads as another prayer was offered. Food appeared. The children ate. Clover picked at the offering. She could not concentrate. The presence of Jim's enemy pulled at her. She sensed his meticulous brain ticking through the deed he had accomplished, reveling in his sin. She dried her eyes and slowly studied the room, table-to-table, head-to-head. Who? Who?

A pair of bright green eyes met hers. A young policeman in full dress uniform quickly lowered his gaze to his untouched food. She understood his embarrassment. His face was wet with tears, his grief real and unpretentious.

She continued to search the room. Her enemy was invisible, smug, and arrogant. She could not stay in the same room with him. She pushed her chair back and began to stand.

Elizabeth Morton reached out with one cold hand and stayed her movement. "Lisa's going to need us more than ever now," she said. Her face was sickly gray. "It's so sad." She appeared much older than her fifty-plus years. "Such a terrible, terrible loss."

Dick took his wife's free hand. "Come, Elizabeth, Clover has the right idea. Let's say our good-byes to the family and go home to weep."

"Yes, of course, you're right." Elizabeth stood. "It's time to go home."

"She's not well," he said over his wife's head. "And standing out in the cold wasn't good for her."

"No," Clover answered. "The service seemed extremely long."

"Come on, Elizabeth," he wrapped his wife's cashmere coat tightly around her thin body.

Clover watched as they made their way along the table, murmuring their good-byes, one gracious sympathetic word after another, perfectly presented. She was thankful for good friends. Good friends and their loving family would see Lisa and the children through this. She made her way into the stream of hand-shaking, hugging people until she found herself standing next to the young officer she had spotted earlier.

"I don't believe we've met," he said.

"No." She started to turn away.

"I'm Max," he persisted. "I'm...I was...Jim's partner."

"Oh." She turned. "I'm sorry. I didn't know." She offered her hand. "Clover," she said. "Lisa's sister."

"Yes, I know. Jim pointed you out to me once, on the University campus."

She waited for him to continue.

"We were driving past. You were getting out of your little red car and I...made some comment...complimentary of course." His smile was strained. "Jim told me who you were."

"I'd like to talk more to you," she said without thinking. "Could we go somewhere? I mean for a drink or something."

He was genuinely startled. "Well, yeah. I guess so. Sure. But. . . " He ran his hand over his formal uniform.

"Right. You're not quite dressed for a bar." She decided to go for broke. "We could go to my place. It's just up the street."

"Should we wait for your husband?"

"Ex."

"Oh, I'm sorry. I didn't know."

"How about you? Your wife?'

He shook his head. "Still single."

"Well, then..." She slipped her arm through his. She was grateful for his support as they left the room.

∽

They walked to her apartment where she poured two glasses of the perfectly aged scotch Dad Billingsley had given her the previous Christmas.

They sat together on her ruby couch in silence until the warm glow of alcohol began to have its effect.

"Tell me about detective Jim," she said. "I've only known the family guy. We never talked about his job."

He emptied his glass. "Not much to tell."

She poured him three more fingers of scotch. "How long did you work together?"

"Not even a year. I'm a rookie." His voice broke. "Jim was my first partner."

"Did you like him? I mean did you like the way he worked? The way he did his job?"

"Heck, yes. He was a straight guy. Cool. Honest."

She smiled. That was Jim. Always decent. "He was like that with his family too."

"Yeah. He talked about them a lot."

"About Lisa?"

He nodded. "And about the importance of a having a good family life to keep you strong at the job."

She studied him as he spoke, watched the light brighten and fade in his eyes. She could not imagine him intentionally hurting or savagely mutilating another. "Did he ever step out of character? You know, maybe drink too much or chase a few skirts?"

"Jim Armstrong? Heck, no. He was always on me about maintaining a good profile in the community, keeping the slate clean."

"How about the cases he was working. Anything that might attract the wrong kind of attention? Maybe somebody out to get him?"

He shook his head. "He had a knack for dealing with all kinds of people. Could strike up a conversation with the highest and the lowest. Never knew anybody to get his goat."

"Every cop has someone he crosses. There's got to be at least one of those."

"Not Jim. He was fair and he was honest. Everybody on the street had at least a bit of respect for him. That's what's so unbelievable about this. If somebody could do this to him, not one of us is safe."

As he became increasingly talkative, she listened for discrepancies in his stories, but, while at times the macho swagger of a cop showed itself in the reflective pool of alcohol, avarice never surfaced from the depths of the man.

The bottle of scotch was nearly empty and he was saying something about Jim's kids, about a soccer game they'd seen together, when she began to cry again. Hard as she tried she couldn't hold back her grief.

He pulled her to him and cradled her head against the rough fabric of his uniform. Standing in the rain had perfumed it with the musky aroma of damp wool Lisa had described.

She sat upright and trailed both hands down the front of his jacket, pausing now and then to wipe tears from her cheeks. "You're so kind. I hope your girlfriend appreciates you."

He shook his head. "No girlfriend."

"Will you be alone tonight?"

He nodded.

"Stay," she said, before she could quell the impulsion. "Stay with me tonight. I can't bear to be alone."

His eyes opened wider for a moment, then softened. "Sure," he said. "Sure."

They stood.

"Let me take your coat," she said. "It's still wet."

He shrugged free of his jacket and handed it to her.

She carried it to the closet. She felt him close behind her as she slid her hand over the plump quilted hanger that held her mother's sable coat. The fur slid to the floor. Her hand shook as she settled his jacket over the smooth silk. "There," she said as she breathed in his scent of aftershave and scotch.

His chest warmed hers. His cheek was dry against the wetness of hers.

She placed her palms against his shirt, slowly raised them to his neck until her body fit against his. His lips were warm and tasted of oaken kegs aged to tangy perfection. His hands moved with a smooth knowing that excited her. He pressed her to him as his tongue caressed the soft flesh of her lips.

Desire filled her with a suddenness that set her limbs trembling. She broke away, took one of his large hands in both of hers and led him to her bedroom.

Clothing slithered and fell to the floor. Sighs soothed the air. She pulled back her crimson sheets and waited. His weight settled on her. She rose to meet him. His supple body moved with none of the hurried movements she had expected from such a young man. She had forgotten the sinuousness of youth. She gave herself lustily up to it.

ᄋᢈ

Sated, they spoke for hours in the broken tones of lovers who know they will again become strangers with the light of day. In a haze of purple, she slept against his muscled back.

When she opened her eyes to brilliant yellow sunshine, his side of the bed was empty.

He left no note.

She was renewed by the unexpected pleasures she had found in what would have been a sleepless and painfully lonely night. And she had partially solved one small part of the puzzle of Jim.

In the afterglow of lovemaking, Max had told her of a pimp named Sammie who tattooed his name on the upper arms of his girls and of the serial killer who was picking off Sammie's harem one-by-one. She now knew where to begin her search.

She showered, donned athletic shoes, and power walked the six miles to the law school where she immersed her grief under mounds of student papers accumulated in her absence. It was late afternoon before she called home.

"Come for dinner, Clover," her mother said. "The Morton's will be here."

"Is the dress code in effect?"

"It's always in effect on Friday night."

"I'll politely decline," she said. "How's Lisa?"

"She's holding up. The children are keeping her focused. She'll want to see you."

"Tell her I'll be over right after dinner. I love you, Mom."

"I love you, too, dear. We'll all be happy to see you."

෴

Clover found her sister sitting on the sun porch watching the children play soccer under the security lights of the back lawn. She sat beside her. "What are you thinking?"

"That I'm alone. That I'll never find Jim's kind of love again."

"You have his children."

"Yes. But not him."

"Have you had any thoughts of why this might have happened?"

She shook her head. Her lips were pale, her face pure white in the fluorescent glow.

"He didn't give a hint, one small clue?"

"He wasn't talking much, Clover. He was withdrawn. No, not withdrawn… he was preoccupied." She looked away. "I was afraid. I thought he'd found a lover."

"Lisa!"

"Really. I really did. I drove out to the house because I was sure he'd lied to me. I didn't expect him to be there. I thought he was off with her somewhere." She hung her head. "I was checking up on him."

"Why?"

"Because he was acting weird. He was different than he'd ever been. He yelled at me." She looked up with red-rimmed eyes.

"Nobody has ever yelled at me." She played with a corner of the upholstered cushion. "Isn't that what you would think?"

"Did you really believe it? In your heart?"

Her eyes were very wide and very blue. "No," she whispered "Never. Not in my heart."

"There! See! You know he'd never have another woman. He could hardly handle you."

Her eyes brightened momentarily. "But something was on his mind."

"And we have to discover what that something was."

"Maybe his job." She waved in response to one of her daughters on the lawn.

"Was he upset about that?"

"Not upset. He was working on something. Something really important. Sometimes he'd be up, like everything was going great. Then, he'd get really quiet and sullen. When he got like that even the kids couldn't talk to him."

"When did that start?"

"About the time we began moving stuff to the new house. I thought he was worried about money. Or maybe he didn't like leaving all our good neighbors, like the Mortons. I mean…who knows…what goes on in a man's mind?"

"And before that he was okay?"

"Yeah. Well, sort of. He was spending a lot of time downtown. Late nights. Lots of sleazy stuff. He'd come home tired and beat and he'd say things like, 'Honey, you don't know how bad life can be. You don't know how lucky we've been'."

"What did he mean?"

"He never explained. He'd say this stuff, then, you know, he'd hold me…and pretty soon, you know…we'd didn't need to talk anymore."

"Sure," Clover smiled. "Didn't or couldn't?"

She giggled. "Couldn't. We'd get too busy."

"So you two were still 'busy' together, even though he was mad and sullen?"

"He wasn't always sullen, but he was stressing-out. Well who wouldn't stress out? Five kids, a new house, all the junk to move... all the expense. Everything costs money."

Yes, even barren wives cost money. The intrusive thought of her painful divorce surprised her. She wouldn't go there. She concentrated hard on Lisa and Jim. "What specifically made him mad?"

"The bedspread."

"Bedspread?"

"I saw it on sale. I wanted our new bedroom to be special. After all, it is the most important room in the house." Her lower lip began to tremble. "Jim had borrowed the Morton's truck. He ran over to Dad's to pick up a case of that wine they order from Oregon. He wanted to put it in the back of Dick's pickup before he returned it."

"Nice gift."

"Well you know how kind Elizabeth and Dick have been. We were going to have one last meal together. We were all so tired."

"I know. I went home exhausted and I only watched the kids. You guys did all the hard work."

"I decided to get some burgers and shakes from Tiny's. Mom stayed with the kids. The diner was busy, so while I waited for my order, I wandered over to that new linens place and picked up the bedspread."

Clover waited for her to continue.

"When I came back, Jim was standing at the living room window. He was clenching and unclenching his fists...and staring."

"At what?"

"Nothing. It was dark. He was staring at nothing."

"And?"

"I pulled the comforter out of the bag and I sneaked up behind him and I tried to kiss his neck." She began to shake with dry, wracking, tearless sobs.

Clover wanted to comfort her, but couldn't take a chance on interrupting her thoughts. She leaned forward.

"He started to yell. He yelled and yelled."

"What did he say?"

"Don't do that, Lisa! Don't ever do that again!" She laid her head against Clover's shoulder. "I tried to apologize. I showed him the bedspread."

"And?"

"He screamed, 'Not now, Lisa! I've got stuff on my mind! Big stuff!' He said that, Clover. He yelled it."

"What did you say?"

"I didn't say anything. I was so hurt. I turned around, grabbed the bag for the comforter, and I ran. I took it back to the store. I didn't mean to make him mad."

"Did he apologize?"

She shook her head. "He left a note. It said, 'Forgot something at the new house. Be back in a bit. I love you, Jim'.

I never saw him again." Tears streamed from her eyes.

Clover could hold back no longer. She had to comfort her sister. She wrapped her arms around her. "Shh. Shhh," she crooned. "Poor, Lisa…shh."

CHAPTER FIVE

The next evening, dressed in her oldest jeans, a faded sweat shirt, and a pair of scuffed athletic shoes, Clover slung a backpack over her shoulder and took the bus to the downtown station Max had said was the meeting place for Sammie's girls.

Once inside she bought a ticket for the last interstate departure, a Styrofoam cup of bitter coffee, and a racy tabloid.

She settled herself into a stained chair near the back of the room where she could observe the activities of the terminal.

Two rows from the front, a large man alternately stood and sat as he carried on a schizophrenic conversation with himself.

In the corner opposite the ticket counter a young couple intertwined in passionate good-byes.

At the very front, between the restrooms and the dim coffee shop, the pulse of the city's nightlife surged and ebbed – restroom to coffee shop, coffee shop to cigarette machine, cigarette machine to restroom.

Outside the smudged windows, city office workers scurried past with sightless eyes. They clung tightly to their briefcases as they hurried toward the safety of the suburbs where the clicking, clashing dances of cockroaches wouldn't be seen or heard.

Across the street men lined up for an overnight space in the Christian shelter.

As the suburban folks disappeared, the inside crowd became noisier and more unkempt. Money exchanged hands. Same sex pairs disappeared into restrooms. Party girls in sequined spandex perched on the pedestal seating of the coffee shop. Some of them eyed Clover.

She took on an air of innocence as she turned the pages of her tabloid.

An out-of-sync movement caught her attention. A fast moving woman, her oversized glasses barely visible under a mass of uncombed blonde curls, jerked the crowd apart with an umbrella stroller. Her shoulders drooped under the weight of two large bags. Her eyes darted rapidly back and forth across the crowded room. One bag's broken zipper allowed soiled baby clothing to hang precariously from its top. Glass bottles clanged together with each step she took.

In the worn pouch of the stroller an undersized toddler, his arms and legs folded protectively across his torso, sat ramrod stiff. His thin body swayed on the stained canvas like an Indian guru. His large, unblinking eyes moved neither right nor left as the woman cut through the mass of humanity.

With a savage thrust, the woman shoved the stroller into a corner, tossed both bags against its wheels and half-walked, half-ran into the restaurant behind her.

The child, frozen in his assigned position, kept his owl eyes focused on the blank wall. He did not whimper or cry at his abandonment.

Back in an instant, his mother shoved cigarettes and a small package into a bag, turned the stroller sloppily on one wheel, hoisted both bags back onto her shoulders, and scurried toward the street.

As his rigid body swung wildly in his tiny nest, the child neither blinked nor started.

Clover saw his alert eyes move over the crowd at the same time the word, Sammie, tattooed on the upper left arm of his mother came clearly into view. She stood to follow the woman and child, but was blocked by the schizophrenic man who picked that moment to jump to his feet and begin posturing.

A new girl stepped into the waiting area. About thirty pounds too heavy for her shorts suit, she hurried forward on stiletto heels.

As she stepped over Clover's pack, her white thighs jiggled. Dirty toes squeaked against the leather of her strapless shoes. Her body settled with a solid thump into a seat two chairs away. A Sammie tattoo adorned her upper arm.

Clover leaned toward her. "Are you looking for someone?"

The girl took her in with one piercing glance. "Are you selling?" She turned her attention back to the crowd.

"No."

"Then mind your own shit."

"I like your tattoo."

"Fuck you."

"I just saw someone who had one exactly like it."

The girl turned fully toward her. "A blonde with a kid?"

"Yeah."

"Was she here?"

"Here and gone. Just missed her."

She stood and peered out the window. "Shit!" She threw herself back into the chair.

A shiny black Lincoln backed into a bus space outside the big windows. A muscular black man stepped from the passenger door.

The girl slithered down into the seat. "If he sees me, I'm dead."

"Trouble?"

"My man. And I'm not supposed to be here."

Clover stood and moved between the girl and the window. "I'll block his view. You hit the restroom."

As the girl scurried away, Clover studied the man outside. His shirtless vest belied the cool fall weather and called attention to his hairless chest and abdomen. A plastic cap covered his kinky hair. Sunglasses covered his eyes. As he turned to raise a fisted salute to someone on the street, his black leather-covered buttocks exactly matched the bulging black tire at the back of his vintage continental. The muscles in his arm and back rolled slowly over strong bone.

He strode into the terminal. His eyes scanned the room. Apparently finding nothing of interest, he turned and strolled back to his car. As it pulled away Clover read its vanity plate: "Sam me".

❧

The restroom reeked of musk and urine. She peered under each scarred door, until she spotted the dirty toes and strapless heels of Sammie's girl. She tapped once. "He's gone."

"Wow, girl! You saved my frickin ass!" The girl moved to the smeared mirror to check her face.

Clover escaped the stinking room and returned to her seat. Her pack was gone. "Well, damn it!" she shouted. "Where's my pack? Who took my pack?"

A few disinterested faces turned. The schizophrenic man hefted a sand-filled butt-can and emptied it on the floor.

"Who?" he shouted, "Who?" He pushed Clover aside and ran from the building.

Sammie's girl came to her side. "For Christ's sake, quiet down. Have a smoke." She held out a crushed pack of cigarettes.

Clover shook her head. "This really pisses me off!"

"Ah, hell. It's my fault. If you hadn't helped me, it wouldn't have happened. I owe ya one."

"I wanted out of here tonight. Now I'll have to go back."

"I'm Sandra. How about I buy you a cup of coffee."

She followed her to the counter. The cup the waitress placed in front of her had a smear of lipstick on its rim. She stuck a stirring stick into the black liquid and swirled it slowly. "Name's Clover."

"Hah! Like in the Bible. 'On cloven hooves'. Meant the devil, didn't it?"

"Who reads the Bible?"

"I did. In a former life."

"Yeah. I guess we all have one of those. A former life."

Sandra dragged deeply on her cigarette, stubbed it out, tore open several packets of sugar and emptied the contents into her cup. "Too bad they all ain't good."

"Is your friend with the kid in trouble?"

"Ain't we all?" She scanned the room before lowering her voice. "But she's in the worst kind. She's messing with Sammie."

"And Sammie doesn't like to be messed with?"

"He can be nasty bad. He says that when Squeak gets hungry enough, she'll be back. But he knows that Squeak's my friend. If he catches me trying to save her ass, he'll beat the fuck out of me. He's been keeping me on a pretty tight string."

"Maybe I can help."

"Don't think you're big enough to beat up Sammie."

Clover laughed. "Wouldn't know where to begin. But maybe I could help you hook up with your friend."

"Why would you want to do that?"

"Cuz big guys like Sammie throwing their weight around piss me off. We women have to stick together."

"You a cop?"

She laughed again. "No. I'm definitely not a cop."

"You sound like a cop. You don't belong here, do you?"

"No."

"Well, I ain't gonna pry. If you ain't got no cop connections, I could use some help. Squeak has a telephone that she's at some times. If you could call her and make a connection, maybe I could get some money to her. I ain't got much, but at least she could feed the kid. She's on her own now and it ain't easy with a kid."

Clover nodded.

"Here." She pressed a matchbook into Clover's hand. "I got it memorized. I call her Squeak cause when she answers that phone she makes little peeping noises. That's how I know it's her. Tell her

Sandra wants to help. She'll talk. Tell her that I can meet her behind the Commerce Tavern about six on any Tuesday."

"How can I get back to you?"

"Same way. I'm always at the tavern at six unless I got a customer. I ain't got no phone."

She dialed the number many times that week. A few times kids answered, once a woman said, "hello", and promptly hung up, but never had she heard a peep from Squeak.

Saturday, after another sleeplessness night, the security of her mother's coat provided no relief from the restlessness of her soul. Drawn by a nagging intuition of something that she must have missed, she drove back to the clearing where they had found Jim's car.

The yellow taped perimeter now extended fifty yards into the surrounding trees. On the recently logged hillside, stumps of varying heights clung tenaciously to the earth. Tree limbs stood in tall piles waiting to be burned. Garbage lay dismally abandoned in a heap along the roadside. Clear Creek meandered through the down-slope of the illegal cut.

She stepped over the yellow tape and picked her way through the sheriff's flagged excavations. At the clearing's western edge a new power pole sprouted from a sand-filled base. The spot was inviting. She moved to the pole, leaned her back against it, and slid to a sitting position. The midmorning sun warmed her. She closed her eyes and laid her forehead on bent knees. He had been here many times. She felt his essence, his evil emanating from the pock-marked ground.

Relax. Count. Meditate. Think. Rhythm and number, three and one and three and one and tree and sun and tree and sun and three and one. Images rose slowly behind her closed eyes, trees and sun, tires and mud. Two then one. Walk don't run.

The call of a crow disturbed her concentration. She began again. One and two, one and two, sun and shoe, fun and goo, gun and zoo.

The crow called again.

She opened her eyes, leaned back, and gazed at the top of the pole. Start from the top. She closed her eyes again and visualized the pole. Ten and nine, shoe and shine, climb and line, climb and climb.

A new sound began. She snapped forward. A vehicle approached the clearing. She measured the distance between herself and the trees, jumped to her feet, and scampered into dark undergrowth.

The naked lady van pulled crosswise to her car blocking her exit. Plumber Casey. She watched him step out. His tight jeans and bright blue shirt showed off the width of his shoulders and the narrowness of his waist. He seemed a different man than the one in the coveralls and camouflage. He turned to study the road behind him, before bending at his waist to peer into the open window of her car. His back and buttocks were well muscled and firm. He could easily have overpowered Jim. He straightened, shaded his eyes with one hand and seemed to look straight at her. She closed her eyes and held her breath.

"Clover?" he called. "Clover?"

Friend or foe, stay or go?

"Clover?"

Friend, she decided. She stepped into the clearing.

"Hi," he called. His voice was surprisingly light for a man suspected of murder.

She walked closer without speaking. He was freshly shaven. His eyes matched the blue of his shirt. She breathed deeply. The sight and scent of an attractive man never failed to soften her mood.

He folded his arms and leaned against her car. "I'm glad I ran into you. I didn't really thank you for your help."

"It's a weakness of mine."

"Yeah?"

"Let's just say I know what it's like to be left standing alone."

"If it hadn't been for you, I'd be sitting alone – in jail."

She smiled.

"Truck's gone," he said.

"I thought it would be."

"Looks like they've hauled off everything they found."

"Yeah. No use looking for anything new."

"Why are you here?"

She shrugged and met his eyes. "I hoped that there would be some clue here, that I might find something. Sometimes if I chant and concentrate really hard I see things more clearly."

"Yeah?"

She followed his gaze to the spot where the truck had been. "He had to have had help."

He rocked heel to toe on his boots. "Not necessarily."

"No?"

"I think he hiked to the house from here. Alone."

She stared at him, unbelieving. "In the dark? In the rain?"

"Yes."

"Really?"

"It's a possibility. He could have parked here, hiked up to the house, killed the guy, took his truck, drove it here and torched it, then drove back to town in his own vehicle. No one the wiser."

"You seem to be awfully sure."

He studied her face. "If you think I did it, you're wrong. I've been wracking my brain since they accused me. The guy, that Jim, seemed pretty nice, for a cop. And he wasn't on edge. He didn't act like someone who was afraid of being snuffed."

"You were the last person to see him alive."

"No. The killer was the last. I just happened to be there near the end. He trusted me in the house. Said to lock up when I was done. Maybe if I'd stayed longer it wouldn't have happened."

"I'm not sure I believe you."

He turned away and scuffed his foot into the moist earth. "My luck is like that. Always has been. I blunder into things. Like I'm star-crossed or something."

She stared up at him for a full minute. "Me too."

"Then you might in time believe me?"

She nodded.

"Well, that makes two on my side."

"One and two, one then two."

"What?"

"Something that just came to me. Who's the other one?"

"Maggie."

"Maggie's a good judge of character."

"Even Jenny has doubts. And her parents! Wahoo. Now there's a pair that has me bound for the electric chair."

"I'm sure the Linds can be difficult."

He flashed a grim smile. "Jenny was such a trip when I first met her. Funny. Crazy. A blast to be with. Now everything has changed. Maybe it's because she's so pregnant, her hormones or something. I don't know."

"It's difficult to live under someone else's roof." She moved closer. "Even harder if you have to depend on them. Even when they're generous and kind, it can be tough."

"Do you women get weird when you're pregnant? I mean fly off the handle and criticize everything?"

A shaft of pain pierced her heart. "No experience."

"Me either. Virgin in a whore house."

"How long would it take to hike to the lake?"

His eyes followed the line of trees that ran up the hills to a high ridge. "There's a trail, goes up past the old logging camp and into the old growth. Man in good shape can easily run it. Want to take a look? "

She checked her watch. "Why not?"

She was surprised at the well-used condition of the trail. "Who keeps this up? "

"My club does a little maintenance. We use this area a lot for maneuvers."

"The survivalist group. You like that stuff?"

"Keeps me in shape. It's a lot of fun."

"Are you good at it?"

"Fair. Well...maybe fifty-fifty. No, actually I get hit so often the guys have nicknamed me 'crucified Casey'."

Clover laughed. He was refreshingly honest. "How long have you been at the Lind's?"

"Nearly six months."

"How long will you be staying?"

"Until the baby's born and probably then some. Jenny's so damn scared, and my business hasn't been the best yet. Guess I should be grateful they'd take us in."

"The Linds were old when they had Jenny. They've always doted on her. They must be pretty hard to please."

"They've made it clear that I'm not good enough for her. Things get pretty tense at times."

"Even people who like each other have problems living side by side, day after day."

"So you're not married?"

"Divorced."

"Thought so."

"Why?"

"You act like it."

"Act like what?"

"Like a woman scorned."

"Hey, now . . . ."

He laughed. "Got you! It's not as bad as it sounds. Only that it seems like women get tougher after a divorce, more independent, feistier."

She liked his laugh. It was easy and heartfelt. "And you've so much experience with women?"

"Women like me. They like to talk to me. Actually, as a plumber, I'm pretty much a captive audience, like a hairdresser or something. I get caught with my head under a sink and pretty soon the woman of the house is spilling her guts. I get to hear all about their problems, their love lives. Grunt once in awhile. That's all it takes. Seems like the plumbing is always the first thing that goes after a man walks off the premises."

"Well, I haven't had any plumbing problems yet."

"Give it time."

They were laughing again as they topped the first ridge where the path became wider and opened into a large meadow.

"What is this place?"

"This is where the office of the old logging camp used to be back during the Second World War. They cut at least a five-mile swath of prime forest and used the wood to build army barracks. See." He pointed toward the valley floor and across to the next ridge. "The green is a different color over there. Second growth. Forty-to-fifty-year-old firs and scrub alder. The bigger, darker stuff is old growth. Worth big bucks. Was only saved because the war ended."

"Was it a big camp?"

"I dunno. Have to ask Maggie. She grew up here. Her dad was a foreman, or something. The Lind's make a party of talking about Maggie."

"Seems like my dad said there were quite a few buildings in that camp."

"Yeah. I think some of them were big jobs, you know, for the loggers. Most of the old foundations are left and a couple of old wells."

"How'd they get the logs out?"

"Pulled them over the ridge to Long Lake. Floated them down river and out to the bay."

"Who owns it now?"

"Government, I suppose. This piece backs up to the National Forest. Pretty sure this part is Federal. Along the lake it's private. Maggie owns most of it and some rich bitches own the rest. If you look really hard, you can make out Maggie's place, way over there." He pointed and narrowed his eyes. "See it?"

"Yeah. The red roof high up on that hill."

"That's it. You've got eagle eyes. I think this is one of the few places on the trail that you can see that far. Kind of neat, eh?"

She nodded. She knew who owned the rest of Long Lake. Mom and Dad had bought up most of the acreage years ago and had gifted lakefront lots to both she and Lisa, but she had never been much interested in her piece. Unlike the rest of her family, she had never been comfortable in the woods and had an unreasonable fear of night in the outdoors. She needed light, lots of light. She preferred spiky heels to hiking boots, frilly dresses to raingear, and the comforts of good food served on china rather than tin. Her family had never forced her to accompany them on their frequent campouts, but fully expected that one day she would build a home next to Lisa's.

She concentrated on her foot placement as they picked their way through prickly brush, large boulders, and scrub trees.

"Be real careful," he said. "Here's the first of the wells." He stood before a rock-lined square covered with rotting timbers. "Probably had a shed over it when the place was open, but it rotted away years ago. Someone tried to make it safer with the timbers, but even they're pretty thin now. Listen." He picked up a small stone and tossed it between the open boards. It was a long time before she heard the splash of water.

"Dangerous," she said.

"This one is the deepest, probably used as a water source for the steam engines that ran the machinery. There're two others farther up. Edges are smooth river rock and they're a lot shallower, like holding dams. I've hidden over the edge of one. I got caught and shot both times, so decided it's not worth the chance of getting in so far that I might not be able to climb out."

He took her hand as he threaded his way through the crumbling maze to pick up the trail.

She moved closer to him.

"We start climbing again, now, but not for long. The rest of the camp is a little way up."

"How do you remember the way?"

"I use the creek. Listen."

She stopped. She could hear the slow trickle of water.

"It runs year round. Runs really fast after a rain. As long as you keep it on your left, you're heading towards Long Lake. Of course, you have to remember to keep moving upstream. When I can't use the creek, I use the size of the trees. Old growth is all to the west of the creek, new growth is to the east. Even on really dark nights, if you can see the sky you can tell where you are.

They came to more stone foundations. Alders sprouted between the rocks. They passed the remains of a very large building. "Probably the mess hall," he said.

They skirted another shallow well before the trail became steeper. The sun's warmth and the increased exertion caused them to breathe heavily. Near the top, the trail narrowed to a tiny pathway and a valley opened up below them. Maggie's cabin was easily visible now. Clover could see the old truck parked on the driveway and the stony ridge behind the cabin where the land fell off steeply toward the lake and Jim's new house.

K.C. pointed in that direction. "See. The timber was pulled up from the valley with winches and steam engines over a bed of logs. The old logs of the roadway are rotted away, but you can go down in the valley there, between Maggie's hill and this one and you'll find the skid way. There's another old trail from town down there. It comes out behind Jenny's house."

"What's that small building by the creek?"

"That's my club's cabin."

"How far is it from the cabin to town?"

"Oh," he shaded his eyes and gazed over the tops of the big trees. "Three, maybe four miles."

"And how far to Maggie's?"

"If you go down to the cabin, then up to Maggie's, it's about one, no, maybe a half mile. If you go from here and stay on this trail, you'll follow the ridge behind the cop's place. Then if you go up the hill to Maggie's you add another mile."

"Which way should we go now?"

"How long has this much taken us?"

She checked her watch. "About an hour. If we stay on this trail, how much longer to Jim's?"

"Thirty minutes, or so."

"Should we go over that way?"

"It's not a good idea for me to be around there."

"If someone were to jog the trail, how quickly do you think they could do it?"

"We've been sightseeing. If we were in a big hurry, we could probably do it in forty, maybe forty-five minutes. That is, if you're in as good a shape as you look to be."

She warmed to his compliment. "So it could be jogged in pretty good time."

"Somebody who knew the trail well? Yeah."

"So Jim's killer could have come up this way."

"I think he did. Except for right where we're standing, he'd be hidden from view. Only Maggie would see him on this stretch of the trail. If he stayed in the brush, he'd never be seen."

"So where do we go from here?"

"Let's go down to my club's cabin and then make our way up to Maggie's. Maybe she'll look kindly on us and give us a lift back to the clearing."

From her cabin window, Maggie caught sight of bright blue on the trail above the survivalist's cabin. The sudden movement in the forest jarred a chord of memory. Well maybe it hadn't been last week. Seemed a long time before. No. It was last week. Maybe two days before the murder, and in exactly the same spot. Standing right there, later in the day. Much later. Sun had already faded behind the big trees. Had been watching eagles ride the thermals above the valley, caught some movement on the ridge. Must be a deer on the old trail. But it wasn't a deer. It was a man caught momentarily in the eye of the scope. A man in brown, all brown. He'd disappeared into the trees.

Now she sat in the sheepskin-covered rocker and focused her scope on the pair as they picked their way down the rocky face of the eastern ridge. Plumber K.C. and the beautiful Clover. Odd couple to be off in the woods together. She watched until they reached the survivalist's cabin, then hurried to put on the coffee and to pull out the pretty cookies she had frosted by the dawn's early light.

She ran a comb through her hair and checked her shirtfront for stains. "There, my dear, you are presentable enough for company." The medicine cabinet mirror had heard many such declarations in the past fifty years.

They were coming. "Oh, dear. I need a clean cloth on that table." She hurried to the drawer and pulled out a fresh white cloth.

༄

When they reached the survivalist's cabin, K.C. realized that he was indeed very hungry. He fired up the stove and pulled a package of bacon from the propane refrigerator.

Clover mixed instant pancake batter in a tin bowl and lay strips of bacon in an iron pan while K.C. flipped pancakes.

They laid out enameled plates and mugs.

The cabin warmed quickly. She pulled her light sweater over her head and tossed it onto an empty chair.

When K.C. finished his meal, he kicked off his boots.

"I feel like a real pioneer," Clover laughed. "Weary, footsore, happy and very well fed." She pushed back her chair, picked up her used utensils, and reached for his.

"You don't look like a pioneer," he said. "You look like a very attractive, well-nourished modern woman."

She picked up his plate and stacked it on hers. "Thank you."

His face reddened.

She laughed at his embarrassment, threw her hair lightly back with a graceful swing of her head and held her hand out for his cup.

He was flustered by her sudden gesture and blushed again.

"What?" she asked.

His blush deepened to include his neck. "It's pretty hard for me to keep my eyes to myself," he said. "I've never seen a woman look so good without a bra."

Her smile widened as she carried the dishes to the sink. She tossed him a sponge to wipe the table.

He caught the sponge in midair, dropped it onto the table, leaned back and studied her. "Honestly, Clover, I'm having a hard time keeping my hands to myself."

She liked his openness. Honesty appealed to her. She stepped to him. "Well," she said, "if you're having that much trouble, I'd say give in."

He reached out one large hand and brushed her breast so gently that she sensed only the slightest of breezes, a bare breath of movement.

She moved closer and studied him. His eyes were closed. A small smile pulled his lips into an attractive curve. His skin was tan and very smooth. She liked this guy. She really liked him. She reached down, lifted his free hand and cupped it over her breast.

He sighed.

She swayed closer.

His hands slid to her waist. His lips brushed each nipple in turn.

Slowly, ever so slowly, she reached down and pulled her tee shirt over her head.

His hands encircled her bare waist and pulled her closer. His lips teased, fluttered lightly over her breasts and navel.

She moaned, ran her fingers through his hair, raked her fingernails gently over the back of his neck and grasped the folds of his shirt. She arched her back as his lips raised gooseflesh on her soft belly. She lifted his shirt to his shoulder blades.

He raised his arms and helped her free him from the shirt, then stood and pulled their bare torsos together. With one large arm he held her to him, while his other willful hand caressed her bare shoulders, her soft hair, the back of her trembling neck.

She tilted her head and raised her lips.

His kiss was wonderfully warm, soft and quietly demanding.

She raised her hands over his shoulders, pulled his head down to hers and opened her lips so she could taste him.

He groaned, glided his hand over her buttocks. Pressed her against his hardness.

She yielded, matched her hip movements to his.

He traced kisses across her face, light feathery kisses, warm teasing kisses. "I have to have you," he said.

"Yes," she whispered. If her body would never give her children, it could at least give her bliss.

∽

Maggie sighed when she saw the smoke rise from the chimney below. Kids. Never could count on them. With patience born of a solitary life, she sank back into her rocker, listened to the chug of the coffeepot, and closed her eyes. Her rocker soon moved to the rhythm of the perking pot. Give them time. Give them time. Sooner or later they would come climbing up her hill.

∽

He ran one warm hand over her tawny skin. "Solar shower out back, want to try it?"

She pressed comfortably along the full length of him, raised one knee and rubbed it gently over his hip and thigh. "Not sure I've had enough indoor play yet."

He laughed softly. "I think it might take me all day to give you enough."

"Might. But I suppose we'd better get going. We'll have to get you home before someone comes looking for you."

"I've tried to be faithful to Jen."

"You're doing okay."

"After this?"

She wasn't sure why she had seduced him. She supposed she was trying to get even with Jenny for all the grief she'd given her in high school. Maybe. Maybe she had become expert at recognizing good lovers. It didn't matter. She smiled, kissed the tip of his nose. "I'd classify this as a friendly interlude. I wouldn't consider it infidelity."

"Depends on how you look at it."

"Nobody else needs to look at it. This is something unplanned and great fun. Why analyze it?" She snuggled against him, ran the tip of one finger across his face, traced his nose and cheekbones. She tasted his lips again. And again. She felt his response against her belly.

He entered her with the slowness of a seasoned lover.

"You aren't going to tell me that Jenny Lind taught you all this."

His laugh was muffled as he buried his lips in her hair.

"No. But we had something like this before she got pregnant and before we moved in with her folks. Now she won't let me near her."

She shifted her weight and slid away from him, scampered out of his reach.

He lunged for her but missed. "You don't want to talk about Jenny."

She shook her head. "Doesn't seem appropriate. But if you want to join me in the shower, I bet we could finish this on the grass."

Maggie opened her eyes. The smoke had lightened from the chimney below. They should be on their way soon. She trained her birding scope on the cabin door and watched with concern when no one appeared. She was about to pull on her shoes and trudge down the steep trail to check on them, when they suddenly emerged into the back yard of the cabin. They were quite naked, quite playful. She watched long enough to know that the encounter was mutually acceptable, before she turned the birding scope to the wall. Children. Naughty, naughty children.

She had dozed off again when the dogs began their warning barks. She stood by the window and watched the pair climb the last stretch of hill before the cabin.

They paused momentarily while he checked Clover's hair and brushed some unseen evidence from her jeans. As they neared the edge of the yard they walked side by side, she with her hair still damp from the shower and he with the look of a dew-freshened poppy. They greeted her cheerily.

She waited for some show of embarrassment, some lies of explanation. There were no excuses for their sudden and sodden appearance at her door.

She liked these two, she decided. She would take them under her wing for they were very much like her. "Well, my goodness! What a nice surprise," she cried. "Come in. There's fresh coffee and I've made some cookies. Come in!"

She settled them at her white covered table and hovered over them until Clover, despite a renewed appetite, remembered her manners and stopped eating after three cookies.

"Maggie, come sit down. We're fine. These cookies are wonderful. Come sit and have some coffee too."

Maggie sat. The two women watched as K.C. finished the entire plate of cookies and two cups of coffee.

"Hiking sure did give you an appetite," Maggie said.

"I don't think it's the hike," he said. "I think it's how good the cookies are. Man, I just ate them all."

"K.C. and I came up from the clearing where the truck was," Clover offered. "We decided that it would be possible for someone to hike into Jim's house. We think he could make pretty good time if he were in good shape. He could have left his own car in the clearing and then driven Jim's back down. What do you think?"

"I think you young people are right on the money. I did see someone on the trail behind the Armstrong's a few days before all this trouble. I've been racking my brain, trying to figure out which day it was, but I still haven't been able to put a date on it. A man it was. And dressed all in brown, like a uniform or work clothes."

"Survivalist." K.C. offered.

"No. Not camouflage. Matching pants and shirt, but I saw only the back of him before he dropped down the trail towards the other ridge."

"Do you think it was the same guy you saw leave Jim's?"

"I don't know. Both times were so quick. And my eyes aren't what they were. Oh, if only I weren't such a silly old woman! The dogs wanted to go when Jim was hurt. If I'd been a few years younger, I would have let the dogs go and I would have followed them. It was me that stopped them."

"Maggie," Clover took the old woman's hand. "If you had gone over there, you would have been a victim too. Nobody would have expected you to go. If you had been hurt we wouldn't know anything about how Jim died and we'd have very little hope of finding the person who killed him."

"Oh, dear. You don't know how I've been kicking myself. I sat right here and watched that evil man drive away. But, I thought he was Jim. I really did. He was the same size and the same build and he was wearing Jim's jacket."

"His jacket? He wore Jim's jacket?"

Maggie nodded. "One of those football ones, college probably. He did play football, didn't he?"

"Yes, in high school," Clover said softly. "He was so proud of that jacket. But I hadn't seen him wear it in years."

"Well he wore it the day long. I know because I watched them all. They were working so hard. The movers brought the biggest stuff. Then pretty little Lisa and the kids arrived with their car stuffed full. And then the Billingsleys. Oh, and the Mortons. Well, no, not both the Morton's, only Elizabeth. Elizabeth rode with the Billingsleys. She brought a big basket. I thought it must be lunch because everyone disappeared inside.

Now that I think of it, Jim drove Dick's bigger truck and the Billingsley's drove his smaller truck. Later, Lisa and Elizabeth left in her van. They didn't return.

After they and the Billingsleys left, the telephone company came in, then the plumber." She smiled, "I mean you, K.C. I didn't know you then, but I saw you come and go. And then Jim left. After that, for a long time, the place was deserted. Then along came Jim again, and the rest you know."

"And you don't think anyone stayed at the house. You didn't see anyone drive in?"

"No. I'm sure of it. No one else came or went. Unless, of course, you two are right and someone hiked in through the woods."

"Everything seems to fit." K.C. said. "Now we can be pretty sure how he got in, but I wish we could figure out why."

CHAPTER SIX

Clover sat on her crimson couch and tapped in the telephone number again. "Squeak?

Silence on the other end. Then a small voice. " Cheep, cheep, cheep."

"Is this Squeak?"

"Who are you?"

"A friend of Sandra. She asked me to call. She wants to help, but needs to meet you."

"I can't meet nobody. I got my kid to think about." Her voice held the insistence and rhythms of an old telegraph.

"She says she can give you a little money."

"Is this a trick?"

"No."

"Sounds like a trick. Is Sammie with you?"

"No. Honest. Sandra says to meet her behind the Commerce Tavern any Tuesday night around six o'clock."

"I got a problem with that."

"She said Sammie's busy other places on Tuesday. She said she wanted to give you some money, to feed the baby. Does that fit?"

"Maybe. See if this fits. You go to the Commerce, pick up the money and I'll meet you."

"When?"

"Today's Tuesday. Ain't it?"

"Where?"

"You get the money then you call me. I'll be here."

"What if she won't trust me with the money?"

"Ya do drugs?"

"No. Do you?"

"Not so much. Anymore. Since I had the baby. You sure you're not hurtin for a fix?"

"Not a user."

"Good. Hurtin people can't be counted on. Call me later." She clicked off the phone.

༄

Clover had only a few hours to find a suitable car. Her convertible would stand out on the street. She needed to blend in.

The cowboy, Roger Parrish, owned some kennels. She pulled out the directory and searched the yellow pages.

Parrish Kennels and Stables, Registered Shepherds, Arabian show horses. Guard Dogs. Obedience Training.

Hah! That was the gist of it, if she were as obedient as a dog, he would like her a whole lot better. Well, she needed his truck and she could not be shy about it. She donned the Shakey's Bar and Grill jacket she had found in a thrift store and smiled at her image in the mirror. She could pass for a street kid.

༄

His house, a one level ranch with a wide porch that overlooked a green pasture, reminded her of Montana. She pulled to one side of the drive. The howling of dogs from a series of low wooden buildings greeted her.

Parrish's old truck stood under a carport. Several signs repeated the message introduced at the top of the drive. **Private Property. Guard dogs on duty. Honk your horn. Do not leave your vehicle.**

The large shepherd, Duke, bared his teeth in a dangerous smile at her window. She laid her hand firmly on the horn.

He stepped from the house, strolled down the wide porch stairs, and, with an almost imperceptible hand signal sent the dog into the house. "Well, if it isn't Miss Lawyer herself," he drawled. "What brings you all the way out here?"

"The need for a favor."

"Really?"

"Do you mind if I get out? It's rather difficult to talk up to you."

He snickered. "I'm sure it is." He opened her door, bowed facetiously and motioned her out.

She obeyed as rapidly as the dog.

"Can I offer you some tea?"

"Yes. I'd love some."

He turned and strode to the porch without looking back.

She followed.

"You have a nice place here," she tried. "Peaceful. Except for the dogs."

"I can take care of that." He whistled a high piercing wail. The din stopped immediately.

"You seem to have a way with animals."

"I believe in well trained dogs."

"Women, too?"

He turned. His face became unearthly still as if all his forces were congealed into one strong emotion. His eyes burned into hers.

For a moment she hesitated, measured the distance to her car.

To his credit, he realized that she had answered flippantly and with good humor. A wide, genuine grin softened his face. "Slick mouth on you."

"It fires before the brain."

He held the door wide and allowed her to enter first.

"Do you live alone?" she asked.

"No. I have lots of dogs and horses."

"I can see that."

"Does that seem strange to you?"

"No. I live alone. Completely. No dogs. No horses."

His look said you would, but he smiled again and held a kitchen chair for her. "Would you prefer a mixed drink?"

"Tea. I would love some tea."

"Good. I have a pot ready. I was about to sit down and have some."

To her surprise he placed a tray with a white china pot, lemon slices and tiny sugar cubes on the table.

"Were you expecting someone?"

"No...Oh, the tea things. Sometimes Maggie stops about now. I thought you were her, until you beeped. Maggie never beeps, she isn't afraid of dogs."

"I don't think she's afraid of much." She watched as his rough hands carefully poured the hot tea. His fingertips were darkened with the soil from his land. He was relaxed and sure of himself as he handed the full cup across the table.

"This isn't a social call, is it?"

She tried the tea. Too hot. "Not exactly. I'd like to borrow your truck. I'll only need it for a few hours."

He stirred three cubes of sugar into his cup, lifted the spoon to his lips and tasted. "I'm not in the habit of loaning out my truck. Especially to strangers."

"I know that it's brazen of me to ask, but I'll trade you my car. Only for tonight."

"You're little puddle-jumper is not quite my style. I don't think my knees will fit under the wheel."

"It's about Jim. I have to meet someone in town and my car is too flashy."

He pushed his chair back and appraised her coolly. "And after I give you my car, will you ask for anything else."

"Now that you ask, yes. I'd like to work with you. I need some help with this case. I have a plan."

His laugh rocked the small kitchen. "What's in it for me?"

"Finding the man you've been hunting."

"Why me?"

"You're strong. You're smart. You have connections with Sheriff Swenson."

"This isn't a woman's game."

"I'm not playing games, Mr. Parrish. I'm deadly serious about this. I intend to find this man."

"How do you know it's a man? Many a woman has threatened to cut off my balls."

"Maggie saw him. She saw a man on the trail above Jim's house a few days before the murder."

"Survivalist. Paint-ball jockeys are always up there."

"Maybe. But I hiked the trail today. It's not a bad climb, from the clearing where Jim's truck was burned, to the house. I think the guy was checking his timing because he was planning to murder Jim."

"Why would he plan it?"

"Because Jim was getting closer to him. Because Jim would be able to identify him as the man who is murdering all those prostitutes."

"You've done your homework. Why would you need me around?"

"I need a partner. Actually, I need a pimp."

"A what?"

"A pimp. I need a man who is streetwise enough to play the role. I'm going to walk the streets until I find this jerk."

"So, you're going to be turning tricks on the seat of my pickup?"

She laughed more easily now. He hadn't laughed at her or discarded any part of her plan. "No. Tonight I'm going to make my first contact on the strip. I have a line on a pimp named Sammie who had been working with Jim. Apparently Sammie has lost so many girls it's putting a dent in his profits. Jim was getting somewhere. I believe he found the killer, but the guy knew it. I want to talk to the girls, find out what information they share, and get to know their johns. Roger, I think I know this guy. I think you know him too. I think Jim trusted him, but got caught being a nice guy. I think he lives out here."

"What makes you believe that?"

"For all these years, Lisa, Jim and I were like this." She twisted her fingers together and held them up as tears filled her eyes. "I know he wouldn't have allowed himself to be trapped, if he didn't somehow disbelieve what he had learned. I think he agreed to meet the guy at his house. I'm going to find him."

He reached into his jean pocket, retrieved a set of keys, and placed them on the table between them.

❦

She circled the bar twice before she found a dimly lit parking space three blocks away. As she climbed the steep hill overlooking Commencement Bay, loitering men whistled in appreciation of her tight black pants.

"Hey, honey," someone called. "If I had the money, you wouldn't be walking long."

She forced a smile, lifted her shoulders, and hurried on. Her breath came in short gasps. Her forehead tightened. A heightened sense of danger quickened her pulse and triggered every nerve in her body. She grew faint as she reached the concrete steps of the Commerce Bar and Grill. She stopped to take several slow breaths. She stepped into the room.

A country cowboy crooned from speakers along one wall. Body odor, stale beer, and cigarettes perfumed the air. Every eye turned toward her.

As she moved down the length of the bar several men laughed and tried to pat her leather pants. She beat at their hands and giggled. "Stop it. I'm looking for someone."

Sandra stood up from a booth.

"Sandra, you she-devil. What are you doing here with all these good-looking men? Ain't you got no sense?"

Sandra grabbed the sleeve of her jacket and dragged her into the booth.

Clover fell onto the vinyl seat. "Jesus," she mumbled.

"Hey, Sandra," someone called from the bar, "does you girl-friend sell it too?"

"Shut up ya stupid ape."

"I need a drink," Clover gasped.

"What kind?"

"Anything. Something. Seven and seven."

The girl called it to the bartender.

The glass felt greasy in her sweating palm. She touched it to her lips, realized some were still watching, so upended the glass and drank fully.

She turned to Sandra. "So? What's up?"

Sandra's laugh boomed. "You're a real shit, ya know?"

"Yeah, well what did you expect?"

"I didn't expect you to show up here."

"Aren't you going to ask me why?"

"I'd guess you made contact with Squeak."

"I did. But before I tell you about that, I need some help."

"I ain't got no money, honey."

"I want to meet Sammie."

"Why?"

"Jim Armstrong was family."

"Dead man."

"Yes. And I think the guy who killed him is the same one who's been knocking off girls down here. I think I'll know him when I see him." She hurried on, "I want to walk the street with you."

"You're crazy."

"Maybe."

"Definitely. Look at you. You're white as a sheet and shaking all over. You wouldn't last a night on the street. And Sammie will never go for it. Ya think he's going to pimp for you? You think he'd make room for a newbie like you? You think I'd make room for competition. There ain't enough business out there, sweetie."

"I got my own guy. But I still need Sammie's help. Do you want to help Squeak and her kid, or not?"

"You can get to her?"

"Yeah. Will you hook me up with Sammie?"

"You go and you keep your mouth shut, and I'll try. You got a number?"

She wrote in on a bar matchbook. Sandra handed her a roll of bills.

"Thanks, Bitch." She tucked the bills into her bra.

Two guys trailed her from the bar. Her knees buckled as she climbed into the cab of the truck, but once she'd locked the door she began to laugh. She felt more alive and powerful than she had in years.

❧

Roger Parrish wasn't sure why he'd agreed to lend the gal his truck. Something about her plan made sense and she'd been resourceful enough to set it in motion on her own. He liked independent women, especially when they were as good looking as Clover Winters. Not that there was a chance in hell a Billingsley would lower themselves to his economic level. Still, she wasn't born a blue blood and she *had* shown a certain degree of street smarts.

Duke had taken a shining to her, hadn't growled and paced, and had stayed by her side at the table. Dogs were smarter about people than people were smart about people, but he had an idea that Clover Winters could be pretty smart about them too.

Maybe he shouldn't have allowed her to go alone tonight. No, his presence would stop the gal's bonding process cold. This much he knew, if Clover Winters could make a connection with the scrappy women on the strip, she had what it would take to make her plan work.

He was quite familiar with Sammie from his days on the force, although it had been at least six years since he'd had any contact with him. Would Sammie take advantage of the woman? Would he even consider letting her talk with his girls, let alone walk with them? If he was desperate enough to not lose any more women, he might give the plan a try.

Guess he'd wait a few days before he'd take a drive to the strip on his own. Sammie had lost enough sales force to consider the plan. A serial killer preying on prostitutes was never good for a pimp's business.

∽

A bold red sign advertised the lack of cash kept on Quick Mart premises. Clover pulled in at an angle. When she turned off the ignition, the windows instantly fogged. She restarted the engine. She'd have to keep it running to be able to see the girl. She leaned her back against the door and studied the parking lot.

Sammie's black Lincoln cleared the curb and cruised slowly toward her. It stopped with its high beams trained on the dumpster near the building. She sat up straighter and prepared to slide the gearshift lever into reverse.

The car turned and drove past.

She ducked her head against the rain and jackrabbited into the store. There were no customers in the narrow aisles. No woman, no baby. She paid for two candy bars and a cold pop.

As she returned to the truck, she saw movement between the dumpster and the recycling bins. She started the engine. Another movement from the dumpster. A newspaper fanned repeatedly. She drove slowly toward it.

Owl eyes came out of the darkness.

She could make out the stroller and several bags heaped against it. She leaned over and threw open the door. "Get in. Quick."

"I can't. The kid." The girl's hair dripped water onto the seat.

"Give him to me. Throw the stroller in the back."

Squeak thrust a stiff plastic bundle into Clover's outstretched arms and heaved the bags onto the floor.

Clover caught a flash as the stroller sailed through the air and into the pickup bed.

The girl brought the smell of cigarettes, sour milk and mold into the truck's interior. "What the hell were you thinkin? Parkin so close to the front door? I couldn't come out. I'd be dead meat out there." She took the bundle from Clover and laid it on the seat between them.

"I didn't know where you'd be."

"Can we get out of here? I saw Sammie cruisin for me. No tellin where he is now."

Clover backed the truck around and turned up the heater fan.

Squeak spread her hands over the blowing air and shook her wet hair. A cascade of raindrops spotted the windshield. "God, this is nice." The skin of her neck shone sickly white. She was thin. Frighteningly thin. The knuckles of her pale fingers appeared too large for her tiny hands. Her cheeks were sunken and contained an unhealthy flush.

"Are you hungry?"

"I'm always hungry." She lay back on the seat. "This is heaven."

As Clover pushed the candy and pop toward her, the bundle between them began to move. The girl picked it up and slowly unwrapped the toddler.

He studied Clover with an intensity that unnerved her. "He stares like an alien," she blurted.

The girl's laugh was as harsh and grating as a crow's call. "Maybe he is one. Don't know where he came from." She tore open both candy bars and began to eat. "I thought sure he was Sammie's, but he didn't come out with enough blackness to be his." She downed the pop in five swallows. "He's smarter than Sammie anyways, knows when to keep mouth shut. Knows we're on the lam. You got anything else to eat?"

Clover spotted a fast food drive through. She pulled in. "What do you want?"

"You buyin?"

"Yeah."

"You got my money? You ain't buyin with my money, are you?"

Clover pulled the roll from her bra and handed it over. "What do you want to eat?"

"A shake. A great big chocolate shake."

"How about a hamburger?"

"Yeah. A burger with the works and fries. A big extra large order of fries. And a shake."

"What about the boy?"

"He only likes milk."

"You have milk?"

"No."

Clover ordered two cartons of milk for the boy and a coffee for herself.

Squeak rummaged through one of the bags, found a cloudy plastic bottle, and poured in the milk. Her hands shook half of the liquid onto her jeans as she twisted a rubber nipple into place.

The boy leaned back on the seat and sucked eagerly.

Squeak took a few bites of the burger, swallowed a handful of fries, and began to search her bag again. She located some macerated pieces of aluminum foil, wrapped the remains of the food carefully, tucked them in among the empty bottles, placed her shake on the dash, pulled a grimy towel from the second bag and began to dry her hair over the heater vent.

"Where are you staying?" Clover asked.

The girl's laugh was boisterous. "Honey, you can drop me anywhere. Home is where I end up. I ain't particular."

"You don't have a room?"

"Nope. Been on the run since summer. Things were fine until this damn rain started."

"What about the shelters?"

"You can bet your sweet ass, Sammie checks every one of them every night. I'd be a sittin duck."

"How about a motel? Just for tonight? You can't stay out in this weather with the boy."

"Let's see what Sandra came up with." She tore open the envelope. A stack of bills fell into her hand. "Ones. Jesus. All ones. You got a cigarette?"

Clover shook her head.

"Don't smoke?"

"No."

"I could tell just by lookin at you."

The toddler handed his empty bottle to Clover. "Does he want more?"

"Probably, but he can't have none. He'll shit his pants if you give him more."

She placed the bottle in the open bag. The child watched the progress of her hand, but didn't protest.

"Is there enough money for a place?"

"Nope. Take me over towards the freeway. Lots of good overpasses. I can usually find somebody I know there."

"You can't stay outside tonight. Not with the baby."

"Why not? We been doin it all the time. We'll make out."

"Until when?"

"Til Sammie calms down and realizes he needs me to work. Then we'll have a nice room again."

"What if he doesn't calm down?"

"I dunno. He's still lookin for me. That means he still loves me. It's the boy he don't want." She had found a cigarette but the truck lighter didn't work.

"I know a place. A lady who will help you."

"Nah. I ain't a charity case. I can earn my way. I get good money when I'm working. I can't stand no do-gooders."

Clover started the truck and drove into the street away from the freeway.

"Where are you going?"

"Out of the city."

"Did you hear me say no?"

"I heard you, but I didn't hear the baby."

"Bitch. Let me out. I can make my own way."

"I'm taking you to a good place. Guaranteed no do-gooders. If you don't want to stay, I'll drive you back." If she could make it to Maggie's remote cabin, the girl would have to stay.

Squeak pushed her weight against the door, but didn't try to jump. She leaned her head against the seat and quickly fell asleep.

The boy looked up and smiled broadly. He was still smiling when they pulled into Maggie's yard. He had not yet made a sound.

Maggie was at the door as soon as the truck lights caught the house. "I thought you were Roger. Is he here?"

Clover stopped on the stairs and spoke as rapidly as possible. "No, Maggie. I borrowed his truck and now I have a big favor to ask. I need a place for a girl down on her luck and her kid. The kid's a mess."

The girl climbed out of the truck and stared up at them. Her washed-out blue eyes and her skinny face revealed distrust and dislike.

Maggie shook her head.

Clover returned to the truck and lifted out the child.

The old woman's face softened. She stretched out her arms. Clover carried him into the light.

Now fully awake, Squeak scampered up the stairs.

"How old is he?" Maggie asked.

"Don't touch him." Squeak grabbed for the child.

Maggie stared her down.

Squeak's eyelids fluttered. "Year, maybe a year and a half."

They moved into the cabin.

"Looks like a skinny little rat," Maggie said. "What have you been feeding him?"

"Milk. He don't like nothin else."

"You tried anything else?"

"Hard candy. He likes to suck on candy."

"What else?"

"That's all. That's all he wants."

"Had his shots?"

"What shots?"

"Baby shots. Vaccinations?"

"Who gives teeny babies shots? That's mean."

"Doctors do."

"Ain't never needed a doctor."

"Who delivered him?"

She stood defiantly now, hands on her hips, unlit cigarette dangling from her mouth. "I did. Me and the girls. Don't need no doctor to help having kids."

Maggie sank into her rocker, turned the child over on his stomach and laid him across her lap. He remained folded up, leg over leg, arm over arm. The back of his head was bald from rubbing against the back of the stroller. "Can he walk?"

"Not yet."

"Does he talk?"

"No. He's a real good kid. Real quiet."

"Can he crawl?"

"Yeah, he crawls when he gets on a floor. Put him down, you'll see."

Maggie placed the boy on his back on her rag carpet.

He moved his head in a queer, ragged way, carefully turning his eyes right and left. The vibrant smile that Clover had seen in the truck suddenly illuminated his face. He unfolded his arms, then his legs and with a sudden burst of energy he rolled onto his belly and crawled straight to the big dogs that lounged by the woodstove.

All three adults raced after him.

Squeak snatched him as he reached out to grab a handful of fur. "He's been on the lam too long, that's all. Ain't many places a kid can crawl around in when you ain't got no walls."

CHAPTER SEVEN

Roger Parrish had decided he would not go along with Clover Winters' plan. She could use his truck, but he'd be damned if he'd use her. He could talk to Sammie and get his reaction, but he was pretty sure the answer would be a flat no.

He changed his mind when Owen Swenson, his face the color of wood ashes, his eyes hang-dogged and old, stopped in with the findings from the investigation of the clearing where they had found Jim's truck.

"Dogs," the sheriff said. "And cats. Seventeen of them. All of them mutilated. Someone tossed them out and covered them with leaves.

But, that isn't the worst, Roger. We found a human arm. Female, judging from the size and shape. All her fingertips were missing. Like someone had used a machete and womped them clean off. I could use a drink, Roger."

"Sit down. I'll fix you some stiff coffee." He poured one for himself, too. They sat across the table from one another and stared silently until Swenson finally spoke again. "You know what young Armstrong was working on, don't you?"

Roger nodded.

"You want to know what I think?"

"Yup."

"I think this guy's a real whacko. And I think he's local. And I think he's somebody we all know and probably like and that Jim Armstrong was going to identify him."

"Yup."

"You agree?"

He nodded.

"Have any ideas about how we go about catching him?"

"The Winters girl. She figured all of this out before either of us. She wants to go out on the strip. She wants me to go down there with her every night and work the place."

"What? Just sit there and watch? He'd pick up on that real quick."

"She doesn't want to watch. She wants to walk the walk, and talk the talk. She wants to play the prostitute and have me play her pimp."

"You know I can't go along with any amateur fool plan like that. Is she nuts?"

"A little nuts, maybe, but not stupid. I think she has the right idea. Between the two of us we know everybody who lives out here. We could see who's frequenting the girls, could have you check them out."

"Nope. No go. Too risky."

"Not at all? You won't think on it?"

"No. The answer is no."

Roger shrugged and drank the last of his coffee. "Then we'll need you to turn your back. I'm going to find the guy who killed my dogs, my horse, and Jim Armstrong. If it looks too dangerous or stupid, I'll be the first to call uncle. Who can it hurt?"

"The gal, for one. And you."

Roger Parrish turned on one heel and opened the door of his truck. Duke leaned forward to lick his face. "Yes, Duke," he murmured as he pulled the door closed after him, "I could use a good washing. This whole place makes me feel dirty."

He had made the deal. He was sure Sammie had consented only because police surveillance on the strip was nixed with the death of Jim Armstrong. The department was unwilling to risk another officer's life for the critters that paced the dirty sidewalks. As long as the monster stayed out of the neighborhoods where good folks lived, they could afford to ignore him.

Girls were everywhere; every shape, size and color, hawking their wares under the direct tutelage of Sammie. Clover would be just one more apple on the tree.

He and Clover would be allowed to try their plan, but with some down home rules. She was not to ever sell for real, and he, Roger, would never interfere with Sammie's workings on the street.

Several times a night, Roger would have a fake john pick up Clover. But even for that, Sammie would give the final nod. Sammie needed that small bit of control even though he wouldn't know any of Clover's customers. And, for her safety, it would first take a nod from he, Roger, watching from his parked truck in front of the Christian shelter. If there were any altercations or problems relating to Clover, Sammie and his gorked-out homeboys would do the interfering.

There would be no quibbling about the arrangement. It was the best he could get. Still, he didn't trust Sammie and didn't know Clover well enough to ensure she would obey. Her footprint on the strip would be a small one, but they were in.

He started the finely tuned engine and carefully pulled away from the Sea-Tac strip. They would begin their watching that very night.

∾

"Here, try this top of Squeak's. God you have nice tits. I wish mine didn't jiggle so much."

Clover took the chemise from Sandra and pulled its clinging silver material over her head. Now that the deal was set and Sammie was willing to let her and Roger hang a shield on the strip, she couldn't let false modesty hold her back.

"Let your belly show. Men like nice flat bellies. Too bad you don't have your button pierced. Yeah. That's it. See how the cloth stands out a little when it hangs off your tits? Makes a man want to run his hand up under there and feel what's he bought."

Sandra stood back and studied Clover carefully. "We'll have to shorten the skirt. No. No! You can't roll it up, you've got to show everything; look like you've been squeezed into it and are dying to be squeezed back out."

Clover walked past the long marred mirror and studied her reflection. "You can see almost everything when I walk," she moaned.

"That's how it's done. Let them see just enough to want to see more. Higher heels, that'll help. Here try mine." She slipped a set of three-inch heels off her bare feet. "That's it. Now don't walk, you gotta prance. Bounce so your skirt lifts."

Clover flounced past the mirror again. What she saw made her face go hot with embarrassment.

"That's it, girl! You go now!" Sandra cheered.

She stopped in front of the glass and at first frowned, but a smile began to tug at the corners of her red mouth. She was no longer herself. She was a woman of the streets, cheap, tawdry and exciting. "Where's my coat?"

"No coat, honey. Get used to it. From now on everybody's gonna see everything you got."

They parked at the Welcome Motel not far from where Sammie stood in the dim light of a park and ride. Clover threw her forbidden coat into Roger's truck and hurried to follow Sandra. As she passed in front of the truck she could feel Roger's eyes burning through the thin material covering her butt.

And, as she passed the lot, Sammie groaned appreciatively, "Baby!"

Her transformation was complete. She raised her chin defiantly and walked on.

A car pulled over "Hey, babe, you want a date?"

"Ask Sammie," she flung the words over her shoulder. Sammie would pretend to control her pickups while Roger coordinated several decoy trysts each night to make her appear the real deal.

Sammie shook his head.

"Name your price, man."

"You ain't got enough for that one, honky," Sammie yelled.

Clover pranced, toe-to-toe, and swayed seductively onward.

"Hon-ey!" Sandra cheered. "Ain't you a classic!"

"Shut up, slut." Clover countered.

"Go fuck yourself." Sandra moved toward the brick face of a building.

Clover tried to follow, but the girl waved her away.

"Stay in your space," she hissed. "I gotta do some real work."

Nervous excitement quickly subsided into a monotonous din of cold anxiety. The constant flicker of car lights, the pulsing music booming from vehicle interiors and portable stereos on the sidelines, the constant raucous calls and her need to swivel and check with Roger or Sammie, the standing alone each time Sandra climbed into a car, all assailed her with mind-numbing persistence.

When a mid-sized sedan pulled up with another middle-aged clean-cut male who requested a "special deal", she looked to Roger who was hanging out of his truck window joking with some of the girls.

He nodded.

Her knees weakened with relief. She looked to Sammie. "Go for it, bitch," he shouted.

She fell into the car, pulled the solid door closed behind her, and smiled gratefully at the man. "Up the street," she said as she resisted the impulse to pull her knees up and collapse into fetal position. "Turn right on 188th and left on 192nd.

He avoided looking at her. He didn't speak as he made the turns.

"Here," she said. "Pull in beside that building and park anywhere in the alley."

"Is this where they really do it? Here in a school zone?"

She shrugged. "I don't know. This is where Roger arranged for me to go. Did you bring the coffee?"

He turned off the ignition and handed her a thermos from the seat between them.

"Thank you, thank you, thank you." She kicked the painful shoes from her feet and wriggled her toes. "Man, that's hard work." She poured coffee into the thermos lid, sipped, and then remembering her manners, offered the cup to him.

"No. Thanks."

She studied him above the cup. "Afraid of germs?"

"No. Of course not. I'm coffeed-out." He flipped on the radio and began to search for a station. "Rock? Talk? Bee-bop? A little country?"

She shook her head. "A little peace and quiet."

"Not a bad night. A little cold. You must be glad it's not raining."

"Yes."

He wouldn't look at her.

"I'm not a real hooker, you know."

He nodded. "Sure look like one though."

"Looks can be deceiving."

"So what normally happens now?"

"Normally?"

"Yeah. You know. If this was a real pick-up?"

"I don't know. I'm a decoy. Not a McCoy."

His laugh was tinny.

Jesus, she thought, I look, therefore I am. She closed her eyes and allowed her head to fall back against the seat.

He pounded his fist gently on the steering wheel, stared at the window into the darkness.

She drew her knees together, laid them sideways on the seat, and faced him. "Turn the heater on, would you? I'm really cold." Something about his stodgy, goody-two-shoes attitude, his inability to treat her, as he would have if he'd met her at the Billingsley's, filled her with slow rage. She wanted to reach out one bare foot and fondle his genitals, to see the reaction on his face, to make him sexually uncomfortable in his smugness. She was surprised at the intensity of her emotion. "We don't have to stay here very long. These things usually take about ten minutes."

He turned his head to begin backing out.

"On the other hand, it's really cold out there, and it feels good and warm in here, you know?"

He nodded, but continued to back out.

Bet you wouldn't be in such a hurry if I could offer what the others do, she thought.

When they reached Sandra, she jumped from the car without another word.

She didn't have any words for Roger, either, when their first evening was done. She pulled her coat protectively over her bare shoulders and rotated her neck in slow circles.

"You did all right," he said. "Looked like the real thing out there. Maybe you missed your true calling."

"My feet are killing me. My back feels like it's going to break and my fucking head is ready to split open."

"You don't just look like a whore. You also sound like one."

"Fuck off!"

He smiled. "Well said."

∽

Clover kicked off her conservative heels and tucked her feet under her skirt. The leather of her chair felt warm and comforting on her toes. She had promised to call Maggie before leaving the law school office. She punched in the number.

"Maggie, it's Clover."

"This is really hard for me, Clover. I do not like this woman and the way she ignores the boy. It's not right. I can't do this for very long."

"I'm sorry I had to dump them on you, Maggie. I didn't know what else to do. You don't know how much I appreciate what you're doing."

"Now you're buttering me up. Why should we take care of this woman? She's not worth the time of day."

"I mean every word I say, Maggie. I'm not buttering you up. It's not the mom I'm worried about. It's the kid. Squeak would survive an atomic bomb blast."

"Don't call him 'the kid'. She calls him Owly."

"Yes, I know his name is Owly. I didn't mean to depersonalize him."

"Owly is a terrible name for him."

"Yes, I agree."

"Don't agree. Stop calling him that."

"What would you have me call him?"

"Victor."

"Victor? That might be appropriate."

"Now you're trying to disarm me."

"No, I'm not."

"And don't try to change the subject."

"I'm not trying to change the subject. I don't know what to do. Sammie is looking for her."

"Who is this Sammie? Will he be looking out here?"

"No, I don't think he would ever come out there. How in the heck would he find you?"

"I can't guard the phone every moment."

"Sammie's king of the street, Maggie. No one messes with him."

"What do you plan to do with her?"

"Give her a little time, maybe find a shelter far away."

"Why can't you talk sense into him? Or, better yet, call the cops on him?"

"There is no talking to him. You don't approach a guy like Sammie and bargain."

"What does he have against the baby?"

"He believes Squeak knew all along it wasn't his kid."

"It has a name."

"I'm sorry, I didn't mean to say 'it' again. I meant to say Owly."

"Victor."

"Maggie, can you keep them safe until I can figure out what to do with them? I'm going to see the folks for dinner tonight. The Mortons will be there. Elizabeth knows the system."

"Good. She'll know where we can send this witch. But this poor little tyke…"

"At some point we'll have to involve Child Protective Services."

"I'll keep them two more days. After that it will be up to you. Say hello to Lisa and her children. Now there's a real mother, if you know what I mean."

"Thank you, Maggie. I'll do that."

☙

Clover bowed her head at the silver-laden table, as Dick Morton offered prayers for acceptance, divine guidance and wisdom.

One of the children snickered.

Clover peeked sideways. Two giggling siblings tossed a green olive back and forth between their laps. Gratitude for the flexibility of children filled her. Now if only Lisa could get back to her old self. She reached out and squeezed her sister's hand.

Mom Billingsley handed the knife across the table. "You look so wonderful when you do the carving, dear. Will you do the honors?"

"As only a surgeon can." Dad Billingsley began to slice slender morsels of beef from the huge roast.

"Oh, Dick, remember how you used to pretend to be a doctor?" Elizabeth, on Clover's left, turned to her. "He was the funniest man. We would go out with new friends and they'd introduce him as 'Doctor Morton' and he would play the part to the hilt. I mean to a tee. No one, not a soul, would ever see through him.

He would tell doctor stories to all those strangers and stay in character all evening. Then at the end of the night, I would tattle. 'He's a telephone repairman'.

Most people could not believe it. He is such a good actor!" She patted her husband lovingly. "I think he liked the attention."

Dick smiled at his wife, "The respect is what I liked. Best role I ever played."

"I doubt that you'd like the actual job as well," Dr. Billingsley offered. "Indoors all the time. A lot of paperwork. On call twenty-four hours a day. Nevertheless, if you'd like the title, it's yours!" He stood and lifted his glass of Madeira. "A toast."

They stood and raised their glasses.

"To a better year next year. To making the best of the rest of this year. To good friends who stand beside us, no matter what the adversity. To the very best of friends."

Glasses tinkled.

"And may each person sitting here today discover their life's most fulfilling occupation and become marvelously successful," Dick added with a beaming smile. "As I have."

Clover reached past Elizabeth and tapped her glass to Dick's. "To good friends and wonderful families."

The men retired to television football games while Mrs. Billingsley retreated to the kitchen, ostensibly to oversee the kitchen help, but in reality to wipe the tears from Lisa's eyes before the children noticed.

Clover stood at the large windows and gazed into the blowing wind and rain.

Elizabeth moved to stand beside her. "It's difficult with the holidays approaching. After a loss like this."

"No way out of it, though. We have to stick together and get it behind us."

"Yes."

Clover placed an arm around Elizabeth's waist. "Lisa goes on for the children."

"She and Jim were so in love, so committed."

"She's a Billingsley. She'll persevere."

"That's what makes big families so nice."

"Did you come from a big family, Elizabeth?"

"Oh, heavens no. It was only Mother and I. Dad was killed at Normandy. Mother raised me alone."

"She never married again?"

"No. Actually she was quite disappointed when I met Dick. I think she expected it to be the two of us always."

"That must have been hard for you."

"It was difficult. Sadly, we never really had a chance to thresh the whole thing out. She became quite ill while Dick and I were dating. She's quite demented now."

"I'm sorry."

"Oh, no, my dear. It's okay. I mean it probably turned out for the best anyway. I doubt that she would ever have accepted Dick."

"I hope Lisa will marry again. I don't think she'll be happy alone."

"She has the children. What about you, Dear?"

Clover felt the familiar clutch of her heart. Children would never be hers. She wished she could confide in Elizabeth, but this was not the time. "When the children are grown they'll have lives of their own. Lisa should have a life, too."

"Dick says he's sure she'll be snatched right up. She's so sweet and has such a darling figure."

"You let Dick get away with saying such things?" Clover teased.

"Oh, yes. There's no use pretending that men don't look. Dick always notices other women. I appreciate his openness about it. I have no worries, he likes the way I look just fine." She blushed.

Clover laughed.

"He says wonderful things about you, too, you know."

"Really?"

"He thinks you're drop dead gorgeous with that lustrous hair and divine figure. He especially admires the way you use the color red. He says your nails excite him because they're so vivid, so perfectly done, and so wonderfully red."

"You could do yours this way. It's really inexpensive and easy to keep up."

"Oh, heavens, no. Dick admires glitzy young women, but he would die if I so much as opened a bottle of nail polish. He loves me exactly the way I am."

Lisa tapped Clover's shoulder and handed over the portable phone. "Old Maggie. Sounds important."

Clover carried the phone to the mudroom.

"She's gone!" Maggie shouted. "She called that ape man and he came and got her."

"Oh, no, Maggie."

"Yes, and good riddance to her. I don't need her kind around. Never will amount to anything. Left the baby. Walked off and left this beautiful baby."

"She plans to come back then. I'm sure they needed to talk."

"Oh, no. She intends to stay away. She flung everything out of her bags that was for the baby and left the stuff in a big heap in the middle of my kitchen. She called me an old bitch when I tried to talk some sense into her flighty head. She said I could have the kid and good riddance to him."

"Poor Owly. Is he crying?"

"Crying? Crying? Why would he be crying? Good riddance, I say. This little mite will be better off without her. And, remember, Victor."

"I don't know who to notify. I'll ask Elizabeth."

"Don't tell anyone! You let things be for a while! You give this little guy some time to fatten up. He's sitting here, smiling up at me, while I spoon mashed potatoes and gravy into his tiny mouth. You just leave him here and keep it quiet until we see if that little slut comes back."

"Maggie, she might never come back."

"So be it."

"Maggie, give me a minute."

"Clover, let it go. Be a good girl and be quiet now. I'll tell you when I need yours or Elizabeth's help."

৶৽

"Don't fold your arms. That makes you look like a school-teacher. You can't show anyone you're cold. Flaunt it. Sell it. See?" Sandra swung her plump arms, swayed her ample hips, tipped her nose into the air and rolled her eyes to take in the whole sad world around her. "Dare them to ante up. You gotta seem like you're enjoying yourself. It will keep you warmer.

Yes. Yes. That's it. God sometimes you act like you were born on the streets."

"I probably was, but right now I feel like I'm fourteen again and the boys are calling each other fuzz nuts. I feel light and free."

"You ain't free, honey. You're chargin for it."

They laughed and flailed their arms as they paced the sidewalk.

"He won't come while you're here, you know that, Sweetie, don't you?"

"Yes, he will."

"He won't, honey. He won't. Already he knows you're here. We ain't had anyone come up missing for a month. He knows what time you start and what time you finish, what you wear and when you go to take a piss."

"How could he? I never do it the same."

"Only because, I don't do it the same. And do you know why I don't do it the same? Cause Sammie tells me what and when to do everything. And if Sammie tells me, who tells Sammie?"

"Sammie tells himself. Sammie schedules the whole damn lot of us."

"And suppose Sammie writes it down somewhere. Who's to say this guy don't see it?"

"Sammie write? Sammie can't even read."

They giggled, posed, and giggled again.

"You might be right, Sandra. He has stopped for a bit, but these guys get all pent up when they don't get any. He can't last long."

"Maybe he moved his operation."

"That would make Sammie happy."

"Sammie's happy anyway. He's got Squeak back to manage his business again."

"Have you seen her?"

"They were holed up at his place. He's thinking of sending her up to Anchorage. He's got six girls up there and he wants to move in more. That Alaska oil pipeline has got business goin all over the place."

"You sure she's all right?"

"Honey, she's all right. She'll be lookin out for herself. She's afraid that old lady will have her arrested for leavin the kid."

"And old Maggie is afraid that she'll come back for him."

"She really likes him, huh?"

"Yeah. She acts like a wicked old witch, but she's soft as mush inside."

"Kind of like me."

"Yes, Sandra. She is like you, but you're better looking."

"Ya gotta forgive Squeak. She can't keep the kid. Sammie would do something with him. Squeak kind of liked the old lady. She thinks the kid will be okay with her. She knows people."

"So you have seen her."

"Yeah. She cries all the time. She really does love that kid."

"Maggie would have helped them both."

"Squeak don't let nobody get too close to her. She's scared of closeness."

"She didn't have to get too close. There were acres and acres of woods at Maggie's, she could have made it there."

"She's more scared of woods than she is of Sammie."

Clover understood that irrational fear.

"She grew up in the woods, someplace in Oregon where there were lots of trees and loggers and stuff. Her dad and brothers were loggers."

"So she has a family. A home somewhere?"

"Hah! That's a good one! Hah!" Laughter jiggled her bare belly.

"What's so funny? What'd I say?"

"A family? A home? You're like from a different planet. All Squeak ever had was a house full of brothers and uncles and a father who sold her for a bottle of booze. They used her since she was a little kid and when they thought she might have a disease, they dunked her in a tub of bleach water between guys. The smell of bleach still makes her gag and vomit. But it was clean sex, you know?"

"Jesus."

"Yeah, honey, you call on Jesus. He's just a'listenin up there. Listening and laughing and knowing every time a little sparrow falls."

"No wonder Sammie looks good to her."

"Yeah. Well Sammie took a liking to her. Sammie's an improvement, ya see? Sammie at least takes care of her."

"But Sammie uses her too."

"Not the same way. Sammie only hits her if she does something to piss him off. He gives her time off. And he takes her places.

She didn't mean to fool him with the kid. She really thought it was his. Just happened it wasn't. Without Sammie, Squeak can't make it. She had to choose, ya see?"

"I do see. But I also see a lot of problems for the kid. Maggie is over seventy-years-old. I'm not sure she can keep him. Legally or otherwise."

"Yeah, but she has you and she knows about kids. None of us know the first thing about takin care of a kid. Squeak was sure you could handle it."

Roger's truck moved slowly toward them. He pushed open the door. Clover reached inside, pulled a small package from the seat, and handed it to Sandra. "A little Christmas present."

"A present? My God, girl, I haven't had a present in an awful long time." She stood in the harsh light of the streetlamp holding the package with both hands.

Clover turned away from the girl's tears. "Go on. Open it."

She tore open the wrapping and lifted out a long, wide, gossamer scarf. "It's beautiful!"

"And warm. It's musk ox wool from Alaska. The Billingsleys found it when they cleaned out my Mom's room. It's been sitting in my drawer for years. It's as warm as a coat. Let me show you." She shook the scarf out in the wind, draped it over the girl's shoulders, and crossed it over here chest.

"I don't have nothing to give you."

"You already gave me many gifts. Look at all that you've taught me. Why I'd only be half a woman if it weren't for you, girl." She hopped into the truck and didn't look back. She was afraid she would see Sammie taking away the present.

છ૭

Roger had carved Owly a rocking horse with a ragged mane and a real horsehair tail.

Clover brought him educational toys: red, yellow and blue plastic sorters and fiddlers and large colorful snap-togethers.

Maggie shortened his new name to Vic and filled a dresser drawer with tasseled fuzzy socks, tiny sweaters with pockets that he stuffed full of trinkets, jeans with rabbits on each knee and a hat with sheepskin earmuffs.

Squeak sent nothing.

"Can't really blame her," Clover apologized. "She's the real victim."

"Victim? Who walked off and left whom?" Maggie snorted.

"She knew you would take good care of him."

"Sure. Any port in a storm."

"Well, she was right, wasn't she?"

"Has nothing to do with anything."

"Never see her," Roger said. "I've watched every night. She's not around."

"Sandra says that she's up in Anchorage, that Sammie will bring her back in the spring." Clover kissed Vic's outstretched hand to make him giggle.

"Winter streets in Alaska? That seems like pretty stiff punishment," Roger said.

Maggie picked up the boy, sniffed his diaper, and placed him back on the floor. "There's not enough punishment in the world for a mother who would drag a baby through alleys, starving him nearly to death, keeping him in a stroller twenty-four hours a day."

Clover handed the child a toy. "He doesn't seem to have been affected by it."

"Humph! You think he's perfectly normal? You think he's already forgotten the past. Well, you watch this!" Maggie dragged the umbrella stroller from behind the kitchen door. With a loud bang, she snapped it open. "Come here, baby Vic. Come to Maggie."

The small boy dropped his plastic truck, grinned widely and toddled unevenly across the floor. His eyes were bright and lively. His blonde curls bounced as he hurried to Maggie's open arms.

She lifted him, kissed his forehead, and hugged him to her ample bosom. 'Let's put you in your little chair for a minute, shall we, Sweetheart?"

As she placed him in the stroller, his arms folded across his chest. He brought his legs up and folded them into an unnatural position across his body. A veil descended over his laughing blue eyes. His smile disappeared. He became an owl-eyed package once again.

"Jesus, Maggie, take him out!" Clover crossed the floor in seconds, but Maggie was already lifting him to her. He snuggled against her, his body limp.

Maggie stared coldly at Clover. "Now tell me his mother is a nice person."

"She did the best she could."

"She could have given him for adoption at birth."

"She wanted to love him. No one ever loved her. She thought she could convince Sammie to accept him. When he didn't, she had no money and no one to turn to."

"There are plenty of other choices she could have made."

"She's not capable of making choices, Maggie. I wish I could help you understand. The only choices she ever really made in her life involved Owly."

"Victor."

"Victor. She decided to run with him, and she decided to leave him with you. They were her only choices."

"A lot of women have hard lives, few of them abandon their babies."

"My mother did," Clover said quietly. "And now I might be closer to understanding why."

"You making excuses for them, Clover."

"I've seen how they live."

"They aren't tough enough to put someone else's welfare before their own."

"No one showed them how. Squeak had this baby without a doctor, without anesthesia, without even an informed person to help.

Sandra and the other women did the delivery. They hid her in a sweltering attic room for two days during the worst heat of summer.

When she saw how white the baby was, she was shocked. She told Sammie that sometimes it was normal for a mixed baby to look white for a time. She kept shaving off his blonde curls.

When Sammie realized he was entirely white, he went into a rage.

She took the kid and ran. No money, no shelter, and little food for her or the boy. No place to hide. The other girls smuggled money to her when they could, but when Sammie found out, he beat them. They stopped helping. Except for Sandra. Every dime she managed to keep from Sammie, she gave to Squeak."

"She could have gone to a church or to a shelter."

"Not in Tacoma or Seattle. Sammie had someone on the lookout at every one. He even knew what dumpsters she might use to look for food."

"Well, I gave her a chance. I took her in and what did she do? She called the boogieman and told him to come get her. Do you know what she said to him? When she opened the door she said, 'Are you here to fight? Or are you here to fuck?' He answered the second and the little slut walked off laughing."

"She doesn't know anything else."

"What about the real father?" Roger asked.

"He could have been anyone."

"I'm going to keep the boy." Maggie announced.

"You can't, Maggie. It's not legal."

"He's not registered anywhere. He has no name, no birth record, no identity. Do you want to be responsible for putting him into the system? He needs a home. I have a home. I'm going to raise him the same way I've raised lots of other kids. I'm not going to let him get lost in a system that has too many problems to care. I don't want him to become like his mother."

"You're no spring chicken, Maggie." Roger said.

"No, I'm not. But that's where you come in. You're going to help me."

"Me? Hell, I'm no good with kids. Dogs and horses is all I know."

"That's a start. You're going to have to learn pretty quickly, Roger, because we're going to give this kid a chance. And don't anybody tell me we aren't."

CHAPTER EIGHT

She could not remember another January without snow. She and the women donned fake fur jackets, but made no other concessions to the weather. On the windy street corner they danced and clapped their hands to stay warm. Clover envied the other women's frequent sorties into warm car interiors.

One night, near the end of the month, Sandra suddenly stopped dancing and whispered. "Now look over there. That little girl. What do you think she's doing?"

A girl, no more than twelve, wearing tight jeans and a leather jacket, paced back and forth in front of the pawnshop. "Looks like she selling," Clover said.

"Jesus H. Christ! Just what we need. Where's Sammie?"

"His back is to us."

"If he sees her, she's in for it."

"In for what?"

Sandra's words matched loud rap music that bellowed from a passing car. "Why, Honey, he'll be sweet as pie. He'll take her home and feed her, then in the night, when she's safe and warm, he'll fuck her and he'll beat her. Come this time tomorrow, she'll be walking just like us."

Sammie and his homies were smoking a bowl and paying no attention to the street.

"Give me a cigarette, Sandra."

"This is no fucking time for a smoke."

"Give me one, damn it." Clover's fingers shook as she cupped the lighter. She turned slightly toward Roger, inhaled deeply, and with a flick of her thumb sent the cigarette skyward.

Roger drove to her. "What's up? What'd you see?"

She leaned into his window. "Go over to the pawn shop and pick up that kid. Get her in your truck and get her the hell out of here."

"It's Sammie's street. Let him take care of her."

"Fuck Sammie. Get her out of here."

He shrugged, "This has got nothing to do with us."

"Do it, Roger, please."

He glanced at the girl, then at Sammie. "We promised we wouldn't interfere with his business."

"She isn't anybody's business. Yet. Please. Roger?"

"God damn it, Clover. This is asking too much."

"Please?"

He put the truck in gear and started down the street.

"Keep moving," Sandra hissed. "Don't watch."

Clover waved at a passing car. It pulled up to her. She laughed loudly and leaned into the window.

"Hey, babe, want a date?"

She glanced at Sammie.

He shook his head.

"Sorry, Sweetie, I'm booked."

Sandra took the date. Roger and the young kid had disappeared.

Clover stood alone and shivering in the night until Roger once again opened his door. She climbed into the warm interior.

"Look, Lady, this isn't a social welfare agency. There are places for kids like her. Institutions. Police departments. Don't ask me to get involved in any social responsibility programs again." He slammed the broad side of his palm against the steering wheel.

"You see any social services people down here? I don't. Take me to her and it's out of your hands."

He turned down a side street. "Yeah. Well tell me what is in my hands? We're supposed to be finding a murderer here and instead we're opening orphanages and schools for misguided girls."

"I think it's more like, one baby, one girl. You've got to keep things in perspective, Roger."

"You need to listen to your own advice."

"I can't turn away from this."

"Miss Idealist. Grew up with everything given to you and you think you can understand the down and outs. My God, you believe you can help these losers. Go ahead. You try. See where it gets you." He stopped curbside at a small restaurant. "She's in there."

Clover jumped from the truck and ran into the place. No girl. She could hear a male and female bantering back and forth in the kitchen. She went into the bathroom and checked the stalls. No one.

In the main room she found a middle-aged woman wiping down the counter.

"What do *you* want?"

"I'm looking for a young girl, blonde. My friend brought her in a few minutes ago."

"Yeah. And she left, Thanks-be-to-God. She sure as hell don't need the likes of you."

"Did you see which way she went?"

"We don't provide our customers with personal services, like some."

"I'm trying to help the kid."

"Sure you are."

"Honestly."

The woman shrugged. "Didn't see where she was going and I didn't ask her where she'd been."

Disheartened she returned to the truck.

∽

Sandra had returned when Roger dropped Clover off. "She booked?"

"Yeah. Roger took her to a burger place, paid for a meal and she took off."

"Soon as she gets hungry again, she'll be back."

"She's only a baby. Why would she try this?"

"Already been used, Honey. Knows where men keep their brains and their loose change."

"Too young."

"Never too young. How old were you?"

"Thirteen, I think." Clover had a vague feeling that she should remember more.

"Did you want to?"

She turned away from the street and ducked into the shelter of the building. A car horn honked. "Come over here, Baby!" a drunken man demanded.

Clover looked to Roger.

He shook his head.

"Go fuck yourself!"

"Did you want to?" Sandra persisted.

"No, and yes. At first I was scared and fought a little."

"Was it rape?"

"He was older. A friend of my adopted dad."

"That classifies as rape, if you're middle class."

"Yeah. I guess it does." She moved closer to her friend. "I never thought about that part. Afterwards I was ashamed."

"Because he forced you?"

"Because he was a friend and in the Billingsley's house. And because I liked it."

"Yeah. That's the rub. It's nasty. But it can seem nice too."

"I was too young to do anything else. I sure couldn't tell my dad. How old were you?"

"Four."

"Jesus!"

She became defiant, swung her hips freely. "The more you learn, the more you earn."

"Was that only one time?"

"No. It was all the time. A live-in friend of my mom's. She'd go to work, he'd go to work on me."

"And you didn't tell her?"

"What's to tell? I didn't know it wasn't normal. 'Tony loves my little Sandra', Mom would say in a little girl voice." She shrugged. "Tony loves my little Sandra'. I thought that's what love was."

"When did she find out?"

"Never did. Far as I know, she's still with him. I ran away when I was ten."

"Where'd you go?"

"A friend's house. They let me stay with them for a while. Until I started doing their old man. Like I said, I thought that was love."

"Did you run away from there too?"

"No. My friend's mom caught the old man and me doing it. She had the police take me away. They sent me to a reform school."

"What happened to the man?"

"Nothing. Nobody ever said anything more about it. The mom said I stole a bunch of money. Out I went. My friends at that reform-a-tory taught me how to make money off of that kind of love. One of them introduced me to Sammie and here I am."

"Sandra?"

"Yeah?"

"How old are you?"

"Eighteen."

"Ever think about getting away from here?"

"Yeah. Yeah. I think about it all the time. All it takes is some cash and some gumption. Now where would I get enough of those? Even if I could buy a ticket, I don't know if I have enough of me left to get on the bus."

"You might be good at a lot of other things. You're a good person. You care about other people. Isn't there somewhere you could go?"

"I have a sister. She's a lot older. She went and lived with my real dad when old Tony tried messing with her. She went to college. She's married. Respectable. What would she want with me?"

"Maybe she'd want a sister."

Her laughter tinkled through the cold air like the sound of falling icicles. "She doesn't know where I've been, the things that I've done."

"Do you know where she is?"

"Yeah." She pulled a faded, flattened envelope from her spandex top and handed it to Clover. "Don't let Sammie see it. He has a memory like an elephant."

Clover slipped the envelope into her pocket.

∽

One week later as the full moon washed the wide strip in pale light and turned the sky and Mount Rainier slate blue, Clover ran on cold stiffened legs and reached the girl before Sammie got a look at her. She pressed the small knife she had taken from her mother's sable coat into the girl's side.

"Move!" she hissed. "Move with me or I'll kill you."

The girl hesitated. Her indigo lips under the fluorescent lights were chafed and splitting. Her cheeks were dirty. Her clothing reeked of smoke and the stale odor of incontinent mice.

"Walk! Don't look back."

The girl began to move ahead woodenly.

As they stepped into the busy alley, horns brayed.

Clover's heels beat with military precision on the pavement. She glanced over her shoulder. Sandra and the others blocked Sammie's view.

She shoved the girl ahead. The small knife felt awkward in her cold hand. The girl swayed against it and cried out.

"Just keep walking. Go. It's not far."

They marched five blocks in silence. She shoved the girl through the squeaking door of an all night convenience store. A wave of onion-scented air blew against her face. She pushed the girl into the back corner where tables and chairs sat along shelves of stale chips and candy bars.

"Pick out some food, whatever you want."

The girl didn't speak but pulled a large bag of chips, two Twinkie's and a candy bar from the shelf.

"Thirsty?"

"Yeah."

"Coffee?"

"Coke."

"Sit. I'll pay. Understand?"

For a moment the girl hung on to her selections like a dog whose food dish food had been challenged.

Clover wrested them away. "Sit. I'll be right back."

The girl slouched into a chair.

As the clerk rang up each item, Clover flung it back to the girl who shoved handfuls of chips into her mouth.

"You'd think she hasn't eaten for a very long time," said the Indian clerk.

"Yeah. Yeah. Give me a coffee, would you? Three creamers and four sugars."

"She is okay, you are sure?"

"Just a hard working girl like the rest of us. Worked up an appetite."

The man ducked his head and retreated behind the donut case.

The girl had eaten half the bag of chips and was carefully tucking the remainder into her shirt as Clover pulled in a chair.

"What are you doing here?" Clover asked.

"I'm looking for work."

"What kind of work?"

"You know," she shrugged. "Anything."

"Do you know what anything means?"

"Yeah."

"Do you have any experience at 'anything'?"

"Enough. Is this, like, a job interview?"

The coffee left a bitter aftertaste. "Where are you from?"

"Everywhere."

"Cute."

"Did you want some of this?" She offered a half-eaten Twinkie.

"No. Where's everywhere?"

"East of the Mountains."

"How'd you end up here?"

"I was going to Kurt Cobain's house. To see the place, you know? This is where my ride left me off."

"Did you see the place?"

"Yeah. Nothing to see."

"Where are you going?"

She shrugged. "Someone said I could pick up some work here."

"You running from something?"

"Hey! What the hell? Who are you? A social services broad?" Her laugh was sharp and loud.

"Do I look like social services?"

"Yeah. A case."

They both laughed. The girl's face softened and grew younger.

"You got a name?"

"Pick one."

"Tell me the real one."

Mindy."

"Nice name. I'm Clover."

"That your real name?"

"Yes. Is Mindy yours?"

"Name I picked. I like it."

"You got a place to stay?"

"Sure. Have a lot of friends in town."

"You wouldn't be interested in the couch at my place then?"

"What are you? A les' or something?"

Clover shook her head. "I thought you looked kind of cold and beat."

"What's the cost?"

"For one night? Nothing. But I don't take in long-term boarders."

"How do I know you ain't gonna rob me or murder me in the night?"

"What am I gonna get? A half a bag of chips and a Twinkie?"

Her laugh was genuine. "You got an old man?"

"Not at this moment."

"Okay. You look honest enough."

Clover studied the girl who lay fully dressed, except for shoes and socks, curled in fetal position on the couch. Her bare, dirt-encrusted feet were folded together as if in prayer.

Towels, toothbrush and comb lay unused on the coffee table.

She would let the child sleep and hope that she would still be there when she got back from the law school. She had allowed her search for Jim's murderer to take precedence over everything she'd thought was important. Now with two reprimands in her file, she could not miss another day and expect to keep her position.

If Mindy disappeared with her TV, VCR or jewelry, it would be a small price to pay for her safety from Sammie, or worse, from the obsessive killer who had not struck in three months. The mutilator would not remain dormant. His bizarre passions could not be held in check much longer.

A shower revived her. She pulled on her robe, combed her wet hair and returned to the living room.

The girl sat upright on the couch in a half-sleep.

"I have to go to work," Clover said. "You want breakfast?"

"What do you want from me?"

"Nada. Not a thing. I thought you could use some sisterly help."

"Are you a freaking feminist or something?"

Clover laughed. "You could say that, I guess."

"You turn tricks in the daylight, too?"

"No, I have a different day job."

"You're a freaking cop, aren't you?"

"No. I work at a school."

"You got kids there or something?"

"No."

"Don't you make enough at your night job?"

"Only the pimps get ahead on the street."

She swung her eyes around the apartment. "Yeah, well, you look like you're doing all right. This place is over the top. You like red, huh?"

"I told you. I'm working two jobs and now I'm hungry. You want a bagel?"

"A bagel? You are a frigging social worker, aren't you?"

"I've been accused of that a lot lately. I'm a teacher's assistant at a law school. I help professors strut their stuff. Grade papers, prepare classes."

"You must be pretty smart."

"Yeah. I guess I am. I have a feeling you are too."

"Smart enough to make it on my own."

"Probably. Look. I have to go. You can stay. Have a bath. Wash your clothes. Watch some MTV. I get back about three."

"And in the meantime, am I going to have any surprises? An old man who just happens to pop in? The cops?"

"No surprises. Will you stay? I'm trying to help you."

"Okay. I hear you. Okay."

CHAPTER NINE

K.C. Casey knelt in the sunken tub. The knees of his coveralls were soggy. He worked the drain snake around and pulled out a mess of long black hair, super-fatted soap, and flakes of skin. Old man is faithful, at least in his bathroom. He discarded the mess in his plastic pail and inserted the snake again.

The young wife sat comfortably on a fancy iron bench. He could feel her eyes on him. "Well it isn't that he's mean to me or anything," she was saying. "I mean he's sweet, just sweet to me. But, you know. It's so boring to stay home all day. I say to him, 'what should I do?' 'Nothing', he says. 'Go shopping'."

She shook her long dark hair and bumped the side of her head with a closed fist. Her hands were slender and graceful with oval, gold-plated nails. "Shopping? 'Do you see that closet full of clothes?' I say. 'I practically have a whole junior's department right here.' 'Call some friends', he says."

"It's hard to talk on phones, you know? It's like every time the phone rings it's for him and it's business, business, business. So I tell him that and what does he do? He goes out and buys another whole system. Puts all white pretty phones with gold dials in just for me. Sweet, you know?"

K.C. grunted and opened the hot water faucet fully. The water burned his knees. Damn. Still blocked.

"Maybe I should have a baby," she continued. "A baby would keep me busy. You have any kids?"

"Almost." He flashed a smile. "Got one in the oven. Should be here any day now."

"Oh, you're so sweet! That's probably what I should do. But then, you know, my husband's so old. I mean he's got grown kids my age. I don't think he's too interested in another family. He says I'm the only family he needs."

K.C. fished another lump of hair from the line and tossed it into the bucket. He flooded it with hot water.

"Is it getting better?" She leaned toward the tub. Her perfume was spicy and mild.

He breathed deeply and inserted the line again. "A little. It's really plugged."

"Yes, I know. I've been telling my husband but he never uses the Jacuzzi. Always showers, you know. Too busy to relax and enjoy the cozy things. It's always business and more business."

"Pays the bills."

"Yes. Especially these high plumbing bills." She laughed.

He pulled another plug and replaced the snake.

"You happy with your wife?"

He gazed up at her as he continued to thread the snake. She was too pretty to look at for very long. "I don't know. I am and I'm not. That's how marriage is. I guess."

"You mad cause she's pregnant?"

"Oh, no. Nothing like that. We're living with my in-laws. Doesn't make life too easy."

"But you still really like her—even though she's big and pregnant?"

"Yeah. I still like her."

"Good! I'd hate to think you'd find her repulsive."

He laughed, emptied another glob and turned on the water. The drain ran freely. "There," he said with satisfaction. "Got it that time."

"You're a genius!"

He pretended he couldn't hear over the running water. He wound up the snake and picked up his bucket.

She left the room.

He reassembled the drain mechanism, stepped from the tub and directed the showerhead to rinse the sides. He could sense her presence behind him. He turned slowly.

She was standing inside the doorway. Her short red chemise caressed the silken skin of her upper thighs. Long black hair glistened richly. She took his breath away.

She smiled. Shrugged her delicate shoulders. "It's a good way to pass the day," she said, asking.

Shouldn't. Shouldn't. Shouldn't.

Her bare feet padded across the floor. Her small firm breasts pressed against the roughness of his coveralls.

His hands reached behind her and touched the round smooth softness of her buttocks. "I'm kind of dirty."

"I think we could try out the tub. You know. Now that it's working and all. I've always wanted to try the tub."

"Can I shower first?"

She shook her head against his chest. Her hair was flower-scented and exquisitely soft. "I think I'll like you dirty."

≈

His voice boomed through the phone. Clover held it away for a moment then screamed into it. "What have I done, Roger? Tell me exactly! What have I done?"

The secretary in the next office stared at her through the glass.

"Screwed the pooch! Screwed up the whole God-damned thing!"

She lowered her voice. "Calm down, Roger. I can't understand you when you shout. Roger? Roger? Roger, shut up!"

"Don't tell me to shut up!"

"Oh, for God's sake. Be rational. Tell me what I've done."

"Pissed off Sammie."

"Oh. Poor Sammie."

"Maggie's right here, Clover. She says don't bring that girl here. She doesn't want anymore of your saved souls. Do you hear?"

"Who said anything about Maggie's?"

"We're just telling you, Clover. Maggie doesn't want her."

"Know anybody who does?"

"Sammie. Goddamn it! Sammie wants her."

"You stupid, stupid ass, Roger Parrish! Stupid! Stupid! Stupid!"

"Look in a mirror, Babe. Then decide who's stupid."

"What? What will I see? A dumb broad who wants to save one kid from the clutches of Sammie and his ilk? What, may I ask, is wrong with that? Would you want your sister to work for the guy? Your cousin, maybe? Tell me, Roger! If he's such a good employer why not get some of your female relatives down there and fix his personnel shortage!"

"Hey! Who asked her to come down there? Who made her volunteer? She wasn't drugged! She wasn't gagged and bound!"

"You! You, Roger! And all the other guys who can't see reality! You and your strong, manly attitude. You put her there, Roger! But, God-damn it, I'm going to take her out!"

The phone clattered as she slammed the receiver into its cradle.

∽

The girl had showered and laundered her clothes. She sat waiting on the couch.

"Hey! You cleaned the whole place."

"Least I could do. To pay for the bed."

"Thank you. I stopped by a friend's restaurant and picked up some burgers and sweet-rolls."

"You don't have to feed me."

"Now what kind of a hostess would I be, if I didn't feed my guests?"

"I'm not a guest."

Clover took out two crimson plates and unwrapped a burger. "Sure you are. I invited you." She offered the plate to the girl who did not take it. She placed it on the table and prepared another.

The girl joined her at the table, took a small bite from the burger. "Why are you doing this?"

"To keep you from Sammie."

"Sammie? Sammie who?"

"Sammie the Pimp. The one who runs the section of the strip you were trying to walk."

"Don't like the competition huh?"

"You're not competition, sweetie, believe me."

"I need to talk to Sammie. I need to get started somewhere."

"You don't get started with Sammie. You get finished."

"Yeah, well. Maybe. I've got to get started somewhere. I'm going to starve to death if I don't get work."

"How old are you?"

"Eighteen."

"Don't feed me any of your crap. You're lucky if you're over twelve."

"Twelve? I'm not twelve!"

"You act like twelve."

"I don't act like twelve. And I don't look like twelve! Everybody says I look older than thirteen. Everybody!"

"They're pulling your leg, honey. You look every bit of thirteen."

"Thirteen? You said I looked twelve!"

"Yeah. But that was before I knew you were thirteen."

"Well…" Her eyes blazed with anger. "You tricked me!"

"Nah. A lucky guess."

"What're you going to do? Call the cops?" She pushed her plate aside and stood.

"What for?"

"To take me in."

"Why? Did you commit a crime?"

She looked away.

"Well did you?"

"If you call running away a crime."

"Some people would."

"Do you?"

"Depends on what you were running from."

"Yeah. Well I have my reasons."

"And it wasn't only to see Cobain's place?"

"Nah. That just gave me someplace to go."

"So. Okay. I believe you had something to run from. Now the question is, where will you land?"

"I don't know. I can't think that far."

"I'd like to help."

"Why?"

"Payback. When I was in trouble some really nice people helped me."

"But you're still out there hooking."

"That's another story, but I can't tell you about it yet. We hardly know each other.

"That big, mean, guy your boyfriend?"

"Roger? No. We have a working relationship."

"He's your pimp then?"

"Something like that."

"If it works for you why can't it work for me? I'd work for him."

"He's a jerk. You don't want to ever work for a jerk."

"I have to work for somebody."

"I think I have a job for you and a place to stay."

"Doing what?"

"Can you cook?"

"Cook?"

"Clean tables? Wash dishes?"

"Like in a restaurant?"

"Yes. I know a lady owns a coffee shop kind of place. She could use some help and she has an extra room. Her kid died. You might be good for her."

"You serious?"

"Yeah." She opened her hands, palms up in supplication. "Think you could do it?"

"I can't substitute for a dead kid! Is she going cry all over me? What about the cops?"

"She stopped crying years ago. She's not going to latch onto you like some reincarnation or anything. She knows what it feels like to be kind of lost. And there aren't any cops out there. Only a sheriff."

"Won't he ask questions?"

"Yeah. But I think Tiny can handle him. You help her out, she'll be fair with you."

"Does she have an old man?"

"No. She lives alone."

"Okay. I'll try it."

"Clover! My God in Heaven, I'm so glad you're home!" Maggie's voice shouted from the phone. "The stupid kid is in it again! He's in deep shit this time! He found a body. No not found exactly. He expected to meet her and instead found her body."

"Maggie, slow down! I don't understand. Who found a body?"

"K.C. He was going to meet some girl in the woods. When he got there she was dead. Oh God, Clover. We can't get him off this time. This time he's really done it."

"Where, Maggie? Where did he find her?"

"The illegal cut. The same place we found Jim's car. Don't ask me what the hell he's doing hanging out around there. But that's where he was. He came running in here all lathered up. Wild-eyed. Said he found a friend of his naked and dead in the clear-cut. He kept saying, 'I didn't do it. I didn't. It's so awful! Awful!'"

"Where is he now?"

"With the sheriff. I had to call Swenson. I didn't know what else to do."

"Did you see the body?"

"No. Victor is sleeping. I can't leave him and I can't drag him out to see a body. I couldn't get any sense out of K.C. I had to call Swenson. It was the only thing to do."

"Have you called Roger?"

"Yes. He said he was going to try and beat the sheriff to the clear-cut."

"Do you think he made it?"

"Yes."

"How can you be sure?"

"Because I didn't tell Swenson where the body is supposed to be. I said I didn't know and that he needed to get right over here to get K.C. As soon as I made the call, I called Roger."

"Thank you, Maggie."

"What can we do?"

"Do you believe K.C.?"

Silence stretched between them. Then, "Yes."

"Do you know the girl?"

"I have no idea. He just kept blubbering, 'Jenny. Jenny. Jenny will never understand. Jenny will never forgive me.'"

"He isn't a murderer, is he, Maggie?"

"I didn't think so. I guess I still don't think so. But nobody believed that Ted Bundy could do those things either. Oh, Clover! I don't know what to think. I just know that he's gotten himself into a big mess now."

"I'll have to hear the whole story. I don't believe I'm wrong about him."

"Well, young woman, if you'll stand behind him, I will too.
"I'm going over to Roger's place."

∽

Roger Parrish knew he had been right from the beginning. "The kid's a God-damned pervert, that's what he is! He isn't innocent! He isn't dumb! He isn't even a kid! He's a sexually perverted psychopath! Don't give me any more shit about knowing him or liking him or standing behind him! He's a shit! A royal, God-damned shit!"

"Roger, please stop ranting and think! I need you to think."

"Think? I don't need to think! The last thing I want to do is think! My stomach is still churning. The Goddamned perversion of it! I witnessed the work of a raving maniac! What a fucking mess!"

Clover grabbed the whistling kettle and poured water into the teapot. With shaking hands, she placed cups on the table. "Roger. Come on. Sit down. Have some tea. Please."

He paced across the floor twice, then pounced into a chair, but was up again immediately. He slammed open the cupboard behind him, pulled down a bottle of rum, and poured some into both cups without asking.

"Maggie sent you out there so you could see, Roger. You need to remember details. We need to write them down."

He sat in the chair. His face fell into a gray anxious mask. "No need to look for any clues. They've got him. Open and shut. He planned to meet her there and he killed her."

She shook her head.

"He did it! I have no doubts. I saw her. Jesus! The guy is crazy. Admit it, Clover. He's crazy."

"Did you see her car?"

He nodded. "And his van pulled right in behind it."

"Was her car damaged in any way?"

"No. Oh, no. She got out of the car willingly. Left her purse on the seat. Her make-up kit was still open on the dash. She fixed herself up for him!"

"Doors on the car weren't locked?"

"No. I'm telling you. She felt safe. Left everything right there."

"And the van?"

"Locked."

"Why would he leave the van and run to Maggie's"

"So he'd have a witness and a sympathetic ear. In case the girl told anybody she was going to meet him."

"Maggie said he was hysterical. That he was in a complete panic."

"Clover, listen to me. Don't look for excuses for him. He's a perverted jerk!"

"I need to know facts, Roger."

"Facts! Okay, facts! Fact one: Why would he leave the van there? Her body is only a half-mile up the trail, closer to the clearing than to Maggie's. He killed her away from the van. I don't think he planned it, but got carried away when he was alone with her.

Fact two: He went up there with her. Her clothes were all together, thrown in a heap, partially covering some of her body. Shoes and all. Thrown there, like he'd undressed her completely before he murdered her. No blood on the clothing, clean and together.

Fact three: It was a hell of a lot harder for him to run up the trail to Maggie's then to go down the trail to the van. If he was in such a hurry to find help and not an alibi, he would have run back to the van and driven to town."

"Did you recognize the girl?"

"The girl? What girl? All that was left was a body. Parts of a body. He cut off every part he could. Toes, fingers, ears, nose. Should I go on? Do you really want to know the details?" He was on his feet and running toward the bathroom.

Clover placed both arms on the table and lowered her head as she listened to him wretch and gag. A chill entered her body at the nape of her neck and ran down her spine to her toes. It could have been her lying on the trail in the woods. Why hadn't he done the same to her when he had the chance? What had saved her?

Nothing. Nothing had saved her because K.C. wasn't capable of such brutality.

She raised her head and filled her lungs with air. She had shared an intimate day with him, had shared his body. He hadn't frightened her. He didn't do this. She was sure he didn't, but she was also sure that whoever did was much more clever than she could hope to be. The mutilator had outmaneuvered them. She rose from the chair and hurried to her car.

᧟

The winter moon shown eerily on fresh yellow police ribbons strung across the rutted gravel road. She pulled to one side, behind the county vehicles and began walking slowly toward the clearing. Something cold left a clammy wetness as her hand brushed against shrubs lining the road. She rubbed it off on her jeans.

K.C.'s plumbing equipment spilled from the open doors of his van. One metal box lay on the hood of an expensive silver import immediately to the van's front. Shadows and beams of light moved across the clear-cut.

She paused and studied the scene until she recognized the burly outline of K.C. He was cuffed to the door of the sheriff's jeep. Swenson had his back to her. She moved closer.

"K.C."

His face was streaked with lines of sweat and tears. He tilted his head toward her.

"You all right?"

"No. I'm in a mess. This is deep, deep shit."

"I know. I've called your lawyer. He's on his way."

"What can he do? It's open and closed. I was here."

"I don't believe you hurt anyone."

"Jesus. No!"

"I believe you. I'm on your side."

"Don't stick your neck out, Clover. It won't do any good."

"Maybe, maybe not. Did you know her?"

"Yeah."

"Real well?"

"Kind of."

"How well?"

"I did some work at her house last week. She did some work on me."

She nodded. "That all?"

"Isn't that enough? She called me yesterday. Said she had some leaking pipes and needed some follow-up. We decided to meet here. I thought we could have a nice walk in the woods where no one would see us."

"Kind of like Déjà vu?"

"I suppose."

"Anybody else know you were coming out?"

"I called her back from a booth downtown. Her husband wasn't home."

"Could her husband have followed her?"

"I don't know. Someone cut her up."

"Roger told me."

"I saw her fingers. Laying on the trail. I thought it was a joke. Like the clothes. Jesus!" He began to sob.

"K.C.? What about the clothes?"

"She told me on the phone that it would be like a scavenger hunt. 'I'll leave a trail. You try to find me.' She was just a kid. I thought it was cute.

When I got here the first thing I see is her skirt. Blowing out into the road from a tree branch. So I run up and pull it down and start up the trail. I find her jacket. Her necklace. This is exciting, I think. What a clever girl. I can hardly wait to find her."

Next it's her blouse and bra and shoes. I'm getting really excited. I practically run up the trail. I go about another half mile and I find her panties. When I bend over to pick them up, I see the fingers. Oh, Jesus! I raise my head and there she is draped across a stump."

"What are you doing here?" Swenson moved between the two. "Get the hell out of here!"

She did not move.

"Don't you know you can end up dead? Where the hell's your Harvard brain?" he stormed.

She remained silent as she watched him place K.C. in the jeep.

"Go home, Clover. Get out of here. Leave this work to us men."

She turned and walked back down the dark road to her car.

༄

Mindy lounged on the couch surrounded by crimson pillows and the blasting beat of MTV. "Phone's been ringing all night. I let the machine get it."

Clover waved and moved quickly to the answering machine.

"Can I get you a coke or something?" the girl offered.

She nodded as the machine began to give up its messages.

"Clover? Lisa here. Folks want you over for dinner Saturday. Can you come? Long time since we've seen you. Everybody misses you. I miss you. Call me."

"Clover? This is Maggie. How's the boy? Have you seen him? He's in real trouble isn't he? We've got to help him. Call me."

"Look, lady! If you want this partnership to work, don't walk out on me. And give up on the plumber! They've got him cold! Bastard deserves whatever he gets!"

"Clover? This is Sandra. Why aren't you out here workin? Sammie's mad. Roger told him about the girl. Get your ass over here!"

"Clover. About the girl. Bring her over Sunday. I'm off. We'll have some time to get used to each other. I'm kind of nervous about it, but Maggie helped me, and maybe now I can help someone else. Call me."

Mindy offered her a can of pop. "She sounds okay."

Clover gratefully accepted the drink.

"Oh, yuck! What have you got all over yourself?"

She followed Mindy's gaze to her cream-colored pants.

"Jesus! Am I bleeding somewhere?" She checked her arms, ran her hands over her face and neck, and finding nothing, thought of the cold wetness she'd felt on the trail. She must have rubbed against blood on the way into the clear cut.

If K.C. went straight from the body to Maggie's, how'd blood get out to the roadway?

"I've got to go."

"Where? You just got here."

"I've got to go check on something."

"Again I say, where?"

Clover liked her spunkiness. "I have to go up to the woods."

"Shouldn't you wait until it's light?"

"No. It will be too late then. It might rain."

"I'd go with you, but I don't walk in the woods when it's dark."

"I used to be afraid of the woods too, but now I know that the worst you'll meet in the woods is a bear or a coyote. I'd rather face them then the guys I see on the street."

"Yeah, well, at least you get paid on the street. Okay, I'll get my jacket."

༄

One deserted police car blocked the road. "We'll have to walk from here."

"Where's the flashlight?"

"No need for one. Sit here for a minute. Your eyes will get used to the dark."

"I want a light. I won't go out there without a light."

"A light will attract attention. We don't need to let the world know we're here."

"We shouldn't be here. Don't you see the yellow tapes?"

"Wait. Study the trees and the road. Pretty soon you'll be able to see fine. We've got a nice bright moon."

"How far is it?"

"Quarter mile."

"Please. I don't want to go."

Clover pulled out her keys. "Okay. You wait here. Keep the doors locked."

"No. I'm scared."

"Your choice." She strode up to the cop car and checked for a deputy. The car was locked up tight. Apparently Swenson had no fresh staff to guard the site. She had walked no more than ten feet before she heard a car door slam behind her.

Mindy hurried to her. "Can I hold your arm?"

"Yes." She turned her head slightly, stopped, and listened. It had not been Mindy who slammed the car door. Maybe there was an officer stationed here after all.

"Someone is coming," Clover whispered. "When we get around the next turn, we're going to go off the road. Stay quiet and follow closely."

Mindy moved closer. "Who is it?"

"I don't know. Hush. Follow me."

They rounded another curve. The ground softened and rustled under their feet as they moved off the road and into the trees. "Hold still. Don't move. Put your head down and breathe through your nose. Slowly."

Both of Mindy's hands dug into the softness of Clover's upper arm.

Clover tapped lightly on the girl's hand until she relaxed her grip.

Soft footfalls moved toward them.

She needed a weapon. Her left hand closed on a Devil's club stump. The needles sunk painfully into her flesh.

Her quick intake of breath caused the stranger to pause.

Mindy began to whimper.

"Once they pass, we'll run to the car."

The girl's eyes were wide and white in the darkness.

"Close your eyes. I'll tell you when."

The stranger was in sight now. Medium height and build. A gun held close to their body. Clover half closed her eyes and breathed deeply. They couldn't outrun a gun. The figure grew large and stopped on the road in front of them.

The girl gasped and pulled away. The gun swung towards them.

"Maggie?"

"That you, Clover? Who you got with you? Come out where I can see you."

Clover dragged the girl to the roadway. "Jesus, Maggie! You scared the starch out of us!"

"You should be scared. I passed here not fifteen minutes ago. Saw a light. Drove home for the dogs and my gun. When I saw your car. I thought he'd gotten you." She clucked her tongue. Three dogs came silently to her side. "Did you see anyone?"

"No one."

"What are you doing here?"

"When I came earlier, I rubbed up against something on the road. I didn't know it was blood until I got home. I hoped the sheriff would still be here so I could lead him to it."

"Well we've let God and everybody know we're here. Might as well put on the light and go find it."

⁓

At that exact moment Jenny Casey was giving birth to a healthy, screaming, eight-pound girl. Although her parents had demanded anesthesia long before it was necessary and insisted on being by her side throughout the delivery, they were not an adequate substitute for her missing husband. Settled in a clean bed, she now cried for her absent husband.

"We couldn't find him, honey, " Mrs. Lind said. "We tried everywhere. His radio is off."

"He was going to help Mrs. Mulroon. He was going to work on her sink. Did you try there?"

"I've told you, Dear. He was there and left. Mrs. Mulroon went on and on about what a wonderful boy he is, and how he ate the big meal she put out for him."

"And that's probably why we haven't heard from him," her father added. "He isn't hungry."

"Daddy! Why do you hate K.C.? Everybody else seems to like him."

"No use going into that now, Jenny."

"He's the father of your grandbaby. Now you'll have to be nice to him."

"We'll thank him for that." Mrs. Lind placed the warmly wrapped infant into her daughter's arms. "Now, we've got to go, Darling. You rest and do what the nurses tell you and we'll be back in the morning. We'll find K.C. and we must think of a better name for this beauty."

"She's Katie, Mother. K.C. and I have already named her."

"We'll talk about it in the morning, Dear". She leaned down and kissed her daughter's forehead. "Good night, Dear Mother."

"Night, Momma. Daddy."

Her mother's voice carried back from the hallway. "We'll have to be firm," she said to her husband. "Katie Casey will never do."

Jenny Casey turned her head into the pillow away from her new baby girl and began to sob.

∽

Clover hurried to the Lind's as soon as she received their call. She parked on the wide drive and had not reached the second porch stair when Mrs. Lind pulled open the door.

"Come in, dear. Come. Come."

Mr. Lind's house slippers made a slithering sound as he moved across the marble floor to take Clover's jacket. He led them into the formal parlor.

"Oh, my dear," Mrs. Lind began. "We are so upset. It doesn't seem possible. How will we tell Jenny? She had a beautiful baby girl, you know. We're going to call her Amy Lind. Her father wasn't there for her birth. He's a worthless boy."

"We've been going over the possibilities. We've discussed our responsibility in this." Mr. Lind interrupted.

Clover poured cream into her coffee and four teaspoons of sugar. She caught Mr. Lind's disapproving glance and added another teaspoonful. "I've talked to several friends in the legal community. We have a commitment from one of the best lawyers in the state. I've brought his name and number so you can talk to him if you'd like." She offered the slip of paper across the Chippendale table.

Neither new grandparent reached for it.

She searched their faces. Silence lengthened and jelled in the cold room.

Mrs. Lind finally spoke. "We've not discussed a lawyer. We assume he'll be given a public defender."

"He didn't do it."

"Certainly he did," Mr. Lind said. "Absolutely. He's guilty."

"I don't believe that."

"He's an odd one. Never looked me in the eye. Always on edge. I'll testify to that."

"He really didn't do it, Mr. Lind." The slip of paper with the lawyer's number remained under her fingers.

"My dear, Clover. We have so much more experience in these things. We've been unhappy with this boy since Jennifer brought him home. We welcomed him into our home having no idea of this dark side he so carefully hid. You can't expect that we would actually hire legal guidance for him, can you?

He's simply different from anyone we would have chosen for our Jenny. Now he's done this terrible thing and our only concern is for our daughter and our grandchild. Perhaps, with your background, you feel some sort of connection, some sort of sympathy…but, dear, you must know that Jenny comes first with us. We will protect her."

"Do you want your granddaughter raised with this dark thing hovering over her for her entire lifetime? What kind of life will she have?"

"A good life. We'll protect both our girls. We'll take them away and soon all thoughts of this horrible man will disappear. We'll settle them abroad. The child will never know about her birth father. We'll find a more suitable father for her."

"K.C. didn't do this, Mrs. Lind. I have proof that he didn't. He has friends who believe in him, who will fight for him, if you won't. I'll say one thing more and then I'll go."

She spilled her coffee on the perfect tabletop as she wrapped her fingers around the slip of paper. "You don't deserve him to be the father of your grandchildren. I find it hard to believe that you can sit here and judge without listening. You can all go to hell. I can find the door."

❧

She drove directly to St. James Hospital and took the elevator to the sixth floor. She paused long enough to observe the small baby with a head full of dark curls and the big blue eyes of her daddy before she followed the hurrying nurses toward sobs emanating from a suite at the end of the hall.

Newspapers were spread over the bed and the floor of the room. One nurse tried to gather them up while another struggled to restrain Jenny from throwing more. On seeing Clover, Jenny lifted a pillow and held it over her face with both hands.

"Jenny."

Her body writhed and turned away.

"Jenny. You have to listen to me. You have to talk to me."

She shook her head.

"Jenny, please. K.C. didn't do this. You know he couldn't do anything like this."

She turned back and lowered the pillow to reveal one puffy, red-rimmed eye.

"Please? Just listen?"

"Have you seen him? Have you talked to him?"

"I talked to him last night."

"What was he doing with that girl? Why was he going to meet her?"

"That's not a question I can answer, Jenny. You'll have to ask him. I can tell you that his only concern is for you. He is worried about you and he wants to hold his baby."

"He wasn't even here! He was out there with her!"

"We all make mistakes."

"Yeah, but we don't murder our mistakes!"

"Neither did K.C."

She turned her face toward the window and stared out at the tree-lined parking lot. "I have to get out of here. I can't stay in this town. I have my baby to think of now. I have to protect her."

"That's true. But she's K.C.'s child too. He's a good man, Jenny. He'll be a wonderful father. Don't you want your little girl to have a good father?"

She continued to stare out the window. "It's too late for that. The damage is done. I can't love him anymore."

"I know it's hard to think about loving him today, Jenny. When you learn the truth, you may find that it's not as bad as it seems."

"The newspaper says he was going to meet that girl. And he admitted that he was. He said so, right to the police. And here I was, having his baby, all alone in the delivery room, and all he could think about was getting a piece of ass! I'll never forgive him for this! Never!"

"You have good reasons to be mad, Jenny, and hurt. I know he loves you and I know, too, that he can be a jerk at times, but he needs some help and Maggie and me seem to be the only people in his corner right now."

She closed her eyes.

"When you're feeling better and you can look at things differently, you might change your mind. Call me if you do. Will you do that much for K.C.? Leave some room in your mind that it may not be what it seems? Will you Jenny?"

Jenny Casey shook her head.

༄

Clover and Mr. Hollingsworth, death penalty expert and opponent, walked through steel doors into the polished corridor that marked the building as a government-run institution.

They were placed in a cold room containing one stationary table, a steel bench and two folding chairs. K.C. waited on the bench. Clover noted the video camera bolted to the high ceiling and was reminded of her senator husband video-taping their divorce proceedings the previous year. She had changed much since that day. She wasn't sure if she'd changed for the better or the worse.

Tears filled K.C.'s eyes. "You're here." He lowered his head onto his folded arms. His shoulders shook with sobs. He lifted his head and met her eyes. "I didn't think anybody would come."

"Couldn't stay away," she said. "The atmosphere here is so irresistible."

He attempted to smile.

"This is Bruce Hollingsworth. He's going to be your new lawyer. He specializes in death penalty cases. We need his expertise. We don't have much time and we've got a lot of questions. Are you ready?"

CHAPTER TEN

"You're a complete fool, Clover. You know that don't you?" Dick Morton raised his eyebrows but kept his voice low and intimate.

"I don't think so, Dick. I think I have pretty good instincts about people."

"Psychopaths aren't people. They're soulless beings driven to distasteful deeds by distasteful thoughts. Your trust in him won't stop him."

"He didn't do it. None of it."

"He did the nasty with her. He admitted it."

"So, if we had sex it would be a crime?"

He answered with a sly smile and raised eyebrows. "Who else could it be? Who else is a prime candidate? Any ideas, Master Sleuth?" His derision was annoying.

"If you'll excuse me, Dick, I think Mom needs some help in the kitchen."

He laughed politely. "My sweet Clover. I do apologize. I seem to have struck a nerve, or maybe a cord. I'll go lay myself on Lisa. She looks like she could use some cheering up."

As usual, Dad Billingsley had perfectly timed this intimate party to bring her sister back into the world.

Clover's gaze followed Dick's retreating back to Lisa who, although thin and rather lifeless, seemed to be handling things much better. She had managed several conversations through dinner and now, while coffee was being served, made small talk with ease.

Lisa smiled as Dick Morton nuzzled her sister's ear and whispered something that must have tickled her enough to bring a smile to her lips.

A chilling draft in the big room caused Clover to pull her beaded sweater close. She made her way toward the crackling blaze in the fireplace.

Dad Billingsley reached out from a small circle of older men and pulled her to his side. "Clover has been studying the murders for some time now," Dad said. "She feels pretty strongly that the Casey boy has been set-up. The courts must have considered that a possibility since they released him on bail."

"Stupid of them," a tall man muttered. "He'll kill again. Or worse, he'll run."

Clover raised her eyes and met the man's gaze. "They offered him a lie detector test. He took it and passed."

"Psychopaths pass those things all the time. They don't have the same emotions or consciences of normal people. It's all open to interpretation anyway."

"They took body fluid tests," she persisted. "He chose to give specimens. When the DNA comes back it will not be a match. I feel certain of it."

"If that should happen, I might concede that you are right. In the meantime they are taking one hell of a chance on this guy. And that crazy old coot Maggie Bamford will be his next victim. She should know better than to harbor a man like him."

"If the DNA matches, I'll walk down Main Street with a sign of apology on my back. And I'll do it once a year for the rest of my life."

"With him out on the street, your life may be pretty short anyway. You'd better stay far away from this creep. Even his wife won't go near him now."

Another man jumped into the conversation "She's made a wise decision. Putting space between him and the child is the sanest thing she could do. Even if he didn't murder the girl, he admits that he'd had intercourse with her on previous occasions. What kind of man would do that while his wife was large with his child?"

Clover smiled up at the man who she had known very well when she was thirteen. "I don't know Mr. McAdams. Maybe you could explain that to me."

Some of the men didn't hold back their smiles. McAdam's womanizing was well known in the circle of friends.

Doctor Billingsley seemed uncomfortable with the interaction. Could he know of Clover's early experience with the man? She gave her father a quick apologetic glance, and was about to sooth over the awkwardness when the housekeeper came between them. "Clover. Telephone. Someone named Roger."

୧∿୨

When she agreed to stay at the kennels so Roger could fly back east and help his ill mother move from her home into an assisted living facility, Clover had felt confident that, with Maggie's help, she could handle the multiple demands of the kennel, the stables, and her job. It would be a good interlude from the nightly chaos of the street.

However, each night, for hours on end, the restless dogs howled, paced their yards, dug at fence lines, and ignored the few commands Roger had taught her before he jetted off. Most nights she sat in his leather recliner and tried to sleep between arias of the frantic chorus. Five sleepless nights behind her, she sought out Maggie's advice.

"I admit it, Maggie. I'm not a country girl. The nights seem like eternities. I'd rather hear sirens and blaring horns of the city, than this constant howling.

"It's the young foxes being weaned," Maggie reassured. "They always scream the first few times their mothers abandon them to search for food."

Clover smiled as she remembered that she hadn't howled when her mother abandoned her. She had instead learned to pilfer half-eaten sandwiches from a garbage can that was advantageously close to her hanging backpack at the back of her second grade classroom. She had survived several weeks on her own, washing her clothes in the single sink and hanging them to dry on the back of a chair.

It had been Lisa who asked why her clothes were always so wrinkled and Lisa who had requested that her family allow Clover to use their laundry room.

When the Billingsleys had arrived at the door of her tiny room, yes, she had collapsed in a deluge of tears. But, she'd never howled. "It doesn't sound like foxes," she now said to Maggie.

"Take a light and follow the yips," Maggie persisted. "You'll find a fox kit yowling for its mother. Be sure to carry that gun that I gave you. There's no greater equalizer in the woods, especially since you've learned to handle it so well."

Even with Duke at her side and the gun in the deep pocket of her jogging suit, she did not have the courage to seek out the source of the screams. In each early morning light, she chided herself for cowardice.

On the sixth night Duke refused to sleep by her chair. Instead he paced the house with narrowed eyes and his ears raised in alert. The hair on his hindquarters stood erect as he pounced repeatedly at one side window. His snarls and bared teeth revealed a viciousness she had not witnessed before.

"Down!" she commanded and when he refused to obey, she had a momentary urge to open the door and allow the dog to follow his instincts. Instead she turned off the lamps and hunkered under a blanket like a child afraid of the monster under the bed.

She had gained a new respect for Roger who so effortlessly managed the place. His handiwork was evident in the neatly spaced split rail fences, groomed trails, and tidy kennels.

Feeding and exercising the dogs and horses took up most of each morning and her duties at the University took the remainder of the afternoons. This was not a life she would choose for herself, but it did keep her away from the town's fury over K.C. And it did allow her to ride one of the horses through the woods to Maggie's each evening to speak with K.C. and prepare his defense.

Everywhere she went the dog followed closely. Perhaps she should get a dog of her own: one as gentle and intelligent as Duke, but not as large. He allowed her to feel safe.

❧

Three weeks later both Roger and DNA results, from the blood found in the clearing, returned.

"If I wasn't in mourning," Roger said, as he tossed his bag behind the seat of the truck. "I'm sure you would make me eat my fill of crow."

She stood by as Duke covered his master with relieved kisses that were met with an enthusiasm she had rarely observed in Roger.

"I am sorry about your mother, Roger."

He glanced over Duke's big head. "Well, it's done. What's another life anyway? She was old and she was tired and she didn't want to leave her home. I'm glad I didn't have to force her to do that."

"Did she die at home?"

"Yes. What can I say? It was her time."

"Say you're sad. Or you'll miss her. That's normally what people feel."

"I won't miss any of it. I put the house on the market as is. I let the neighbors come in and take what they wanted and I handed the key to the real estate woman. Nothing more to it."

Some of her newly found respect for him slowly melted away. He really was a jerk.

❧

Despite Dad Billingsley's lobbying efforts, K.C. was not forgiven or exonerated from the suspicions of the townspeople.

Without work he boarded with Maggie, helping her reconstruct her sagging porch and adding shelving to the room where Victor slept.

His tenderness with the boy brought tears to Clover's eyes and changes to Victor's hesitant personality. Only the rolling, mellow dogs and the teasingly patient K.C. could make the boy laugh until his now chubby body shook with joy. It was for K.C. that he took his first real steps and it was for K.C. that he finally ventured out the doorway on his own to look up, unafraid, at the huge trees that surrounded him.

∾

Clover's and Roger's return to the strip was met with hostility.

"It's because of Squeak," Sandra explained. "She's gone again and Sammie thinks you have something to do with it."

"Do you know where she is, Sandra?"

"Dunno. She hasn't called me. Every time she's gone before, she's called me. She knows I'd never rat on her."

"She hasn't been in touch with Maggie. She wouldn't run off without at least checking on her baby, would she?"

"I dunno. She was mad at Sammie, but she gets mad at him a lot. She didn't have no other boyfriend that I know of. She woulda told me. I just hope nothing bad happened to her."

"You girls lead dangerous lives, Sandra. I worry about you every time you go off in one of those cars."

"Me? Heck, I can handle anything. I ain't worried."

"Have you thought about the offer from your sister?"

"Yeah. I think about it all the time. All it takes is some cash and the guts to run. Now where would I get enough of those? Even if I could buy the ticket, I don't know if I have enough of me left to get on the bus."

"I could help."

"I don't need no charity. Only take money from turning tricks. Honest money. Good clean money."

"Sure," Clover laughed. "Hard-earned."

"Hard-earned! Hey! You're getting funny, girl!"

A horn honked. Sandra spoke to the driver and slid into the car.

Clover leaned against the building and turned her head to one side. She was tired and discouraged.

"Hey!" The familiar horn of Roger's truck summoned her back to reality.

She strolled over to the pickup and leaned seductively against the cold metal.

"Yeah?"

"Sammie's pissed. Insists I go to Maggie's and see if Squeak's there. I told him Maggie hasn't heard from her, but he's been drugging all day and isn't hearing what I'm saying. He's getting pretty nasty. He knows about that sweet young thing you stole from him. I'm not sure you're safe here, Clover."

"I'm a big girl. I can take care of myself."

"Not where Sammie's concerned. The guy is dirt. You've crossed him. He'll screw you first chance he gets."

"I'm not going to let him scare me off. Somebody has to stand up to him."

"That somebody shouldn't be you."

"That's my decision."

"Look. I'm going to go up to the store and make a call to Maggie. The guy in the store is on Sammie's payroll. He'll snitch. That might calm the bastard down."

Clover shrugged.

"I have a john arranged for you, should be by anytime now. Tall guy in a white camper. When you come back, we're calling it quits!"

"Fuck you, Roger!"

"Yeah. Same to you, Clover!"

Five minutes after he drove off, the camper came into view – a big new RV.

She waved gaily at the man driving and did a little two-step, pulling her short skirt high enough to show her wares. The man pulled over to the curb. "Hey," he said.

"Hey, yourself."

He smiled.

"You want a date?"

His laugh was as tentative as his words. "I'm not sure."

"What? You don't like what you see?" She twirled once and took a deep breath to show off her breasts.

"Looks fine."

"Available."

"Yeah?" A deep dimple creased one cheek.

"Well, honey, for someone as cute as you, we should talk. Who knows where it might lead."

Sammie, standing in the shadows, waved his hand in confirmation. She could see the white teeth of his smile through the darkness.

The driver laughed. "I'm a little lost. I'm looking for the airport and a friend."

"Hey, you got yourself a friend like you never had before." She swayed slowly through the lights of the vehicle and showed a lot of leg as she climbed into its high seat.

He hesitated and took a deep breath. "Which way?"

"Straight ahead. I'll tell you where to turn."

He concentrated on his driving but couldn't make the turn into her usual alley.

"Oh, shit! I didn't realize this rig was so big. Go ahead two more blocks and make a left." She would take him out to the river road where the view was better.

"This area is new to me."

"Don't worry, I've done it all before."

Five minutes later, he pulled into the scenic viewpoint where the rig took up the entire parking area. "So what do we do now?"

"Turn off the lights and we'll enjoy the view."

She liked his hesitant smile. "Did you bring the coffee?"

"Coffee? No I don't have any. I have some stuff for drinks though. You want a drink?"

"Sure. I could use one about now."

He seemed relieved to be moving. He climbed into the back. He was very tall.

"Boy. You're a big one," she said.

He didn't respond.

She followed him down the small hallway.

He stopped and pulled a bottle from the tall cabinet and carried it to the kitchen area where he filled glasses with ice.

She walked past and through to the rear where a bed filled the entire space. "Hey. This is neat." She flopped onto a thick comforter, lay back, and pulled her legs up. She liked teasing these straight guys.

He handed her a cold glass and sat beside her.

"So, how long have you known Roger?"

"Who?"

"Roger. You know, my friend and partner, Roger."

"Oh, that black guy?"

"No. No. Roger."

He was bewildered, totally bewildered.

Jesus! Wrong john! She sat up. Should she explain? Should she ask to be let out into the darkness? An involuntary shiver ran through her. She would not chance walking alone through the jungle of city streets.

He smiled again. "I've never done anything like this before. You'll have to excuse my ignorance." The dimple on his cheek gave him an air of innocence.

Sammie had waved her on. Had he set her up? "First time for everything." She had to find a way out. "So. Where are you from?"

"Now? Portland. I'm on my way to Seattle for a game. Basketball."

"You a fan?"

"Nah. Rookie player. I'll be a pro one day."

"They must pay you pretty well." She studied the room again, playing for time.

"The pays okay. It'll get better."

"What brings you here?"

"I'm supposed to pick up another guy at the airport. I got a little lost. I was going to ask for directions. You waved and I came running." He looked away, studied the wall behind her.

"Do I scare you?"

"You scare the bejesus out of me."

"I don't think I've ever scared a man before."

"I've never done this before. I mean, I could always have a groupie after the game like a lot of the guys do, but I had a steady girlfriend. I've been a little out of it since we broke up. I've never paid for it before. I don't know what girls like you do."

What had Sandra said? 'Half of it is psychology, like going to a shrink.'

"What happened to your girl?" she asked.

"Ran off with another player who got traded. We'd been together since high school. Never thought she'd leave."

"Did you treat her badly?"

The question surprised him. "No. Never. I guess the other guy was more interesting." He reached out one hand and traced a circle on her bare leg. "I'm not a very exciting guy."

She did not move away. "I find you exciting."

"You don't know me."

"Sometimes that can be exciting in itself." She no longer felt a need to escape.

He nodded.

"So why'd you stop?"

"I was going to ask directions. You kind of took over."

"Yes, I guess I did."

He put his glass on the floor, took hers and placed it beside his. "So what do we do?"

She smiled and ran one finger over his lips. "Everything," she said. "And anything. Anything you want."

"I'll take it all."

"It's yours."

~

Her hair was still damp from their shared shower when she jumped from the RV. She waved good-bye and blew kisses into the air as the vehicle disappeared. She felt strangely powerful, as if she'd completed a long journey, a great adventure. She smiled broadly as she sashayed across the street toward Sandra. "Honey," she called. "I just turned my first trick."

"What's that you're sayin?"

"I did. I really did. Don't ask. Don't tell. Don't scold. Don't say a word. Honey, I won't tell you nothin!"

Sandra began to laugh, and then caught herself. "They're all out lookin for you. Goin to be real mad."

She shrugged. "I don't care. Look. He gave me all this money." She held a roll of bills out toward Sandra. "Take it. I don't need it. Take it and go home. Don't go to your place or tell Sammie."

Sandra stared at the cash, but pushed it away.

"I mean it. Take a cab to the bus and get on it." Clover retrieved the guy's business card and shoved the money into the girl's hand. "Will you go?"

"Sammie would kill me."

"Promise me, Sandra."

"Shit, girl, what's wrong with you. You're out of your mind."

"Promise me. Go and don't look back."

"Stop it."

"Sandra, this is your chance. You can just walk away."

"What? Just like that? Just up and go?"

Clover nodded. "Yes. Just up and go."

Sandra glanced quickly up and down the street. She took the money.

"Here comes your man."

"Hurry. Go."

"I say thanks, but, honey, I got to ask. I got to know what you did to deserve this much money?"

Clover laughed. "I did what I normally do, only a little better."

"Shit! Like how better?"

"You'll never know," she swung her hips and strutted her stuff. "I won't tell nobody nothin."

Roger's face was white and strained as he jumped from the truck. He put his hands on her shoulders and looked into her eyes. "You all right, Clover? You're not hurt?"

She heard Sandra's quick giggle. "I'm fine, Roger. No problem."

His hand touched her hair. "Your hair's wet."

She shrugged and looked away. "Sandra, call me, you hear. Call me."

"Where'd you go?"

"Over to the river. I thought he was your friend. Sammie said yes."

"Sammie's mad at us, remember?"

"It was okay."

"What have you done?" he demanded.

"It's none of your business. I'm a big girl!"

"You're a tramp!"

"Hey, now, Honey," Sandra interrupted. "You better watch that mouth of yours around here. Someone might take offense."

Clover snickered.

He turned on Sandra. "This is none of your business, bitch!"

"Well, now, Mr. Big Man, you're starting to sound just like Sammie." Sandra turned her back on the couple and walked into the night.

"You scared the hell out of me. Had me running up and down the streets like a crazy fool, looking into parked cars, shining lights in people's faces." He turned away and ran both hands over his hair. "I'm finished with this. Finished! You can get yourself a real God-damned pimp. You look like you've earned one."

She faced him. "Maybe I have. Maybe I've always needed one." She turned and walked away from his accusing eyes. She was finished too.

Roger Parrish slumped in his chair, an uneaten TV dinner on the table before him. He had never been more wrong about a woman. He'd had his share of unfaithful wives and headstrong girlfriends, but he'd never known one who would stoop to the level that Clover Winters had. He'd thought she was different, but in the end she was as untrustworthy as the rest. Why did he care anyway? She was just a broad with an upscale background and no real core strength. A million out there like her, maybe not as good looking, but with the same manipulative ways. He'd learned long ago to not depend on a woman, so why had he slipped up now?

"I don't know, Duke," he murmured to his dog. "I don't know what makes a woman tick. It certainly isn't their hearts that lead them. Weak. The whole lot of them. Not worth the time of day." With that thought he refilled his glass and chugged the rum.

Sleep evaded her for two nights as she waited for Sandra to call. Finally, on the third morning, she showered, pulled on her jogging clothes and a fanny pack with Maggie's gun, and sprinted off for a good run. After the third lap around the high school track, she felt the pattering anxiety in her mid chest slowly fade away. If Sandra couldn't make the break, then so-be-it, at least she had given her a chance, had gambled on the girl's innate goodness and had provided the means for her to change. There was nothing more she could do.

She did four miles then turned for the run up the hill toward home.

Sammie's Lincoln was parked in front of the townhouse. Sammie paced on the sidewalk. Before she could turn away, he called out. "I want words with you, Bitch!"

She slowed her pace and moved closer. If he was strung out she could easily outrun him. "Sammie? What are you doing here?"

"I said I want to talk to you."

She took several good breaths before she met his eyes. "Well, talk."

"In my car."

"I'm not getting in your car. You want to talk? Talk!"

He reached out one long arm, grabbed her sweatshirt and pulled her to him. His hot breath was metallic.

She swatted at him. "What the hell's wrong with you?"

"It ain't what's wrong with me. It's what's going to be wrong with you! I'd like to break you in little pieces and scatter you all over this sidewalk!"

"Asshole! Let go!"

She felt the force of his blow across her face and down the back of her neck. Her legs buckled. Her buttocks hit the sidewalk with a small thwack.

His socks were mismatched.

"You're ruining my business, sister! And I got the right to make you pay up."

"Touch me again, jerk, and you're going to be paying with time!"

Several neighbors came out onto their decks. "I'm calling the sheriff!" someone screamed.

"No," Clover shouted. "I'm okay." She pulled herself up and faced him full on. She curled and uncurled her fists, then lifted her red fingernails to threaten his face. "Don't touch me again," she hissed. "You touch me again and I'll fucking kill you!"

Her eyes burned into his. Her blood red lips pulled back across perfect white teeth.

He stepped back as she pulled herself to full height and pursed her lips to spit.

With shaking hands she released the Velcro of her fanny pack and pulled the small pistol from its bed. She pushed it against his chest.

His startled expression brought a smile to her face. "Now, fuck-nut," she said. "Tell me exactly what it is that you don't like about me."

"No hard feelings," he tried.

"Not on this end."

"Where's Sandra?"

"I don't know."

"Fuck that!" He raised his fist.

She tipped the gun toward his face.

"Okay. Okay. Maybe you don't know. But know this, Bitch. The deal was, I helped you. You helped me. It ain't worked out that way. The deal is over."

"Yes. The deal is over."

"Fuck it!" He stamped his foot. "I lose a couple of women to a fucking pervert and now I lose just as many to a fucking Mother Theresa. Either way it's money down the tubes. You think I don't know about that girl you stole from me? You think my people don't tell me what's happening on my block?

I got eyes where you ain't got a clue. Stay off my street! Understand? Don't show your white ass down there again. You got the goods now, sister, but next time we meet the odds will be on my side!"

"Fuck you!" She screamed at his retreating back. "Fuck you!"

She held the gun in view until his car sped off down the long wide street, then she tucked it into her pack and turned to a frightened neighbor. "Millie," she smiled. "You got an icepack? I think I'm going to look like a prizefighter in a little while.

၈၅

"I'm okay." She held the phone away from her painful jaw and ear as she tried to explain to her sister.

"That was a stupid thing to do, Clover," Lisa said.

"Yes, I know. But, he hit me. It pissed me off."

"He doesn't sound like someone you should fool with."

"I wasn't fooling. If he came at me again, I would have shot him." She moved the phone to her other ear and studied her face in the mirror. The swelling had lessened; some bruising remained.

"Have you talked to Roger?"

"No. He's mad at me too."

"Why?"

"He's in a snit of some kind."

"Are you going to press charges against the other one?"

"No."

" Do you have a permit for that gun?"

"You don't think I'd walk that damned strip without some protection."

"How long have you had that thing?"

"A while."

"And you know how to use it? The right way?"

"Yes, I took lessons."

"Where?"

"From Maggie. Maggie is an expert with guns."

"Oh, Clover, I'm so afraid for you."

Lisa's sobs softened her. "Lisa. Lisa. It's going to be all right. Please. I know what I'm doing."

"We want you to stop. None of us could stand it if something happened to you."

"I can't stop. It's not only about Jim anymore. There are a lot more people involved. I have to finish this."

Her sister could not speak as her sobs increased.

"Lisa, I have another call coming in, I'll call you tomorrow, okay?"

"Call me. Yes, call me early. I love you, Clover."

"Me too, Lisa. Bye." She clicked the phone to the second call. "Maggie. Oh, Maggie you're like a breath of fresh air."

"The whole town is talking about you, young lady."

"Yes, I know. Let them talk."

"And Roger is mad at you."

"Yes, he is."

"Can you tell me why?"

"No, I can't."

"He says you still drive to that damned strip every night even though he's not with you."

"I do drive over there."

"You have some kind of nostalgia for the place?"

"Nothing to do with nostalgia. I've been looking for Squeak and Sandra. I'm really worried about both of them, Maggie. I think Sandra left the street, but she hasn't called. She said she would."

"It's possible she chickened out."

"Yes, I know, but I'm sure she would call and tell me if that was it. I hope you're wrong. I want to believe that she had the courage to go home."

"How's your face?"

"It still hurts a little, but it's almost better."

"Clover, I'm going to be honest with you. You've got to stop this madness. Without Roger to protect you, you're a sitting duck for some creep. You've got to stop going over there."

"Maggie, I can't stop. How's K.C.?"

"A little better now that he's talked to Jenny."

"He saw her?"

"No. She called him. They're talking about getting back together. She's in California with the baby."

"You've got to be kidding. That's great news. But, California? K.C. can't leave the state now."

"I didn't mean right away. They've got a lot to work out first. But, eventually that's where he'll go."

"Oh, good, you had me scared there for a minute. The last thing we need is for him to jump bail."

"I'm sorry Jenny left town. It would have been easier for K.C. if she'd stayed and backed him."

She could hear the chortle of the toddler coming closer. The sound tugged at her heartstrings. "How's Owly?"

"Victor. Or Vic."

"I'm sorry, Maggie. I slip up now and then."

"He's talking now. Calls me Muggie."

"He calls you Muggie? That's cute. A little speech therapy and the kid will go far."

"Not nice, Clover."

"I'm kidding. You're doing a wonderful job with him."

"Both Roger and K.C. have names too. Roger is Og and K.C. is See. They both spend a lot of time with him." She paused. "It's Roger I'm calling about, Clover. What do you think makes him the way he is? He rides those horses hard and he speaks more to them and the dogs than to anyone else. What is wrong with him?"

"He rides his horses hard because he's angry. It's his nature. I think he was born that way. Whatever it is, Maggie, I'm sure he'll get over it."

"I think you could change that, my dear."

"No, sorry, Maggie, there's nothing I can do to change anything."

"Are you going to that awful street tonight?

"No, I'm not. Tonight I'm going to have a hot bath and catch up on my Law School stuff. I'll call you tomorrow."

"Promise?

"Yes, I promise."

She settled into the tub and ran a washcloth over the tender areas of her neck and ear. She picked up her hand mirror and compulsively studied her face.

She was thinner and more drawn, but except for the remaining slight bruising she was pretty much the same. Was she a whore at heart? Was her decency only skin deep? Did her likeness to her mother run deeper than the classic good looks that had made her life so much easier and so much harder at the same time?

The gun had felt right in her hands and when she pointed it at Sammie, it was all that she could manage not to gently squeeze and put a perfect hole through his pulsing, putrid heart. She had wanted to kill.

That fact both confused and intrigued her. Was she becoming a danger to society or was she a pawn like the other women who walked that cursed street? Did she have the heart of a streetwalker or the nerves of gunslinger?

She opened the drain with her big toe and stood. She was changed. Forever changed. She was wiser, more controlled and less afraid. There could be nothing wrong with that. She wrapped a soft towel around her wet hair and pulled another from the shelf.

The doorbell chimed. To hell with them. She continued to towel the moisture from her back.

The bell chimed again.

She splashed rose cologne on her flushed skin and pulled her heavy terry robe from the hook behind the door. As she tied the robe she laughed at her wrinkled toes peeking out from her crimson scuffs. "I'm coming," she called. "Who is it?"

"Roger."

"Well, Roger. Imagine that."

"Open the door, Clover. I need to talk to you."

She opened the door. "Long time, no see."

He followed her into the room and stood awkwardly.

She turned and faced him. "Did you come to apologize?"

"I suppose. I never gave you a chance to explain. I expected the worst and exploded."

"Oh?" She wasn't sure she wanted him to continue.

"Well, Jesus, Clover. What would you expect me to think? You were gone two hours. You came back looking like you do now, fresh from the shower and glowing."

"Am I glowing?" She shook out her hair and began to dry it with the towel.

He didn't answer.

"And what exactly did you think, Roger?"

She came closer to him. Droplets of water from her hair fell on him.

His eyes darted from wall to wall.

"I thought …You know… Damn it, Clover, you know what I thought."

She would make him have eye contact with her. "You thought I got into an RV with a strange man and drove off with him. You thought that I undressed for him; that I had sex with him; that I did any number of ungodly acts with him; and then I calmly showered and came back. Is that what you thought, Roger?"

He didn't answer.

"Is that the worst that you thought, Roger?" She asked softly.

She was very close now.

She felt his fingertips brush her skin. "Is that the worst, Roger?"

He stepped backwards.

"Is it, Roger?"

"You know God-damned well it is!"

Finally his eyes met hers.

"I'm very happy to inform you, Roger, that you were right on. The worst did happen."

"Bullshit!"

"So I tell the truth and you don't believe me."

"I don't want to believe you."

"Really, Roger, that's what happened. I got into that RV, thinking that it was your decoy. The driver was very attractive. He didn't know anything about me."

"I don't want to know any more."

"But I want to tell you, Roger. I want you to understand."

"I can't understand."

"Try, Roger. Think about this. I get into a vehicle. I think I can tease the man because he's in on the ruse. I strut for him. I am seductive for him. And when I find that I am alone with him and he doesn't know and I'm free to do whatever I please, I strip for him, I become very, very sexy for him."

He was turning away, walking toward the door.

She needed to shock him, to hurt him into feeling. "But really, Roger, that wasn't the worst. Do you want to know what the worst was, Roger?"

He stopped at the door and shook his head.

"The worst, Roger, was that I enjoyed that man. I enjoyed every God-damned thing that I did with him."

He was opening the door.

"Wait, Roger. Wait. The best is yet to come. Listen to this." She reached out to him and touched his shoulder.

He winced.

"The worst and the best, Roger. You'll like this. He paid me. He became the first man that I have ever known who actually paid me for it." She began to laugh.

He turned. His eyes frightened her.

"Shut up!" He grabbed her shoulders and shook.

Her head flailed from side to side painfully, but she couldn't stop laughing. "He paid me, Roger. And I kept the money."

Her robe came open. She could feel his cold eyes on her warm skin. The sweet musky scent of roses filled the air.

She was in his arms. His hands pushed the robe away. He tasted the skin of her neck, her shoulders.

She trembled. Her heart beat erratically under her smooth breasts. He tasted her heart.

She fell backwards on the couch. She felt the weight of him. His flannel shirt was soft and warm. His wool pants burned her flesh. He moved away momentarily and then was inside her.

They moved together, shuddered, thrust and retreated. Again and again. Her robe balled up behind her, bending her back in an unnatural arc. His body hurt her, bruised and burned her and still she responded. Perspiration dripped from her temples, pooled in her closed eyes and still she accepted him.

He groaned painfully, as if his very soul were burning.

She felt a slow lifting of his heavy weight, aloneness, a coldness that she had never experienced before. She lay still until she heard the door close quietly. She turned her face into the sofa and began to sob softly, ever so softly.

CHAPTER ELEVEN

For three days she hid in her crimson cave. She unplugged her crimson phones and pulled down her crimson shades. Each night, sitting cross-legged in the middle of the living room floor with her mother's coat draped unceremoniously over her head, she chanted from dusk until dawn.

When she felt hungry, she padded into the kitchen and nibbled on stale crackers and sipped soda pop. When the pop was gone she drank milk from the carton then tossed the empty container into the garbage and climbed into her crimson bed to stare for hours at her crimson walls.

The world was perverse and humankind was twisted. She belonged everywhere and nowhere. She wandered dry-eyed and sullen from bed to living room, floor to kitchen and back again.

On the morning of the fourth day something in her psyche changed. She opened the front door and was surprised with the scent of early spring and the first pink flush of buds on the rhododendrons. She collected the neglected newspapers, brewed a cup of tea and settled at the small table by the window.

She sorted the papers by date and began to read. A small column on the third page caught her eye. "The nude body of a young white female was found in a wooded area near Mid-valley Elementary School. Two young children playing near a popular jogging trail found the body in a partially covered grave. The woman was described by authorities as five feet, five inches tall, one hundred and fifty-five pounds with blond hair and blue eyes. Police report that she had an identifying tattoo on her left upper arm. The tattoo is one common to a prostitution ring which operates in the SeaTac area. Police will not reveal her identity until next of kin can be located"

She dropped the paper and telephoned Maggie. "Maggie, My God, why didn't you call me? I just read the paper. Who is the girl? Is it Squeak?"

"Where the hell have you been? Everybody's been trying to reach you?"

"I was doing some things."

"I called the law school. They said you were on sick leave. What's wrong?"

"I've had a flu or something, but I'm getting better now."

"I called the Billingsley's and Lisa said not to worry that she had talked to you and you had promised not to go on the strip again. I talked to Roger and he said he had seen you and that he didn't care if he ever saw you again. What is wrong between you two, Clover? And don't tell me you don't know, because that's what he said and I don't buy it."

"I don't want to talk about it, Maggie."

"You'd better start talking to me, girl. You're driving that man to drink and I can't stand by and watch."

"Is he drinking?"

"Like a fish."

"Roger's an angry man, Maggie. His problems started long before I came along."

"But something has happened. I've never seen him quite like this."

"We've been in the middle of a lot of crap lately. Hanging out on the strip has affected us both."

"He's been falling down drunk since he found out about that girl, Sandra."

"She ran away."

"Well she sure didn't run far. Body was right there by the river."

"Sandra's body?"

"Didn't Roger tell you? He came over to tell you."

"We had an argument. I didn't give him chance to tell me anything. Oh, God, Maggie, what have I done?"

"You tell me, girl."

"I thought she had run away. I gave her money to go. Oh, Maggie!" Tears dropped onto the stack of newspapers, spread dark circles over pictures of the local hospital formal ball.

"Honey, you come over here. Can you get in your car and come? I've loaned my truck to K.C. and Victor is sleeping soundly. Can you drive over here?"

"I'll be all right. I gave her money. She had a sister. She was going to her sister's."

"Come over, Clover, please."

"I can't. Maggie, I have to think. I'll call you back later, okay? I'm going to call Lisa."

"You promise?"

She clicked off the phone.

She had showered and dressed by the time Lisa pounded on her door.

"What the heck have you been doing, Clover? The place looks like you've loosed five toddlers to do destruction and dirty deeds."

"One of my temper tantrums. I feel like a toddler with a need to destroy."

"Maggie said you sounded terrible. She's afraid you've had too much to cope with. I brought the antidote." She lifted a pink bakery box high above her head. "Ta-dum! Straight from Henry's and all your favorite kinds; Chocolate Chip, Pineapple-filled, Pecan Nutties, and the crème de la crème, Éclairs with real whipped cream."

"I have no appetite, Lisa. Sorry."

"You look awful."

"I haven't been able to sleep. The maniac out there is tormenting me. I haven't come one step closer to finding him. He's smart,

Lisa. And sometimes I feel like he knows everything I say, everywhere I go, everything I care about.

I tore the place apart looking for bugs, microphones, cameras – anything that he could have used to watch me. I found nothing. Absolutely nothing. I called a security company to add another system to the windows and the doors. I think I'm becoming a little paranoid."

"Oh, God, Clover. I didn't know what I was asking when I made you promise."

They sat on the vanity bench and held tight to one another.

"Oh, God! Oh, God!" Lisa sobbed. "I can't take anymore. It's all too much."

"I know. I know."

"You're such a good sister, Clover. I'd die if I lost you too. I miss Jim so much. God I miss him."

"I do too."

"I've been brave for the kids and for Mom and Dad. But I hadn't thought about you. You're always so strong. I want you to stop, Clover. I don't want you to look for that man anymore."

"He's so close, I can feel him baiting me. I can hear him laughing. I know that he's daring me to come closer. Sometimes I think if I could only concentrate hard enough I would be able to see him."

"I wish I'd never asked you to get involved."

"I'm glad that I got involved. I've learned so much, about living, about me, about men. I think I know why I picked such a loser to marry and why I do some of the things I do."

"I'm scared for you, Clover."

"I think I know why this killer does what he does. I think I might be smarter than he is. I know that I'm stronger willed. He knows that too. He likes the challenge.

I can't stop. If I stop he'll hurt more people. I can't let him do that."

"Let the cops deal with him."

"Lisa. That's how he got Jim."

Lisa's shoulders shook with sobs.

Clover could not afford the luxury of mourning. "The cops can't stop him. He has binges like us, Lisa. Killing is his cookie-binge and he's on a tear right now. He's really needy. And when he's needy he's vulnerable. I'm not going to give up. He's become active after a fairly long pause. What he did to Jim caused too much attention and he had to hold back. Now he can't stop himself. Now is when I have the advantage."

"No, Clover. You have to stop. I can't bear to have you hurt."

She held her dear sister away. "I won't get hurt, Lisa. I'm going to take a couple of days away."

"Where are you going?"

"The law school is sending me to Portland to find a recruiting venue. They're giving me another chance, even after I've missed so much time. I'm going to put all of this out of my head for a while, so I can think more clearly. When I come back, I'm going to start over, fresh and clear. This time I'll find him."

Shame. It penetrated deeply into Roger Parrish's soul. How low had he sunk? Had he forced himself on Clover, or had it been a mutual encounter? He'd never had sex like that before and doubted that he ever would again. He was angry. She had baited him. Was that rape or two consenting adults? He had begun to think of her as family, maybe a sister or a daughter, but watching her strut on the strip had allowed old feelings to emerge.

He had cared about her in the beginning, wanted to protect her at all costs. Now he had pushed past the line of decency.

But then, so had she. Something about the Sea-Tac strip had strengthened her, weakened him, and corrupted them both.

He shook his head to try and clear it. Too much rum, too much thinking. Neither would do him any good. What was done was done. Too late to fix anything.

❧

Clover held the card in one hand and dialed with the other.

His deep voice came on quickly.

"Hey! Hello!" She smiled. "This is Clover from Seattle."

"Clover?"

"Clover. We met on the street and had drinks near the river. Remember me?"

"Oh. Yeah. Wow. How could I forget?"

"Hey, I'm here on business and thought we might get together, if you'd like."

"Yeah. Yeah. I'd like that, but I got a game tonight."

"I meant this afternoon. Thought we could have lunch."

"You mean like nooners?"

"No, I mean real lunch. I'm here on other business."

"I'd like nooners."

She laughed. "I honestly have only lunch in mind."

"Oh. Well that's fine. I could meet you about 12:30."

"Where?"

"Where are you?"

"Over by Lloyd's Center."

"There's a great Mexican place on Broadway, Texas Grill. I might be late. Can you wait?"

"Sure. I'll have something to drink."

"Okay. I'll see you there."

She had knocked back two Margaritas before he ducked through the doors.

He scanned the room and passed her by.

As he walked back through, she stood and offered her hand. "Hi." She barely reached his chest.

"Clover?"

She nodded. "Sit down. I think you might need a drink."

He kept her hand, took in her professional suit and expensive heels with one long look. "Wow. I didn't recognize you. I honestly didn't. I mean…"

"I know. I'll explain if you'll sit down." She drew him into a chair.

"You look so different." He shook his head.

"I'm starving. Can we order?"

She condensed her story into the first course of chips and salsa.

By the time the Enchilada plates arrived he was laughing with incredulity. The attractive dimple in his cheek appeared repeatedly.

Her face flushed with unexpected heat. She had never quite felt this way before. She wondered if he felt the same.

"You know I came back for you that night," he said.

"You did? Why?"

"I had some vague notion of whisking you away. Of reforming your life."

"A man after my own heart." She tried to keep her voice light as her heart raced.

"I drove up the freeway to the next exit and came back around. You were gone. I imagined you already had another date. That bummed me out."

"Yeah?" She held her hands tightly in her lap to keep from touching him.

"A pudgy blond was standing in your place. I decided to ask about you."

"You talked to her?"

"Never got a chance. Another guy pulled in and whisked her away."

Clover leaned forward. "You saw someone pick her up?"

"Yeah. Pissed me off. I figured I'd never find you again."

She held her breath before asking, "Did you see who picked her up? "

"Some middle-aged guy. Forty, forty-five."

"What kind of car?"

"Yellow Mercedes."

She could barely breathe. "Do you remember anything else about the car? This is really important."

"Really? Why?"

She gathered her briefcase and her purse. "Do you remember anything?"

"Sure. The guy was driving slow as a slug. I had to follow him for blocks. He had one of those license plate rims with a message. Said something like, 'lineman for the county.' It didn't seem to fit with the expensive car so I figured he must of played sports at some time."

"Holy fuck!"

"What? Clover, what is it?"

She stood, touched his arm, pulled away, touched him again. "You are the most wonderful man in the world. You are terrific. You are the most attractive guy I've ever met. I think I could love you. I have to go."

"Clover?"

She stopped moving and looked into his eyes. "I'm serious. I've been looking for someone like you for a long time. Does that scare you?"

"Hell, no. I like you too."

She fished in her briefcase and pulled out her business card. "Here. Call me. Please. I'll explain everything. Right now I have to go."

∾

K.C. Casey was on his knees in another stopped-up bathtub. He cursed silently as the snake stopped advancing, and then whistled happily when he retrieved a hunk of gunk from its tip. It felt good to be back to work. He would give Morton a generous discount for trusting him.

"How's it coming?" Dick stuck his head through the door opening.

"Pretty good. But it's stopped up big time. This will take me awhile."

"Fine. Fine. I'm going to run up to the store and get some cigarettes. You mind staying here alone?"

"Not my usual practice," K.C. answered, straightening slightly. "Not a good idea, but I guess since I know you, it's okay."

"I'll only be a few minutes. If the phone rings, would you mind answering? My wife is flying in and she's going to call with her arrival time. She's been gone awfully long. I wouldn't want to miss her flight."

"Should I give her that message?"

"Yeah. Sure. You know how it is. You get used to having them around. It gets a little lonely without them."

"Yeah."

"Oh, sorry fella. I forgot about your wife. How ignorant of me."

"Hey, it's okay. Not your problem."

He heard the diesel engine rattle on the Mercedes as he screwed the snake into the drain and pulled back once more.

A mass of long blonde hair and black gunk clung to the coil. K.C. smiled. Guy hadn't been too lonely.

He picked up the mess, threw it into his bucket and ran the hot water into the drain. It backed up and wet his legs. Christ when would he learn? He stood and crouched over the drain again.

He ran the snake. Jiggled it. Pulled. More black gunk, blonde hair, paint chips. Into the bucket and water on. No go. The water was up to his rubber shoe tops.

Another run of the snake. Black, fetid, putrid gunk, paint chips, kinky black hair. A cloud of sewer gas followed. The stink was over-powering.

He began to sweat. He stepped carefully from the tub, turned on the bathroom fan and opened the window. Could be the vent pipe was blocked. He'd need to borrow a ladder and go up on the roof when Morton returned.

He stepped back into the tub. The snake advanced several inches farther before he hit a solid blockage. There it was. There.

He advanced the snake slowly, pulled back quickly. Black gunk, big paint chips, slimy stuff like old chicken skin, kinky black hair. The bucket reeked. He lifted it from the tub and placed it nearer the window.

He could hear the Mercedes engine coming up the drive.

He replaced the snake and was relieved when it advanced sev-eral more inches. More putrid gunk, black kinky hair, and some-thing white and glistening. Jesus.

Looked like a fingertip. On one end a shiny red-painted nail, on the other, macerated chicken skin.

Holy Christ! Some liquid dripped onto the floor as he studied the slimy mess.

"Hey, Casey, did she call?"

The water gurgled down the drain. He turned the hot water full on.

"No."

"Good. I wanted to talk to her myself." He came into the bath-room. "God! What is that smell?"

"Just your old normal plugged up bathtub smell." He tried to smile, but he knew his lips were quivering and his balled up fist dripped debris on the tub behind him.

Dick Morton's head came up like a pointer after a bird. "Well, hell, let me get it out of here." He picked up the bucket and walked through the door.

K.C. emptied the content of his hand into his toolbox and slammed the lid shut. He ran his hands under the running water before carefully coiling the snake.

He was having difficulty remembering all the things he usually did when he finished a job. He must act normal.

He stepped to the sink and scrubbed his hands with hot water and soap. The odor remained. He scrubbed again, opened the window wider. He was cold now. Goose bumps rose sickly on his neck and forearms. He pushed his face through the window and took deep breaths of the fresh, cold air.

In the yard below, near the edge of the woods, Dick Morton knelt and carefully sifted through the contents of the bucket.

K.C. ducked back into the room and splashed water onto his face. He could not control his shaking hands.

The tub was not completely clean. He used the shower wand to rinse it thoroughly; pulled a rag from his pocket and wiped the floor and sink area.

On trembling legs he walked down the long hallway into the kitchen. He lowered himself onto a chair and prepared his invoice: Cleaned drains, one-hour labor, $48.00. His handwriting was barely legible and wandered wildly outside the lines.

Dick stepped in through the back door. "Nasty stuff."

K.C. sensed the man's increased alertness. "Yeah. They get that way. You get used to it after awhile."

"You find what was blocking it?"

"No. Whatever it was, it pushed on through. Shouldn't give you any problem. Pipes get bigger in diameter as the stuff goes through the plumbing. Should go right into the septic system."

He was more in control now. His hand shook only slightly as Dick took the bill from him.

"You okay? You look a little weird."

"Hypoglycemia. Missed lunch. Gives me hell now and then. I'll be fine as soon as I eat."

"Have lunch with me" He wrote out a check. "I'm a lonely man."

"Thanks, man, but I'm already late for my next job. I'll grab a burger at the drive through." He pocketed the check, hefted his toolbox and the coiled snake.

"Oh, hey! Your bucket. It's by the steps there."

He stooped quickly and collected the cleaned utensil.

He could feel Dick Morton's eyes on his back all the way down the stairs. It was all he could do not to hunch over and make himself into a smaller target. He had to call Clover.

❧

Clover peered out the window and cursed the delay as the train slowed again for a waterlogged section of track.

A few native indigo lilies poked their heads above the soggy edge of a pond. Another few weeks and the area would be awash in blue. Now rain pelted down incessantly as the wind blew small sacrificed limbs of evergreens across the gray waters.

She had a sudden sense of Déjà vu. Had she been stopped on the train in this very spot before today? Is this where she and mother had begun their memory game? She shook the thought away and concentrated on her case against Dick Morton.

How many other women had he deposited with the fishes? Could he have had anything to do with her mother's disappearance? The timeline certainly fit.

Stop. Concentrate on who would believe accusations against the man. Certainly not Mom Billingsley who had described him as a dear friend from the very beginning of his marriage to Elizabeth. And not Sheriff Owen Swenson who played cards with him every Friday night in the cozy living rooms of other community leaders.

She could not take a chance on using the telephone. Dick Morton could have taps on everyone's lines. She needed some evidence, some rock-steady witness besides her basketball player friend.

Involve him now and Dick Morton would make short work of the man. She had to have proof.

She needed someone's help. Lisa. Maybe Lisa would remember what Jim might have discovered that sent Dick into action. No. Lisa would also become a victim.

She leaned her head against the gently rocking headrest, closed her eyes, and gave herself up to the rhythm of the train.

Jim was moving. He had borrowed Dick's truck. Lisa said that he had driven the truck to Dick's garage. When he returned he was in an agitated state. He was distracted and uncommunicative. She said he had stood in the window and stared at the Morton house. Had he met Dick at the Morton's house?

No. Maggie said the telephone company was at the new house before Jim arrived. That would have been Dick and that meant that he had a key or knew of an unlocked door. But then what?

Maggie also said the telephone truck had left long before Jim showed up. Could Dick have hiked back through the old growth forest?

Lisa said Jim hadn't planned to take another load to the new house. Had Jim spoken with and planned to meet Morton? Was there a second person involved? How could she find out without tipping Morton that she was on to him? Where should she begin? She needed to speak with Lisa.

∽

Three hours later, sitting at the Billingsley's dinner table, picking at a seafood salad, and attempting to act as normal as possible, she listened to five kids talking at once. Her brain raced with more questions.

When she and Lisa finally had a short time alone in the kitchen, there were no additional answers. Talking about past events brought Lisa immediately to tears.

Clover said her good-byes and drove the long dark road to Roger Parish's kennels.

She guessed by the way he balanced himself in the open doorway that he had been drinking. The disarray she found in the cold kitchen confirmed it.

Duke welcomed her by pushing against her legs until he had backed her across the narrow floor to the sink.

"I've got to talk to you, Roger."

"I'm all ears." His voice was thick.

"Is it my turn to apologize or yours?"

He shrugged. "I'd say it's yours, but you'll probably say it's mine."

"Okay. I'll start. I was stupid and out for blood. I wasn't fair to you and I egged you on and I'm sorry for that."

"You'll need to say that a little slower if you want me to understand. I've had a few drinks."

"I won't repeat it, Roger. I truly am sorry. I did some pretty stupid things and I don't know why."

"I was just as stupid."

"We both were and probably still are, but you're the only person besides Maggie that I feel I can rely on in this town."

"Should I consider that a compliment?"

"Take it for what it's worth. I'm trying to make amends, Roger."

"Good old twelve-step?"

"No, just one small step. We have to put aside our differences and begin working together again."

"Why? I'm quite happy with the way things are."

"I know who killed Jim and all those women."

"Yeah? Who?"

"Dick Morton."

"Dick Morton? His laughter boomed against the kitchen walls. "Now I've heard everything. Get real, Clover. Dick Morton. That's the funniest thing I've ever heard."

"Listen to me, Roger."

"Go ahead. Tell me more."

"I went to Portland and looked up that guy that I went off with in the RV."

He knocked a wooden chair aside violently. "What the hell is this, Clover, another one of your twisted jokes? A good laugh on old Roger?"

"Please, Roger, listen and then if you want to be mad, be mad. I really need you to listen."

He picked up the chair and straddled it. "I'm all ears," he said again as if it was the only retort he could manage.

"That guy said that he came back looking for me. He said that only Sandra was on the street and she was getting into a car with some guy."

"And how do you know that he wasn't the guy? How do you know he didn't pick up Sandra and do her in?"

"He told me that the car was a new Mercedes, yellow, and it had a license plate holder that said 'Lineman for the county'."

"Lineman for the county?"

"Yes. How could he make that up? He was only passing through. How could he have described Dick's car?"

"I don't think he could have."

"Jim had borrowed Dick's truck. I think when he took the truck back, he discovered something, saw something, or maybe heard something. Lisa said that he was upset when he came back from the Morton's, before he drove out to the house."

"And you think Morton was waiting for him?"

"Yes."

"But we can't prove that."

"No." She breathed deeply. He had said 'we'."

"Jesus, Jesus, Jesus, all this time, right under our noses and we were telling him everything."

"And the things we did not tell him, he learned on the phone lines."

"I'd like to kill him with my own hands!"

Clover wished that was possible, but she knew they could only beat him in the courts. "We have to be sure. We need proof. One guy's word isn't enough."

"We could go over there. Scope out his house when he's out. There's a trail through the old growth that goes to that neighborhood. We might see the same thing that Jim saw."

"What if Jim heard something and there's nothing to see?"

"It won't hurt us to look. No one needs to know."

"I'm afraid to go home. Now that I know, I'm afraid he'll read my mind."

"Stay here. I'll take the couch. That is, if you think you can trust me."

"I never did not trust you."

"After what I did?"

"We did it together, Roger. Whatever that was, it wasn't just one of us. I would have to see a shrink to figure it out. I don't think I want to know. Can we leave it?"

"Let bygones be bygones?"

"Something like that."

"Done."

༄

Duke led them along a trail through dense thickets of blackberry thorns and native holly trees. The vines snagged her hair and pulled at the jacket Roger had retrieved from his closet. She had raised her eyebrows when she pulled the fashionable size five garment over her jogging suit.

"Ex-wife's." He shrugged. "I've had a few."

"That I can believe."

"I thought we were calling a truce."

"Sorry, Roger, it's my nature to be cynical."

"That's why we get along so well." His smile surprised her.

The brisk walk cleared Clover's head.

When they reached the edge of a bluff overlooking the Morton home, they stayed out of sight in a grove of old alder and young maples. Chickadees chattered as the light increased.

Roger paced the small spaces between the trees and whispered to Duke who whined to go forward.

Clover was grateful for the interlude. Breaking and Entering; she would be on the wrong side of the law this time.

She studied the small cluster of homes below. There was Jim and Lisa's dollhouse with the barbecue pit where Jim had served up his famous alder-smoked salmon when she and the senator announced their engagement.

There were dreams down there and small triumphs and the everyday details of family life. Porch lights glowed through the cold morning air.

It was difficult for her to believe that here, in the middle of all the picket fences and manicured lawns, lived a monster worthy of Lucifer's highest ranking. She would never again be taken in by the myth of small town safety. She might never feel entirely safe anywhere, for if Dick Morton could do the things she believed he had done, then the devil did indeed walk the earth and the only sanctity was to be provided by individual strength.

She rose and took a few steps to kneel beside Duke. She buried her face in his wet fur. "Good dog, Duke," she whispered. "We'll be on our way soon."

A car engine sounded below. Elizabeth Morton's car backed out of the garage and moved slowly out of sight.

Clover looked into Roger's eyes without speaking. It shouldn't be long now.

The back door of the house opened. Dick Morton stepped into his rhododendron-studded backyard. For an instant he scanned the hillside above him, as if he sensed their presence.

Clover gasped.

"Don't move," Roger hissed between clenched teeth. "He won't see you if you're still."

Dick studied their position for a long moment. Clover could see his lips move and his breath mingle with the morning air. Was he talking to himself, or was someone else near? She moved her eyes slowly, but could see no other person or animal.

Duke began to growl.

Roger signaled.

The dog silenced.

Dick Morton paced the length of his yard, ranted without words, and threatened the sky with raised fists before he stamped one foot and kicked at a pile of black debris at the forest's edge.

Clover's courage failed and with it any curiosity she had had about Dick Morton's garage. She turned her face and looked for a direction to run.

Roger steadied her again.

As suddenly as he had appeared, Morton retreated into the house.

Clover sat on a downed log and breathed deeply. "It's him, I know it's him," she whispered.

Roger sat beside her. "I've known him about twenty years, but I've never seen him act like that before."

"Where did he come from?"

Roger shrugged. "He married Elizabeth shortly after Dr. Spillmen retired. She was about forty and considered an old maid. She met Dick at some convention back east. Everyone accepted him for what he seemed – a steady, reliable, nice guy."

"That must have been when Elizabeth began to work for Dad Billingsley."

"Yeah, I think so."

"That was about the same time the Billingsleys took me in. Elizabeth was already like a member of the family."

"Elizabeth and Mrs. Billingsley went to the same schools. They go back a long way."

"So Dick did what I did – dropped into a convenient spot and became part of the community."

"I'd be interested to know where he came from. He never talks about his past. It's like he came into being when he arrived here." Roger shook his head.

"He probably did. Don't we all do a bit of reinventing when it's convenient?"

"I have a feeling his reinventing goes a lot deeper than normal. I bet he's got a history that would surprise us all."

"Here he comes. Here he comes." She instinctively lowered her shoulders to make herself smaller.

The yellow Mercedes backed rapidly out of the drive, swung wide and roared off towards town.

Clover held back as Roger and Duke began to make their way down the steep embankment. "We could be arrested for this, you know."

"Can the law-abiding citizen stuff and admit you're scared senseless," He called over his shoulder. "Come on."

She hurried after him.

Roger checked the windows and doors for an alarm system. Convinced there was none, he produced a ring of keys from his jacket pocket and began to try one after another, in the garage door lock. "Lock is old, easy to do." He forced the door up a few inches. "You're smaller," he said. "Go in and hit the opener."

The concrete floor pulled at her clothing as she belly-crawled into the dark space. Dim light came through a small window. Fear clutched her heart. She couldn't do this.

The door closed behind her. She had no choice.

Garden tools hung neatly from pegs on the wall to her right. A series of shelves lined the left wall. Dick's pickup truck took up a third of the space. Overhanging shelves were custom fit above its bed.

She scrambled to her feet, ran to the inside door, pushed the switch, and held her breath. The overhead door mechanism growled to life.

Roger and Duke ran in. Roger hit the button and closed the door.

"We have to think what Jim would have done," she whispered.

"He would have backed the truck in," Roger said.

"But, if the garage was locked, he might have left it out front."

"It was raining. Dick's a perfectionist. He wouldn't want the truck out in the rain. He would have left the door open."

"Boy, it would be hard to back the thing in with those shelves in the way." She climbed into the bed of the truck. "Maybe he knocked something over."

"Too obvious. Elizabeth would have been able to get into stuff in here."

"Not up high. She has a spinal problem. She's always had a problem climbing stairs and ladders. Dad cleans the high shelves in the office so she won't have to deal with them."

"It's a good place to start." He climbed into the truck bed and began to lift boxes from the highest shelf. Most were covered with dust and spider webs. "Hey, here's something interesting. He pulled down a neatly wrapped rectangular object.

Clover gasped. "Jim's coat!"

"Are you sure?"

"Yes. Look, Armstrong on the back." She hugged the jacket to her.

Roger placed a polished box on the tailgate and lifted two brass clasps that held it closed. "My God!"

"What?" She laid the jacket on the edge of the pickup. The odor of formaldehyde burned her nostrils. "They can't be human!"

"He's preserved them! There must be at least fifty!"

"Why would he save fingers?"

Duke growled a warning.

Roger shushed him.

"What is it?" Clover whispered.

"A truck. I hear a truck."

She climbed down and worked her way along the small space between the pickup and the window. "The telephone company cherry picker."

"He couldn't know we're here." Roger shoved the case back on the shelf and stepped down beside her. "Get away from the window."

They huddled together in the shadows behind the truck. Duke leaned against her.

The garage door slid slowly open. Dick Morton dashed into the light, unlocked the entry door, and disappeared inside.

"Go." Roger whispered. "Hurry."

She tripped over Duke and fell on her hands.

"Go!" He urged again. This time Duke moved with her. She skipped down the length of the truck towards the open door. She sensed Roger close behind; heard the door to the house open.

Dick called out. "Who's there? Who is it?"

"Run," Roger commanded.

Together they stumbled through the open door.

"What the hell?" Dick shouted.

She sprinted across the lawn, arms and legs and heart pumping a wild beat.

Roger gained and moved ahead.

Duke reached the cover of the woods first.

The high-pitched whine of a bullet passed near her right ear. She pushed her legs to go faster. The trees were close now, ten feet, maybe twenty.

Roger disappeared.

Gasping for breath, she dove into the brush after him.

"Don't slow down. Don't stop." Roger pulled on her flailing arms.

"I have to catch my breath!"

"No! Come on!"

She followed his gasping chant. "Run! Run!"

She scampered up a leaf-strewn hillside. The ground slid from under her feet. She clawed into the wet mass and pulled herself up. As she cleared the hill, she tumbled forward, off balance. Another rise waited before her.

Roger and Duke were already near its top.

Her side hurt. Close your mouth, she remembered. Breathe through your nose. She couldn't do it. She slowed, staggered, and stopped.

Roger was at her side. He pulled her behind the multiple trunk of a tree. His face was pasty white and wet. "Rest a minute. Get your breath," he whispered. "Stay still and quiet."

Duke dropped onto his belly at their feet.

Dick Morton thrashed through the underbrush behind them.

She reached into her coat and pulled out Maggie's small pistol. Roger snatched it. "Clever girl," he breathed.

Dick Morton quieted.

The sounds of their breathing were loud in the still morning air.

Fear heightened her senses. She could hear Dick's steady inspirations. She leaned her back against the tree, forced herself to relax, to regain control of her emotions. He was smarter. She had a stronger will. She must remember that.

She studied the blackberry-infested forest before her. Dick might work his way around the small valley and sight them from above. They had to move.

A large downed log lay on its side directly ahead of them. If they could get behind it, they could crawl along its full length and be near the top of the small hill before he spotted them.

She reached out and touched Roger's butt. He turned slightly. She locked her eyes on the log and tilted her head. He followed her gaze. It took a moment for him to understand. He nodded slowly.

She scooted down until she was stretched out fully on the roots of the tree, turned onto her abdomen, and began to commando crawl toward the log.

Duke whined.

She signaled him to hush. He took the command as 'come' and leaped forward. "Down," she hissed.

He obeyed.

She heard the crackle of twigs. He was circling to their left. They would have to move quickly. She reached the log and rolled over it, dug her elbows into the wet earth and crawled rapidly uphill. The log jutted over a steep ravine. She could feel Duke at her heels, and hear Roger's rustling clothing behind her.

She tumbled headfirst over the edge.

Her arms trembled as they held her body in a steep angle. Sharp rocks cut into her abdomen and legs. She felt a mist of rain against the back of her neck.

At the bottom of the ravine she raised herself on all fours and scrambled to the left where a large outcropping offered shelter.

Roger and Duke came in beside her. They backed against the rocks.

No movement. No sound except the steady patter of rain.

"If we can stay put long enough, he'll have to go back. Someone is bound to question the cherry-picker parked in the middle of the street." Roger whispered.

"He'll kill us if he can."

"He doesn't know we found anything."

"I dropped Jim's jacket. When he finds it, he'll kill us."

"We'd better move."

Roger led the way, stopping every fifty yards to listen.

"If we can make it to the truck, we'll be okay. We'll drive to the sheriff's office."

Duke sniffed the air, picked up his ears, but gave no warning whines. Clover soon lagged behind, but when the roof of the truck came into view, she increased her pace to catch up.

Duke stopped, pointed his nose into the air, and let out a low growl.

Roger signaled. The dog dropped.

Unsure of which way to move, Clover backed into the trees.

A shot rang out.

She heard the crackling of underbrush and Roger's low moan.

Another shot. Fear overcame her. She crawled to the cover of a thick patch of evergreens and tried to push down her rising panic. Dick would stand in front of her, smile down on her, and pull the trigger. He was smarter. She had a stronger will. Neither mattered.

The silence deepened.

Duke rose and bolted toward the truck. She heard his snarling anger, a thud, and Dick Morton's cry of fright. A gun cracked. The animal howled. She caught a flash of movement as Roger staggered into the woods toward the creek.

"Fucking dog!" The thudding sound of boots against heavy flesh caused Clover's knees to weaken and shake. "Fucking, bastard dog!"

Duke yelped with each thud.

Footfalls came toward her. What was she afraid of? Dick? That creepy, pandering, asswipe of humanity? No, it was not the man that kept her frozen in place. She feared the touch of cold metal against her temple, the dreaded click of the gun's trigger as it sent its bullet home. She couldn't outrun it and she couldn't outsmart it. She sank to the ground, pulled herself into a small snail shape, and burrowed her hands and face into the dank mulch of sacrificed leaves.

He crashed through the brush near her head, but turned away to go after Roger. She lay with one ear to the ground, and listened to his retreating footfalls. Roger had the gun. Roger would surprise him with the gun. She had to get help. She sat upright. She had to move. Now.

She rushed to the truck. Its doors were open, tires flattened, hood up revealing broken wires and torn hoses. She sank to her knees.

Duke's low whine brought clarity. She moved to him. Bright blood matted his thick fur. She glanced up the rutted road. A good half-mile to the highway. Another three or four into town. Morton would expect her to go that way.

Duke whined. The whites of his eyes glistened as he stared up at her.

If Morton came back he would kill the dog. She couldn't allow that to happen. She pulled off her coat, removed her sweatshirt and her bra, picked up a jagged piece of glass and began slicing up the soft material.

CHAPTER TWELVE

K.C. Casey lifted the finger from his toolbox and laid it on the spotless kitchen counter of Maggie's kitchen. The nail's cheerful brightness nestled in gray slime made it appear like an adolescent gimmick or a fifties horror flick. "Couldn't be," he whispered. "Just couldn't be."

He'd been conducting this argument with himself and the finger most of the night. He'd tried to call Clover, but she hadn't answered his messages. He'd waited to show Maggie, but she had stayed in town with Vic who'd come down with the croup. He was reluctant to show his face in the angry town.

If he came forward with his gruesome discovery, who would believe he had fished it out of Dick Morton's bathtub? Certainly not the sheriff. The sheriff would believe that he, K.C., had severed the finger; that he was blowing more smoke and trying to finger someone else. He laughed nervously at his morbid pun and rolled the piece of flesh into a square of paper toweling.

As he scrubbed his hands in the kitchen sink, his eyes wandered to the window that overlooked the old growth. The rain had begun again and now it poured ceaselessly from the steep shake roof and rattled in the gutters on its way back to the earth's floor. He should never have come to this dreary and gray place. He placed the tiny package into a plastic sandwich bag and laid it on the counter.

A strong gust of wind shook heavy drops from the big trees and sent them spattering loudly against the cabin walls. As soon as he could get this thing over with, he would return to California where sunshine, freedom, Jenny and their new baby girl waited.

He dialed Clover's number and stamped his feet when the answering machine clicked coolly on. "God-damn it! Where could she have gone?" He would not leave another message, he had told her everything in the last three.

Pop! No wind this time. Pop! He cocked his head to one side and listened. Maggie's dogs whined softly. "She's not coming, fellas," he said. "She's staying at Tiny's until the kid gets better. You're stuck with me. You've been upstaged by a kid with the croup."

One of the huge Shepherds rubbed against him, whining softly. "What? You hungry? You want out?" All three of the big dogs crowded the door. "Okay. Okay." He opened the door. "Here you go." They ran off towards the big woods.

Pop! There it was again. He stepped to the porch rail and listened. Large caliber. Past the old growth and closer to the town. No games planned for a couple of weeks, but one of his pals might be practicing. Maybe he should drive down, have a look. He pulled on his camouflage jacket.

The rain had lessened. He checked each chained off roadway for tire tracks as he passed, but saw nothing fresh.

The road to the murder site was still gift-wrapped in yellow. Four roads later he recognized the deep rutted tracks of a truck cutting through the mud. He turned and followed the tracks into the forest.

Not fifty yards in, the telephone company cherry picker blocked the narrow road. He backed the van out, parked to one side, and walked into the old growth forest. He picked up his pace when he saw Roger Parrish's truck ahead, then pulled to a quick stop as he realized it had been vandalized. He moved to the truck and peered inside. Empty.

Pop! Gunfire not far off. He turned toward the sound. A bloody rag lay by the flat front tire and a bloody trail disappeared into the forest. Someone had dragged a heavy body away.

K.C. Casey turned, ran back down the road, and jumped into his van. He must find someone to call the sheriff. And this time he'd call his lawyer too. This time he wasn't going to be tagged as the murderer. This time Dick Morton was going to take full blame.

⚬⚬

Roger Parrish had made it to the edge of Clear Creek before his shattered left leg began to tremble and would no longer support his weight. Blood pulsed from a wound above his knee and ran into his boots. He could go no farther. He had bought some time for Clover and now she was his only hope. He would hole up; get a tourniquet on the leg and hold out as long as possible. He scanned the landscape for a likely vantage point and seeing none, plunged into the creek and crawled up the far embankment.

⚬⚬

Dick Morton observed the man's slowing movements that evidenced his fatigue. This kill would be leisurely. He moved cautiously along the creek, staying well inside the cover of the forest. He had become accustomed to the ruminations of women's minds; adept at anticipation of women's tricks. This was an entirely new game to play.

No hysteria noted in the man. He would not plead or show weak anxiousness or try to appease. This one played for keeps and that made the event so much more interesting.

What was Roger thinking now? That he was too weak to continue? That he would need to hole up and make every bullet in his small gun count? He would most likely ambush him from higher ground and wait for a good shot before firing.

Dick Morton would not give Parrish that chance. Judging from the stains on the man's pants, it would not be long until his mind dulled from lack of oxygen. He could get to him while some life still lingered in his withering body. He needed the elation of a good kill. He needed to hear Roger scream as loudly as Jim Armstrong had screamed.

Parrish was a worthy adversary. He might squirm with contempt and shout epithets, but his hatred would be palpable and his will would be magnificent to behold. He must have the chance to see this man's full potential.

He watched quietly as his prey struggled up the embankment, his legs pumping widely, his firm buttocks doing the work that would normally be done by his lower legs. He was well hung, Roger Parrish was. Dick Morton began to snicker. Roger Parrish was beautifully hung, and he, Dick Morton could hardly wait to unhang him.

❦

Clover lay in the small ravine where she had dragged Duke and where he remained, partially covered by a protective layer of leaves. She had no idea where she was; which way she should go; what she should do. She had wrapped the dog's wounds with pieces of her clothing to stop the bleeding, dragged him as far away as her strength allowed and had headed toward the road. Now an hour later, she found herself back in the same spot.

Except for the single shot she had heard earlier, the forest was still. Only the rain pattering down on matted leaves and her anxious breathing interrupted the silence. She was inert, afraid to move and call attention to herself, yet she knew that she must do something soon or the damp cold would render her ineffective. Her thick socks and jogging shoes squished when she walked. She shivered, more from her terror of being alone in the darkening forest than from the cold.

Panic paralyzed her.

She hugged her arms tighter over her chafed breasts. She had used her bra to bind up Duke's wounds. The burning coldness of her nipples was made worse from the rough fabric of Roger's borrowed jacket. She had to do something. She could not hide. She must get to town.

∽

Clover's red sports car was parked in Roger's drive. His luck was definitely getting better. He pounded on Roger's door. A cacophony of barks and yips erupted from the kennels, but not a sound from inside. He stood awkwardly with his hands in his pockets, and waited for the unlikely pair to open the door.

Funny, he didn't hear Duke. He moved down the porch and rose up on the balls of his feet to peer over the café curtains covering the kitchen window. Two cups were on the table. Clover's large leather handbag sat on the nearest chair. Her red leather coat was hanging from the back of the same chair. He pounded once again. Nothing stirred except the kenneled dogs.

He made his way around the house to the bedroom window. Rainwater spilled from the gutters and into the collar of his jacket as he stepped through the shrubbery. The curtains were open. The bed was rumpled and unmade, but empty. Only one pillow lay at the head of the bed and only one side of the quilt was tossed aside.

Clover must have driven in early this morning then gone off riding with Roger.

The dogs bayed at him from their high fences. One lifted his food dish and dropped it with a clang. K.C. walked to the enclosures. All the food dishes were empty. It was not like Roger to go off without feeding his dogs. He must not have expected to be gone long.

The vision of Roger's truck, the bloody rag, and the cherry picker parked recklessly in the clearing suddenly jelled together.

Had Clover and Roger challenged Dick Morton?

He pushed against the front door. It was locked tight. He hurried around to the kitchen door and pushed his weight against it. The door was loose enough in its jam to force open. He went back to his van and pulled out a pry bar. Within minutes he was in the house and dialing the phone.

He could hear little Vic crying as Maggie said hello.

"Maggie, we've got a situation here!"

"Oh, I'm sorry, K.C., I can't hear a thing with this young one crying. Just a minute, let me put him down. Just a minute now."

He could hear her crooning, as the crying gradually became quieter.

"K.C.?"

"Maggie. Maggie. Please listen."

"I will. Have patience. Wait a minute." She dropped the phone again.

K.C. slapped the receiver against the palm of his hand.

"K.C.?"

"Maggie."

"Okay. Okay. Now I can hear. Speak to me."

"Listen. Dick Morton is the guy we've been looking for."

"Dick Morton? My goodness son, where is your head?"

"Maggie, just listen. Please!" He was close to crying.

"I'm listening."

"I found a severed finger blocking his bathtub drain."

"And you expect me to believe this?"

"Yes. Yes. You have to, Maggie. I heard shots and I found Roger's truck beat to hell and a bloody rag and parked behind it was the telephone company's cherry picker.

I'm here at Roger's and so are Clover's car and her jacket and her bag. And Roger hasn't fed the dogs. It looks like they went off in a big hurry. I think Dick Morton has gone after them in the old growth. That's where the shots were coming from."

"K.C., come on. Clover is in Portland."

"I'm telling you, all her stuff is here – her car, her purse, her red jacket. I heard shots and decided to go have a look. Roger's truck is on a logging road completely pulled apart. When I found the truck, I high-tailed it here to use Roger's phone. No one's here."

"You're not hysterical and making this up, are you, Casey?"

"I swear, Maggie. I swear on the life of my baby daughter."

"K.C., I'm here alone with Victor. He's so very sick. Tiny and Mindy have already left for work. You'll have to call the Sheriff."

"No! I can't wait for the old lard-ass. I'm going to check out the woods and see if I can find my friends. Don't go to your house. It's not safe. Have the sheriff go up there. I left the finger on the counter. When he sees that he'll know I'm telling the truth."

"K.C., listen to me. Stay there and wait for the sheriff."

"So he can arrest me for breaking and entering? No! I know what I have to do. I want you to call the sheriff and have him do a background check on Dick Morton. Ask him to check out the logging road before the third curve from town. He'll see all the truck tracks going in. He'll find the telephone company cherry picker and Roger's truck. Tell him I heard shots. Tell him Clover and Roger are in the woods near there and I am too."

"Oh, K.C., I think this is a foolish move."

"Do you have it, Maggie? Will you do it?"

"Yes, of course I'll do it. But I wish you would wait there.

"I can't, Maggie. I've got to help Clover."

∽

Sheriff Owen Swenson cradled the telephone between his left ear and shoulder as he walked to his file cabinet and began to rifle through a drawer. Morton. Morton. Was it under Dick? No. Richard. It was under Richard Morton.

Maggie continued speaking. "Owen, did you hear what I said?"

"Yes. I heard you, Maggie. But I find the whole thing to be a bit far-fetched." He pulled a file from the rack and returned to his desk. "I said far-fetched, Maggie. I didn't say you or the Casey kid were making it up." He laid the file on his desk and opened it with one hand. "Maggie, could you put the kid down or something? I can hardly hear you. Yes, I know he's been sick, but damn it, Maggie, I can't hear a word you're saying and I can't think with all that wailing."

He scanned the first page of the document. "Yes. That's better. Now, Maggie, you listen to me. I'll check it out.

Yes, I will.

No, I don't hold a grudge against the Casey kid.

No, I don't. I'm just doing my job.

Yes, I do do my job, Maggie, everyday.

Maggie, if you're going to bad-mouth me, I'll have to hang up. I'm warning you. Okay, last warning!"

He placed the receiver in its cradle and held his hand on it, as if to hold back the woman on the other end. It began to ring again. "Hey, Larry," he called to his deputy. "Get the phone, will you? I've gone for the day."

He sat at his desk and turned a page in the folder. Complaint from a telephone customer claimed Dick Morton touched her inappropriately when he installed her phone system. Mamie Herreid interviewed, but charges dismissed when she suddenly left town.

Two more carefully typed reports, both from women, both outlining uninvited physical contact. No follow-up indicated.

Probably a lot of smoke. He looked across the small room to Larry who was holding the phone away from his ear. Poor bastard. Well, the telephone company was a short stroll up the street. He could walk over there and be back before Maggie was done with Larry. He'd have a chat with Morton's boss. Maybe have a look at his personnel file.

He tipped his hat to Larry as he quietly closed the door.

∽

Roger Parrish knew he was out of luck. His left arm hung limp and useless at his side as he half-sat, half-lay against a moss covered log in a soggy mass of composting leaves and forest debris. With his good leg he pushed himself into a sitting position. He could not focus sharply enough to discern the difference between the sheets of falling rain and the long fronds of Cedars that swayed in a gentle wind.

The purple gray haze that had begun to cloud his vision smoothed everything flat except the moving form that steadily advanced on his position. Roger blinked, forced his eyes to open wider.

Dick Morton filled his visual field. Dick Morton: smiling, pink-cheeked and appearing as if he was about to sit at his table and join him for dinner. Even now he could pass for a lawyer or a judge taking a moment out from the bench to say hello to an old friend. What a fucking perversion. What a fucking con game.

"Hello, Roger," Morton called out cheerfully.

Roger raised his small gun and fired. The effort caused his arm to shake erratically. The gun slipped in his hand. His stomach lurched. For a moment he could taste the tea and Danish pastry he had shared with Clover before leaving his house.

"You missed, my friend."

Roger lifted the gun and took careful aim between the man's bright green eyes. The retort caused him to slide farther into the muck. He raised his knee and pushed himself upright.

"Missed again."

Bastard wanted to play. He fingered the gun. How many shots had he fired? He tried to concentrate, to remember the pull of his finger on the trigger. He braced his elbow against the log and brought the gun up again.

"It won't do, Roger. You're too weak. You couldn't hit me if I stood three feet in front of you with a bulls-eye painted on my shirt."

"Why?" Roger moaned.

His smile deepened. "It's great fun. Haven't you ever wanted to be a little kinky?"

Roger stared, tried to keep him in perspective, but his eyes wouldn't take his commands and rolled backwards, making him very dizzy.

"What? Did you shake your head no, Roger? You've never wanted to try some of the darker things in life? Some of the forbidden fruits?"

Roger held his breath and squeezed the trigger. A searing pain filled his chest. The Danish and Tea scalded his throat with bilious vomit. He harked and spit. Warm mucous slid down his chin.

"Oh, Roger. You are a mess. Stop it now. You'll ruin my fun."

He straightened his head, forced his eyes open again. "Why?"

"Why what, Dearest?"

"Why?"

Dick pulled a bright white handkerchief from his pocket, shook it out fully, and tossed it toward Roger. It fluttered damply in the wind. "Wipe yourself, Roger. You've spittle on your chin."

"Why? The horses and the dogs? Jim Armstrong? All those women? Why?"

Morton leaned against a tree, crossed one ankle across the other and struck a relaxed pose. "Why not? It's great fun. Airs out all those little corners that get so stuffy in a burg like this. Let's one explore something quite larger than our puny lives. Let's one experience all those dirty, base, perverted, excitingly wonderful parts of the psyche. Really, Roger, it fills in the otherwise endless hours of boredom we are forced to endure. Haven't you ever been bad, Roger? Really bad?"

"Asshole."

"Yes. I've explored a few of those myself." He smiled again. "And you have too, haven't you, Roger? Don't think I didn't hear all that talk about you. Small towns, big mouths, you know how it is. Didn't it have something to do with other officer's wives? Swapping? Sharing? No. No. Neither. It was neither. Obedience classes. That was it. The young officer who was new to the canine patrol. You taught him the works, didn't you, Roger? Doggie style. Everybody doing everybody else. The officer, you, his wife. A happy little train you had going, didn't you?

But somebody got jealous, didn't they, Roger? One or the other spilled it all to the Chief. That was it, wasn't it, Roger?

Granted, not a big deal in most enchanted kingdoms. But in a small town? Whoosh…everything up in smoke. Career, reputation, family. I understand your own mother washed her hands of you. Filth. Dirt. Corruption."

"Asshole."

"Roger, sweetie, you've done it before. Let me help you know the wonderful, painfully exquisite heights of your darker side once again. Let me show you the pleasure you can find when someone fucks every fucking inch of you.

Let me hear you beg me for it, Roger. Or, let me hear you beg for death. Either way it will turn out the same.

Oh, Roger, already I've got the most God-awful, wonderful hard-on."

Roger pushed himself up again. The movement caused chest-crushing agony. He forced his eyes to stay focused on the man. His fingers wanted to relax, to let the gun fall, but he wouldn't allow that.

"Jesus, Roger. You're so God damned boring. Can't you say something?" He squatted before him like a young man commiserating with friends over a pair of lucky dice. "I'll tell you what. I'll give you one last chance to live. We'll lay here on this hallowed ground. I'll butt hole you. You can butt hole me. We'll call it even." He raised his arms and eyes expectantly. "What do you say, old buddy? You game?"

"Go fuck yourself."

He feigned shock. "Oh, Roger, you haven't got the picture yet, buddy. It's you who is going to be fucked. You're the fuck-ee. I'm the fuck-er. You said so yourself. I guarantee you'll find your position quite interesting." He began to move forward, smiling confidently at his prey.

He was growing larger, filling Roger's rapidly shrinking world.

Roger raised the gun. His arm bent closer. Closer. He felt the cool metal against his right temple. "Sorry, Dick," he mumbled. "Sorry to spoil your fun."

As his last lucid act on this earth, Roger Parrish pulled the trigger.

~

The gunshot was close. Clover had stumbled onto Clear Creek and recognized that she was headed in the wrong direction. She was closer to the Survivalist's cabin and Maggie's than to town. Dick would not expect her to head in this direction. The gunshot told her that Roger was still able to fight.

If she stayed to the right of the creek and followed it uphill, she would not have to go into the dense new growth until she was very near the cabin. She could manage this. She moved into the shelter of the tall trees. Another shot. Fear slammed her knees into the thick carpet of pine needles. "Please, please, don't let me die," she cried softly. "I'm so scared."

The sudden loudness of her voice startled her. She covered her face with dirt-encrusted hands and began to sob. She should go on. But maybe it would be better if she found a hiding place and waited for Roger. It would be all over soon. Maybe staying put and hugging a tree was the best action for now.

Another gunshot rang out clearly above the increasing wind. A shake of her head sent droplets of water flying through the air. The loneliness of that one shot stilled something in her, sent a sudden sharp pain through her heart.

She rose to her feet, wiped her face with a soggy handful of leaves and needles. She would cross the stream and go into the cover of the underbrush. She would crawl along the stream until she reached Maggie's door.

∾

K.C. Casey circled toward the gunshots. Whoever was shooting might mistake him for the enemy. Sure-footed and more confident, he followed a human trail along Clear Creek. The water was muddied and disturbed. As he examined depressions made by large shoes and filled with a mixture of blood and rainwater, a single shot rang out. He dropped and rolled down into the creek.

∾

Sheriff Owen Swenson rocked slowly in the swivel chair as he scanned the telephone company file on Dick Morton. Twenty years worth of duties and promotions, the adjectives were worthy of a king: dependable; intelligent; physically superior; great dexterity for fine jobs; flawless driving record.

He found several minor complaints sandwiched within the glowing reports. All were complaints from women and all involved some minor peeping or the perception of inappropriate touching.

Morton's list of community involvement projects was endless: Active member of church; member of the Country Club; Volunteer at the food bank.

"I've never seen Dick Morton at the food bank," he murmured.

The clerk looked up and smiled, "Elizabeth is into that. He helps with the truck work."

The blank pages that followed surprised him. Not one reference check. No background check.

"Didn't you get any references on him?"

"Didn't need any. Personally recommended by Doc Stillwell and Doc Billingsley. Didn't need anything more."

"Well, where'd he come from?"

"I don't know. I never asked. I suppose Elizabeth could tell you that, shall I call her for you? I saw her at the clinic as I came in this morning."

"No. I'll wander over there and have some coffee."

A branch snapped very close. Clover froze in her half-crouched position before crawling into a thick stand of Gorse. She rose slowly to study the tops of the bushes ahead.

Something was definitely there.

She held her breath to steady herself, relaxed her knees and bent into a tighter crouch. She could feel the physical presence of another warm-blooded mammal. The tops of the bushes moved twenty feet ahead nearer the creek. If she could stay still long enough she would be okay.

The movement suddenly turned toward her. Gray coat. Gray coveralls. Coming closer. She began to run, dodging this way and that through the dense brush. Thorns of Gorse tore at her clothing. She scampered over small rocks and fallen tree limbs.

He was behind her, moving slowly, cutting directly through the brush.

She broke from the dense thicket, lifted her knees and sprinted through a clearing. She turned to look, caught the flash of a smile, a hand raised as if in greeting. God, oh, God, what was she doing here?

Her feet thudded against a soft obstacle. She lost her balance, reached out to grab a handhold and recoiled when she touched something cold and furry. She tumbled, slid face first into the slimy floor of the forest, rolled over and kicked at the obstacle that had tripped her. It wouldn't be moved.

Oh, God. Oh, God. Her screams filled the air.

Roger had tripped her. Poor, bloody, emasculated Roger draped over a small log for the entire world to see. And directly in front of her stood crazy Dick Morton, folded over in gales of laughter, stomping his feet and holding onto his stomach as if he had just witnessed a comedy of magnificent proportions.

She scrambled to her feet and began to run again. Branches pulled at her hair, stung her face, and poked into her open mouth. She ran as fast and as straight as her body would allow, but it wasn't enough. She felt his hands on her jacket; smelled blood that seemed to waft from his pores. His body weighed in on her and slowly pulled her to the ground. Small animal sounds emitted involuntarily from her throat: whimpering, pleading, inarticulate.

"Gotcha," he whispered into her ear. "Finally. Gotcha." He moved his hips seductively against her buttocks, slid his arms around her torso and fondled her breasts through the wet jacket.

Her stomach, as if echoing the disgust of her brain, emptied itself onto the pine needles. She could feel the hard butt of his gun against the tender flesh of her breast. She tried to move. It was use-less. He was much stronger than he appeared. She filled her lungs with one more ragged breath and acquiesced.

With animal instinct he felt the change. His grip loosened slightly on her chest. He flicked his tongue into her ear, pushed off of her with one arm, and turned her face up. His lips parted as they came down on hers.

The bite of his teeth caused her to gasp. His tongue darted rap-idly into her partially opened mouth. She gagged and wretched. He didn't seem to notice. His hips thrust against hers, against the wet taut material of her jogging pants.

She tried to turn her face away.

"Clover," he whispered.

"Filthy pig." She pushed against him.

"Clover?" Another voice whispered.

He tore away, pushed one bloody palm against her mouth, came up on all fours and ground his knee into her abdomen and groin. The pain momentarily stunned her.

"Clover?"

K.C.! She opened her eyes, tried desperately to turn her head, to call out. Morton leaned all his weight on her teeth until she was sure her jaw had broken.

She gurgled a warning. K.C. turned.

Dick Morton raised his gun.

K.C. fired first. She felt the shudder of Dick's forty-five. Some-thing hit her face, stung her eyes.

Dick began to laugh. "You stupid son-of-a-bitch! You gonna hurt someone with that toy?"

Her vision clouded. She blinked several times until the specter of Dick, painted red, became clear. He waved his gun gleefully; relaxed his grip on her mouth, removed his weight, and stood. Where was K.C.? She scrambled to a sitting position.

"Gotcha." Dick kicked K.C.'s head. "Nigger." He kicked inert legs. "Hah!"

She crawled toward her friend. A red stain covered his chest. His fingers twitched then were still.

As she reached out to touch him, her head was jerked back violently. She screamed with pain of thudding kicks to her back, her sides.

Dick wrapped her thick hair in both his hands and began to drag her across the soggy ground. She clawed at him, raked his hands with her nails, tried to kick and twist free until she could bear the pain in her neck and scalp no longer.

She took hold of both his wrists and allowed him to drag her away.

CHAPTER THIRTEEN

Elizabeth Morton wasn't at the clinic. A neighbor had called to report strange events on their street that involved the telephone company cherry picker and loud noises in the woods. She had left to check out her home and had not returned.

Sheriff Swenson caught up with her in her spotless kitchen where she was calmly placing fresh rolls and homemade soup into the microwave.

"He usually comes home for lunch," she said as she placed a white bowl of soup in front of him. "He hasn't touched any of this, but we won't let it go to waste, will we, Sheriff?"

"Much as I hate to take another man's bread, I won't say no, Elizabeth."

"Oh, my. I can't bear to look again at the lawn. What would have caused him to drive over my dahlia bed? It certainly isn't like him, but I'm sure he must have had good reason. Maybe he momentarily lost control of the vehicle."

"I'm sure he'll explain when he gets to a phone."

She turned and smiled. Despite her small size and pleasant demeanor, her air was one of superiority. "Dick is a telephone repairman, Sheriff. If there's a telephone line nearby, he has a phone."

"You mean he can plug into any line and call home?"

"Of course. He's always done that."

"Doesn't that interrupt other conversations on the line?"

"Oh, my, no. If the line is busy, I'm sure he simply goes on to another."

"Really?"

"One time, it was so funny. I was talking to my mother in Evanston. She'd been ill, so ill, and we'd been on the line for quite some time. Finally, I said, 'well, mother, if I don't go now and begin Dick's dinner, he'll be home before I've started.' And this other voice, it was Dick of course, said, 'Well, Elizabeth, if you would have given me half a chance fifteen minutes ago, I would have told you I'll be late.' We had such a good laugh."

"So he'd been listening to your conversation for that long?"

"Yes. He's really a trickster, that man."

"It sounds like he is."

She turned suddenly from her work at the stove. "Has Dick done something, Sheriff? Has there been an accident?"

"No. No, Elizabeth. I'm starting a drive for the new department vehicles. Thought maybe Dick could help. Be on a committee."

"Well, of course. Of course he will. That would be such a feather in his cap, wouldn't it? He'd love to do it."

"Do you suppose he'll be here soon?"

"Certainly. And I'm sure he has an explanation for the lawn. Would you like some apple cobbler and some coffee while we wait?"

"Don't mind if I do," he smiled. "I'd like to get a little background information on Dick anyway. I'll have Larry write a little bio for the paper."

"Oh, yes. Dick will like that. Imagine my sweet man with all those big shots. How wonderful!"

K.C. Casey staggered down the bank of Clear Creek, fell to his knees and tugged his red-soaked jacket from his throbbing shoulder. Jesus. A lot of blood. Major vessel. Had to be. He shrugged his arm out of the coat and felt his chest. Splintered edges of metal tore at his hand. His paint ball case. It must have exploded with the impact of the bullet. He pulled open his shirt and probed his chest. Dick Morton would have hit him square in the heart had it not been for the metal case of paint balls that deflected the bullet and sent it deep into his shoulder joint.

He would laugh if it were truly funny. He had been so stupid. In his haste to get into the woods, he had brought only his paint ball weapon. Jenny had been right. He was an absolute idiot.

He unsnapped his vest, slowly undid each cuff and button on his flannel shirt and shrugged both off. When he tried to remove his thermal undershirt, he found it pinned into the wound with pieces of jagged plastic. With pincer fingers he grasped several individual slivers. Rivulets of blood ran down his chest. Too impatient to care, he yanked hard. Hunks of flesh peeled away with his thermal.

He dipped the shirt in the creek and sponged the wound repeatedly until the creek ran red with blood and paint. Now he could see that his collarbone was shattered, but he couldn't tell if the remaining shards were plastic or bone.

He flung his jacket and flannel shirt higher onto the creek bank. A shaft of pain nearly overwhelmed him. He placed the vest against his thigh, snapped it closed, and pulled one armhole over his head. He backed his injured arm into the unlikely sling. The pain became less intense. Slowly he rose to his feet and began to climb.

Near the top of the bank he lost his balance. His injured arm jerked in its socket and sent wave upon wave of pain down his arm and into his fingertips. His vision blackened as he felt himself sliding backwards.

The icy waters of the creek revived him. He again crawled up the bank, collected his jacket and flannel shirt and continued to the cover of the forest. Now safely in the trees, he sat on the ground and pulled a first aid kit from his jacket pocket.

He pushed the watertight container against his thigh until it opened, dumped out a vial of iodine and a roll of bandage. Years of manipulating small pipes made saturating the gauze with one hand easy. He quickly packed it into the gaping hole in his shoulder and pressed it until he could no longer feel the stream of blood flowing over his chest. With his teeth he started a roll of adhesive tape, but when he tried to apply it to his chest, it would not adhere to his wet skin. He tossed it aside and tried a roll of elastic wrap.

Wrapping the elastic around his torso with one hand proved to be impossible. "Fuck!" He tossed the wrap aside.

In another jacket pocket he found loose change, bullets, a stick of peppermint gum and an old rubber band. He rolled his shirt into the smallest parcel he could manage and stuffed it under the sling, against the wound.

His teeth rattled, his jaw quivered. He pulled his jacket over his good arm and flung it over his shoulder. He tried repeatedly, but couldn't connect its zipper or snaps. He unbuckled his belt and pulled it from his pant loops. His sheathed knife fell into the muck at his feet. He placed the belt across a log, leaned against it, tucked the buckle end under his injured arm and pulled the tongue end to meet it. Once he had it connected he could almost close the jacket.

His rifle and stained thermal shirt lay in the creek, too wet to be of any use. He unsheathed the knife and slid it into his boot.

The afternoon was waning. He had to find Roger and Clover quickly or he would never see them alive again.

With new determination he started back into the forest.

Dick Morton's breathing became labored as a sharp rise slowed his pace.

Clover sensed the change and felt a fresh shot of adrenaline surge through her veins. When he stopped midway on the hill to get a better grip on her hair, she rolled into a crawling position and scampered away.

He was on her in an instant. The acrid scent of his sweat burned her nostrils; the pummeling of his fists on her rib cage took her breath away. She felt a dull blow to her head.

All light and noise faded away.

∽

Elizabeth Morton knew surprisingly little of her husband's history before their fateful meeting in Chicago. He was an Iowa boy, she said. Somewhere near Garner, she thought. That was the only name that came to mind. He had no family left and she certainly didn't press him to reveal painful memories.

Swenson whiled away an hour in her pleasant company, but when Dick did not come home, he returned to his office and telephoned the sheriff's department in Garner, Iowa. What could it hurt?

"No. I don't remember a Richard Morton ever living in this town." The sleepy town sheriff was not pleased at being called at home. "No, don't remember him as Dick, either."

He asked about animal mutilations.

"What? Animal mutilations? Who did you say you were?"

"Sheriff Owen Swenson. Washington State."

"That's what I thought I heard. Well, hey, give me a minute. Brain doesn't work as fast as it used to. I do remember something about that."

"In Garner?"

"No. Not here in Garner, somewhere up in the Northwest corner of the state. Give me a minute. It's been years ago. Fifteen. Maybe twenty. They thought they had a bunch of devil worshipers or something. Bunch of horses and stuff had their nuts cut off."

Owen waited.

"Yeah, I'm sure it was up near the twin cities. Let me give you the number up there, just a second."

෧৩

She woke up screaming. A searing, ragged pain pierced her upper jaw, ran straight up her nose and into her forehead. She tried to sit forward but was held back by a restraint across her chest. She opened her eyes and looked directly into the green eyes of Morton. He kissed her nose, smiled and moved away. The instrument he held up to the sky was bloody.

"You broke a tooth. It hurt my tongue when I kissed you. I extracted it for you."

The rusty taste of fresh blood filled her mouth. She tried to spit.

"The bleeding will stop in a few minutes. Here. Open up."

She stared at him.

He cupped her chin in one hand and squeezed. Her jaw opened involuntarily. He placed a large wad of cotton into place and released her jaw. "Bite down, now. Bite down!"

She turned her head away, but was stopped by intense pain in her neck and shoulders. She closed her eyes until the pain lessened then slowly opened them.

He had moved away, was standing with his back to her waving his arms. No, not waving. The man was combing his hair. He was standing in front of a tree on which hung a small mirror and he was combing his hair.

She pushed herself up as far as she could against the pull of the restraint and studied her surroundings.

They were under a small, tin roofed shelter. The timbers were old and rotting, but the space was dry. Her feet and hands were tied with rough rope. A strand, as thick as her wrist, had been wrapped around her chest and secured to a pole at the center of the shelter. Everything had the musty stink of dry rot.

Blood pounded through her head and its rusty taste filled her mouth. She strained to see the forest beyond. A steel basin balanced on a log round beside a stack of pure white, neatly folded towels and washcloths. A large leather satchel sat on the wooden floor beside the makeshift table.

He sensed her movement, turned and smiled. "Just freshening up a bit," he said. "I don't want you to think I'm an animal." He pulled a bottle of cologne from the satchel and splashed some over his face and neck, before checking his image in the mirror.

Something about the space was familiar. She stared into the dim light of the forest. The old logging camp. She recognized the remains of the main mess hall that K.C. had shown her on their hike. She tilted her head back. A rotting utility pole supported one frayed wire and a newer cable that circled down the pole and into the ground where Dick stood. Had he connected a telephone?

"Like it?" He asked suddenly. "It's my little home away from home."

She did not answer. She was thinking of the line from the clear-ing where she had sat on the day she and K.C. had hiked here. She had not recognized the connection then.

"Oh, you won't need to talk. I rather like my women silent and obedient."

He was smarter, but she had a stronger will. She closed her eyes and concentrated on gathering energy and strength. She would not stay here. She would escape.

"Well. How do I look? Am I presentable?" He lifted his hands to the sky and strutted across the small space. "But, oh, my dear, we've got to do some work on you. You are a mess."

Resistance was futile. He lifted her jacket and pulled a tight length of nylon cord around the tender skin of her abdomen.

She watched with open interest as he unraveled the cord and tied it to a steel loop in the floor. He pulled a tight knot. "Old winch hold," he smiled. "Imbedded in concrete. Handy, don't you think?"

He came back to her, untied the restraint from her chest, and carefully freed her feet. "Up you go, " he said cheerfully. "We'll get you fixed up in no time."

He led her to the middle of the enclosure before releasing her hands and jumping out of reach.

She bolted toward the far corner. Her breath left her as the momentum of her dash jerked the rope taut. She pulled at the rope. When she couldn't slide out of it, she ran back to the steel loop and tried to loosen the knot with her bloody fingers.

He stood to one side, arms akimbo, and smiled as she fell to her knees at the center loop.

She would not let him near her again. She was wasting energy. She had to find the right time to fight him. She had to pace herself.

"Now that you've tested the limits of your tether, shall we get started, Clover?"

She raised herself to full height. "Started what?" The blood-saturated cotton fell from her mouth.

"The cleansing. Are you ready?"

She looked full on him. "I'm ready when you are, Dick."

"Take off your shoes."

"What?"

"I think I was clear. Take off your shoes, Clover."

"Go to hell."

"You take them off, or I'll take them off, either way we'll end up in the same position."

She bent over and pulled off the sodden tennis shoes without untying them.

"Now the socks. Take off your socks."

"It's too cold," she protested.

"We'll get you some dry ones. There are plenty of spare clothes in my bag of tricks."

She slipped off the wet socks and placed them into her shoes.

"Wriggle your toes."

"What?"

"I said wriggle your pretty little toes, Clover."

She stared at him.

"Wriggle your toes, what can it hurt? They're cold, aren't they, and stiff from the dampness?"

She obeyed.

He laughed joyously. "Oh, you've done them in crimson, too. How wonderful! Oh, Clover, I think I love you. You are such a free, yet refined, woman."

The man was certifiably insane, but then she must be too. Why else would she stand here calmly and perform for him?

She began to cry. Her mouth filled with bitter mucous and blood. She spit the vile mixture onto the ground. His groan pleased her. She must not show emotion. She must play his game.

"That ruined your image, my dear. Come here and get another piece of cotton." He held a piece of fluff at arms length.

She gathered more mucous and spit again.

"Well have it your way." He placed the cotton in his jacket pocket and took a few steps to one side.

"Take off your pants," he said like a naughty little boy in a vacant lot. "No. No. Wrong. I don't like that."

She stood still.

"The coat. Take off your coat."

She unzipped it slowly, watched every plastic tooth separate from its partner. She could feel her resolve strengthening until she hit the stop in the zipper and looked up.

His leering smile told her she had made a mistake. Her slowness titillated him. If she were to survive, she must become asexual, an automaton, and stone cold.

She pulled the wet sleeves from her shoulders and tossed the coat onto her shoes. She must not show fear.

He was on the move, pacing back and forth just outside the reach of the rope. His eyes focused on her bare chest.

She gathered another wad of mucous and spit.

"Jesus, Clover, would you cut that out? Here place this cotton." Once again he offered her the pad.

She turned away.

He climbed on her back, his arms wrapped under hers; his strong hands forced her mouth open.

She kicked and lost her balance, became ensnared in the rope.

He shoved the cotton into her mouth. "Bite down, " he commanded. His hand moved over her bare breasts and abdomen.

She bit hard on the piece of cotton.

"You excite me, Clover," he mouthed into her ear. "You don't know how much you excite me."

She stilled herself and spat out the cotton. "You do nothing for me."

He shoved her to the ground.

Splinters of old wood stabbed into the flesh of her hands as she tried to break her fall. She lay on the floor breathing hard.

He kicked at her. "Get up, slut! Get on your feet."

She obeyed.

He stood wide-legged and rubbed his chin, like a director contemplating a movie scene. "What happened to your shirt, Clover? Old Roger take it from you? I watched you at his house, you know. I peeked into your windows. I watched you sleep. You are beautiful when you sleep, Clover."

"Did you and Roger ever do it, Clover? Did you ever lay with him?"

She would not answer.

"Take off your pants."

She removed the garment with business-like precision and tossed it on the pile.

"Walk this way."

She would not move.

He pelted her with a sharp stone, then a second. "Walk, I said!"

She stepped toward him.

"Stop. That's good. That's wonderful." He studied her carefully. "You match, you know: your toenails, your fingernails, and your panties. I always wondered how far you went with the red. It's visually exciting, you know."

He fluffed one hand in a circle. "Lose the panties."

She lowered the bit of crimson lace over her ankles and was about to toss them on the pile when he shouted.

"Throw them here."

She obeyed without emotion. Gooseflesh rose on her skin, she shivered with the cold. Her chafed nipples contracted painfully.

"Turn," he commanded. "Turn slowly. That's it. Turn again."

"I'm cold."

"You're hot, Babe. You're really hot. Spread your legs, reach toward the sky."

She folded her arms across her breasts and stood still. "I said I'm cold."

"I don't give a fuck what you are! Spread your legs. Reach your arms up towards the sky." Another stone stung her leg.

She would not recoil or try to protect herself. A large stone hit near her eye and knocked her to one knee. He came at her, kicked her to the wooden floor.

"Now get up and reach toward the sky, bitch!"

She stood slowly, lifted her arms laconically.

"Almost perfect! Almost. The best I've seen yet."

She lowered her arms.

"Come here."

As she picked her way over the litter of stones, her teeth chattered with a rising fear. She focused her eyes on a point in the woods behind him. She would not look into his face.

He placed his hands under her armpits and like a buyer at a horse auction slowly slid them down the length of her. His thumbs pinched the soft flesh of her thighs. "Not perfect. No, not quite."

He pushed her away, reached down into the earth near his feet and scooped up a handful of cold wet soil. "I don't like red nipples. I find them repulsive. I like dark, dark nipples. Black nipples." With painstaking exactness he began to smear mud over her breasts.

She kept her eyes open, willed herself to remain still. Her clenched fingernails bit into the torn flesh of her hands.

"You've never been pregnant, have you, Clover?"

"I never will be."

"Ah! You're one of those imperfect creatures who will never conceive, is that it? An androgynous freak of nature. Model beautiful, but forever barren. If you like, I'll pretend you're normal, although I find it a bit repugnant."

Had she spoken aloud or had he read her thoughts? He knew where to jab, but then, so did she. "Your precious Elizabeth has never had a baby. She must not be perfect either."

"No she's not physically beautiful, but psychologically she's perfection. A Biblical woman."

"Elizabeth would be angry with both of us if she knew what we were doing."

"Elizabeth doesn't mind if I find pleasure elsewhere. She's not very healthy. I wouldn't violate her with my needs. We both understand that perfectly."

Clover began to laugh. Once she felt the release, she could not stop. She laughed as she sometimes did at weddings and funerals, wild cackling laughter, belly shaking baritone laughter. The woods echoed with her high-pitched shrieks and deep moans.

Her head jerked back when he grasped her hair. She felt the wind of the slap before her face jerked violently to one side.

"Stop it!" he shouted.

But she couldn't stop. Something in her had snapped at the thought of frigid Elizabeth holding him at arms length with her high and mighty New England manners and ladylike countenance. "She's fucking frigid," she giggled. "Elizabeth the mighty has pink nipples and an intact hymen."

She did not raise her hands in defense, but allowed him to beat her until he tired and even then she made sure he could see resistance in her eyes.

She would lay down naked on the cold ground, but she would never give up hope.

He stood, gazed down on her with a look so tender that she recoiled as if he had struck her again.

He began to laugh. "You're a wonder, Clover. A beautiful, spirited wonder. You are going to be the most wonderful companion I have ever had. I'm sure of it."

∞

Sheriff Owen Swenson took the call at the restaurant. "And you say his name was Ron Haviland?"

He pushed his plate of barbecued ribs aside, wiped his mouth on a paper napkin, and pulled the long cord of the phone into the deserted back hall.

The Wisconsin officer had pulled a file. Swenson could hear him rifling through it before he spoke again.

"Yes. He was a dental surgeon."

The sheriff raised the napkin and blotted sweat from his brow. "I've got that."

"Found his parents, wife and four sons bludgeoned in the family home."

"Jesus."

"Was questioned once and dropped out of sight."

"Disappeared? Just like that? When was this exactly?"

"September of '69."

" And no one ever saw him again?"

"Went to some kind of medical convention. Says here it was in Chicago."

"Chicago, you say? So you were only able to interview him once before he disappeared?

"Yeah, but there was other stuff that went away with him. We'd been having a series of animal mutilations and prostitute disappearances. They stopped when he left."

"How many?"

"Quite a few over the years."

"Could you fax me a picture of this guy?"

"Have only one. It's old, from the missing-poster we had made up? Would that work?"

"Yeah. Anything you've got. It's a far shot, but I'd like to get a look at him, see if there's any kind of match with what we've got going on here."

"If he's the one, let us know. I, for one, would like to get my hands on this guy again."

"Sure. Yeah, well listen, I sure do appreciate your help."

Young runaway Wendy stood behind the counter and watched as Sheriff Owen Swenson hurried out the front door.

~಄

K.C. Casey had run out of steam. He could feel his heart beating too rapidly and too feebly beneath the blood soaked shirt he had used as a sponge. He was within sight of the club's cabin, but it might as well have been two hundred miles away.

He rolled onto his back and studied the dark clouded-up sky. Typical. So damned typical of his life. He would die out here in this stinking rain and never see another ray of California sunshine.

He'd like to have one more day at the beach, to once more breathe in the heady aroma of suntan lotion and nearly naked bodies.

Up the hill, toward Maggie's place, he could hear a horn honking and dogs howling. He tried to call out, but his lungs seemed to have lost all their air.

Tears filled his eyes as the sound of a car engine faded away.

∽

Dick Morton shoved her through a small door in the hillside at the back of the crumbling mess hall.

The space was dark and filled with the dank scent of mice. She tumbled several feet through dead air and landed with a thud on a cold dirt floor. She heard the door close and his soft tread on several stairs. The dull glow of a single light bulb came on to her left. She scrambled to her feet and darted for the stairs. One jerk of the rope and she was lying face down on the dirt again.

"You're quick, I'll give you that."

She felt cold links of chain fall over her face and settle on her neck. It made small clinking noises as it slowly cut off her breath. She reached up with both hands and tried to pull the steel away.

He pulled it tighter. Her mouth opened. Her tongue thickened. She could feel the painful pressure of her eyes bulging in their sockets before she sank into a void of blackness.

∽

Swenson and Larry turned into the logging road Maggie had described. Sure enough, there was Casey's fun-mobile and, farther in, the telephone company's huge cherry picker.

Maybe the kid was doing telephone linemen these days. Even as the thought crossed his mind, he knew he had to change his line of thinking. There were far too many similarities between the Dick Morton he knew and the dentist from Wisconsin who had disappeared into thin air.

What Elizabeth told him fit the profile. Dick had worked as a lineman before and during a brief stint at college, she had said. He had learned his skill by doing. She admired his persistence and his clear sense of himself. He liked being a lineman, she said. He never regretted leaving college.

Had he regretted leaving an entire lifetime behind? A dentist. Yes, he could see Dick Morton as a dentist. And worse, he could see Dick Morton using surgical precision as he cut off body parts.

He had waited nearly an hour for the picture to be faxed before he told his secretary to watch the machine and to call him at Maggie's.

But Maggie wasn't home. All her dogs were out and he'd had to restrain Larry from shooting them when they assailed the side of the cruiser. They had not gained access to the house, so had driven to Roger Parrish's kennels where they found more howling dogs and Clover's sporty little car. He had peered through the kitchen window and seen the young lady's coat and handbag, just as the boy had described them. Casey's story rang true.

As they neared the turn around, Larry shouted, "Jesus H. Christ! Roger's gonna sure be mad when he finds out about this!"

"I have a feeling Roger already knows," Swenson said. "We'd better get back into town and get a search party together."

He saw the question in his partners' eyes. "Roger Parrish and Clover Winters are somewhere in this forest. And I'm pretty sure the man who's with them is a murderer."

"It's Casey then, for sure."

"No, I've been wrong about the kid. It's more than likely Dick Morton."

He could tell from the expression on Larry's face that he did not believe him. "I'm having a picture faxed of a suspect from Wisconsin. If it shows any resemblance to Dick Morton, we've got a problem on our hands. A really serious problem."

CHAPTER FOURTEEN

When she opened her eyes, his penis was the first thing she saw.

He laughed loudly at her response. "It is big, isn't it, Dear Clover? Every woman has the same reaction when they see old Ronnie. Magnificent, isn't he?" He caressed her face with his erection.

She tried to turn away, but her head was held rigid by something tied across her forehead. She tried to raise her arms, but they too were held tightly in place. Behind her one light bulb glowed eerily and cast moving shadows that reminded her suddenly of something that had happened when she was very young and still had her mother. She had lain in the dark then, as now, but covered with her mother's fur coat. When she had peeked out, she had seen moving, swaying forms of humans moving rhythmically in a dim light. Something bad had happened then as was happening now. What was it?

She felt him against her lips. She pressed her teeth together tightly, but he grasped her jaw near its hinged edges and she was unable to resist.

"Ah, Clover."

Her clenched lips moved over ridges and irregular bulges. She gagged violently. He didn't stop.

"Do you feel that, Clover? Oh, sweetheart, do that again. Can you feel my love knots?"

Her eyes burned. She squeezed them tightly against the sight of his flesh. She wretched again and this time her stomach emptied. Bile filled her throat, burned through her nostrils.

She couldn't breath, but he persisted. Her mouth was lax. She heard the gurgle of a death rattle. Bile burned into her lungs. She felt herself sinking through ragged edges of consciousness.

He pushed his hand against her forehead and pulled himself away.

She gagged and spit, her stomach heaved with uncontrolled retching as waves of contractions tried to empty any fluids she had left. She opened her burning eyes and saw him swaying beneath the light in some bizarre contraction of arms and back. What was he doing? She opened her eyes wider and forced herself to look.

He was rubbing a wide sheet of sandpaper over his penis. His head rolled back on his shoulders as he alternately howled in pain and cried in agony, "I'm a bad boy. I must be punished. I'm so sorry, so sorry."

She closed her eyes and fell back into the abyss.

ɔ∾

Swenson stared at the picture for a long while before tossing it across the desk to Larry.

"What do you think?"

"It's him all right. A lot younger and pudgier, but that's Dick. Would you look at those glasses? I bet he wore leisure suits, too."

"Better get on the wire and call for help. We'll need all the men we can get. And dogs. Probably be best if we get a few of Roger's dogs. They'll be faster at finding their master."

"I'll call the Tacoma and Seattle chiefs and see who they can send."

"I'll call in some reserve deputies. Have everyone meet at the cherry picker. With all this rain, the trail will be damn cold. It'll be dark soon, too. Break into the earthquake supplies and pull out every good lantern you can find. We'll need extra batteries and some highway flares to mark the road."

"Helicopters from the military?"

"Hell, yes. I should of thought of them first. They might not be much help with the wind and the rain and the tree cover. Ask what they think. If they can fly, we'll use them."

"Strange that they've disappeared into the woods like that. Maybe they'll walk out on their own."

"Yeah, well, the longer they're in there, the more chance there is that they won't walk out at all."

He was sitting on a chair of some sort, hunched over, mumbling to himself. Somewhere above, the wind howled through trees with a high keening whine. She could hear the steady trickle of water from a gutter somewhere near. The space was musty, but warmer now. He had taken off his coat and his shirt and seemed to be writing on his chest.

"So. You're with me again? I knew you would be all right once you got warmed up. Is it warm enough for you now?"

She stared at him.

He was bleeding from multiple wounds on his chest and abdomen. He did not look at her, but concentrated on something he held between his legs. "I've been doing my atonement, my retribution, the cleansing of my sins. Only through the blood of Jesus can our sins be washed away. You'd do well to learn the creed, Clover, and to follow it. You'd do very well, indeed."

He came to her, exposed himself like a man she had happened upon once, sitting in a parked car, smiling, penis in hand, his face an expectant leering pale oval.

She closed her eyes.

"Open your eyes, Clover! I want you to see what has been done to me. I want you to know how these years have affected me. They haven't been easy, you know. I do have feelings. I do repent for my sins."

"You'll burn in hell for your sins." She pressed her eyelids closed.

"Oh, surely, I will. But in the meantime, I've come this far, why stop now? My game is up. They'll be no hiding now. My cover's blown. I'll have to give up everything: Elizabeth, my home, my many friends."

"You've killed your friends."

"Some of them, yes. But that wouldn't have been necessary if everyone had not meddled into the affairs of others."

"Murder is everyone's business."

"Oh, ho! A philosopher among us. A person of discernment, of moral rectitude."

"You killed Tiny's daughter."

He giggled. "Yes, that little waif. Nothing to her. Flat as a board. Neck like a chicken."

"Why her?"

"She was playing by the lake. We skipped stones together for a while. Skinny arms."

He opened her tethered hand and placed his partially erect phallus into her palm. "Can you feel those ridges?" He curled her fingers around the organ. "That's my payment. I don't take my pleasures for granted. I pay for them."

He was becoming excited again; she tried to pull her hand away, but was restrained by the tether.

"Do you want to hurt me, Clover? Do you hate me?"

She curled her fingers into a claw and dug her nails into his turgid flesh.

He arched his back and begged, "Please, don't, Clover. Please."

She pushed the ragged nails deeply into his flesh until she felt they were almost meeting.

He tore himself away.

There. Feel some pain, Dick Morton. Feel that, Goddamn it! Her eyes flew open involuntarily.

His body writhed. His face, bathed in the glow of the overhead light, appeared ghostly pale.

She wanted to plunge a knife into his heart. To twist it. To plunge it again. Her bloody hand clenched and unclenched automatically. She burned with the desire to kill him.

His face was close now. His stale breath warmed her cheek. His smile was tender, transforming his features into a gentle child. "Thank you," he whispered. "Thank you."

He climbed onto her. His weight forced the stiffened joints of her hips and spine to splay painfully. A gasp escaped her lips. He stopped it with his tongue.

He thrust himself into her without warning.

She tried to bite, but he stopped her with his teeth and continued to thrust. She tightened her pelvic muscles. The movement caused her hips and thighs to contract painfully.

He jerked on the choke chain, pulled it taut again.

As she again lost consciousness, his chant echoed in her ears. "Bitch. Bitch. Bitch."

∽

A low steady hiss told her she was near someone dying. She was in a hospital room staring at plastic tubes, white sheets, a blipping screen that flashed with a green light, and a pair of large feet sticking out of bedcovers. Antiseptic hospital smell permeated the air. She wanted her mother, wanted to bury her face in her mother's breast and inhale the sweet scent of lemons that marked the woman's daytime hours, but mother was holding the man. She waited for the sound of the suction machine. She would not open her eyes until the nurse sucked out the bloody slime that caused the man to gurgle and sigh.

"Mommy?"

The hissing continued. "Mommy?"

There was no answer. Slowly she opened her eyes, cast about the dim room and remembered. She was in this dark hot hole with Dick Morton.

He appeared to be straightening and stacking along a row of thick shelves. She watched through narrowed eyes as he lined something up methodically in the plank cupboard.

He was naked, extraordinarily pale and spindly for a man who ran five miles every day. The cords of his legs and the tops of his arms were thick and muscular, but the rest of him was bony and long.

He moved with a spider's quickness, back and forth, up and down. The sickly color of his skin surprised her. In all these years that she had known the man, she had never seen him in shorts, she realized, or in a bathing suit, or even a short-sleeved shirt. He had always dressed formally, long slacks, polished leather belt and shoes, starched and pressed white shirts.

When he jogged he wore expensive matching sweats and perfectly white shoes. When he worked, he wore coveralls. She'd seen him like that, shiny black shoes, starched white collar, peeking out from his dusty gray telephone company uniform. All these years she had never really noticed his obsessive prissiness.

She turned her head to follow his movements and realized that she had been moved. Her hands were free and the tether across her forehead had been removed. She was on a rough blanket on the dirt floor. She reached up to check for the chain around her neck.

Her head jerked and her body lifted doll-like from the dirt floor. Her legs and arms dangled in midair and pulled painfully in their stiff and thickened sockets. She heard the screech of metal on metal as she fell abruptly back to earth.

He squatted next to her. "You're drying out," he said. His voice was high and birdlike. "Drink this."

He held a cup to her lips, poured a sickly sweet liquid into her mouth.

She wanted to drink. Her body cried for water, but her throat had closed up. She choked and blew the potion through her nose.

He lifted her into a sitting position and released the tension on the choke chain.

She drank voraciously. Her stomach heaved and tried to disgorge the fluid, but she swallowed hard and kept it down. She needed her strength, but at the same time feared his desire to keep her alive. "Why don't you just kill me?" she asked.

"And spoil our fun? Oh, my Clover, we've just begun our little adventure. I have great plans for us." His voice had returned to normal, but his head moved sluggishly on his shoulders and his hands were slow and had a dreamlike quality to their movements.

She moved her eyes slowly about the room. Kerosene lanterns glowed from the darkest corners and a heater of some kind blew loudly but with a dull flame from near the stairs. Leather cases were neatly stowed on the lower shelves along one wall and a surgical stand with a small metal tray stood under a drape next to a green canister with black lettering.

"What have you been doing, Dick?" She asked in a conversational tone that surprised her.

"Playing."

"Playing what?"

"Doctor."

"And what has the doctor prescribed for himself?"

"You are perspicacious, my dear. I've been tinkering a bit with the Nitrous, taking myself on a little journey while you slept."

"My God, Dick, you aren't telling me you've been huffing?"

"And what would be so wrong about that?"

"It's so out of character for you."

He laughed. "Another little sidelight of my multi-faceted personality. It does a person good to stretch a little now and then."

"That's a mighty big stretch. Where'd you get the tank? Is that telephone company issue?"

"That's the best part, dear Clover. I rob the tanks from Doc Harrison's office. He has a little shed where he stores the stuff. I think he may use a little himself, since he never seems to notice that his tanks are frequently near empty. I imagine he and his pretty little receptionist share a bit now and then. I've always had the most difficult time in his chair while that sweet thing hovers over me. She's so tempting, if you know what I mean."

"Oh, I get the drift, Dick."

He laughed again. "You're so clever and quick with words, Clover. I always did admire your sharp, little tongue. I always imagined you would be the perfect mate for my good friend, Jim. You two always seemed to play so well off each other."

"How can you still call him friend? He's dead! You killed him!"

"He is my friend!"

She caught the edge in his voice. She had hit a chord.

He stepped forward, his arm raised as if to strike her.

She winced and turned from a blow that did not land. Chains rattled as she was swung violently into the air to dangle at his waist level.

She must remain calm. "Did you kill my mother?"

"What?"

"My mother. Did you kill her?"

"How should I know? I can't remember everything."

"Twenty years ago. She wore a red satin dress and matching shoes."

"Can't remember."

"Do you remember when I came to live with the Billingsleys?"

"Before my time. You were already their pampered brat when I arrived."

"We used to play together."

"Who?"

"Jim, Lisa, and me. Why did you kill him?"

"He asked for what he got! He snooped in my garage! He thought I didn't know. I trusted him. I loaned him my truck and gave him my house keys and how did he repay me? He came out of my garage, ran across the street and got right on the phone."

"I saw him running, so I listened to be sure. He called his boss and said he had found something that might be related to the prostitute murders. He wouldn't tell him what, said he wanted to be sure because it was unbelievable to him and would be to others. You see, Clover, he knew. He had found my treasures."

She tried to lift her head to relieve the pressure on her lungs, but the movement sent a sharp pain down her spine and through all four extremities.

"I had to shut him up! I told Elizabeth that I wasn't ready for dinner; that I needed to have a jog to clear my head. She was dismayed, but, angel that she is, she said, 'Fine, Dick. You just run along.'"

Clover fell abruptly to the dirt floor, but no breath escaped her lungs. For a moment trapped air threatened to burst into her chest.

He swung her around like a dog on a leash and pulled her to him. "Kneel!"

She obeyed like a dog.

He fondled her hair, rubbed a hand gently across her forehead. "Jim was often bad with Lisa. I could watch them from my bedroom. They did things that were vile in God's eyes."

Her back was painful. Her body too heavy to bear. She felt herself falling toward him, looking to him for support.

He loosened the neck chain.

Her gasping breath was stopped by the thrust of his partially erect penis into her mouth.

She fell onto him, struggled to right herself.

He took her head in his hands and continued to thrust weakly. "I called him from the truck. I told him that I was on the way to the new house to work on the phone. I asked him to meet me there."

He pulled away abruptly. "I'm tired of you. You're a lousy lay!" He pummeled her head as she fell backward onto the floor.

The hissing resumed. She pulled herself into fetal position and closed her eyes. She wanted to sleep, but throbbing pain kept her vigilant. She pulled on the neck chain until it loosened slightly. When she moved her hand away, it was covered in blood. He would kill her if he wasn't careful. She wished that he would, but in the logical part of her brain something wanted desperately to survive. I am stronger willed, she reminded herself. I have to stay strong. She rolled her eyes to find him.

He was sitting to one side, reading something and eating a sandwich that he held carefully by its baggie wrapper.

"How did you get to the house?" She again surprised herself with her casual tone.

He looked up from his meal and smiled. "To Jim's house? That was the easy part. I did exactly what I'd intended. I went jogging. I parked the truck in the clear cut and ran up through the old growth. When I was done, I drove his car back down, torched it and went home to my supper."

"And you could eat after what you had done?"

"Oh, my dear, I never lose my appetite. For anything." He threw the empty wrapper into a can near his feet and stood.

He had some difficulty manipulating the surgical stand across the dirt floor.

The antiseptic smell was stronger now. "What are you doing?"

He pulled on the ropes until her head was raised off the ground.

Her twisted body moved in the opposite direction. She felt the bite of rope on her wrists, her ankles.

He tied her, one limb at a time to stakes on the ground until she lay spread-eagle with her head suspended inches from the ground.

He stood between her legs and waved a long scissor-like tool.

"What are you doing?" she again demanded.

He dipped the tool into a small basin on the stand and methodically began to paint his erect penis. He moved slowly and deliberately with a surgeon's careful precision. Round and around in small circles, across his abdomen and down into his groin. When he was bright orange from his waist to his thighs, he turned his eyes to her. "Now I prep my patient."

She felt the cold liquid touch her skin, drip down between the folds of her labia. His attention to detail frightened her. She could feel gooseflesh rising on her abdomen and legs. She flinched at the probing of her vagina, at the painful thrust of the steel to her very center and screamed in agony as he thrust into and probed her rectum. He placed the instrument in a tall steel pail and lowered his weight onto her. When she tried to turn her face aside, he jerked on the rope and lifted her neck higher.

He kissed her face. His lips were dry against her skin.

He thrust into her: into every cavity; every wrinkle; every orifice. With priaptic persistence he continued until the part of her that wished to survive moved into a protective haze of pain and semi-consciousness. At least she was warm. Finally she was very warm.

She felt him leave her. She lay on the filthy blanket and stared into the void of partial darkness. The lanterns had burned out; only the light from the single bulb offered any comfort.

While she had lain beneath him, her mind had taken her backward to another time of fear. She had remembered something. A fragment of time. A sense of escape. Something before the Billingsley's. Before her mother's disappearance. She was running beside a train, being pulled along by someone who was in a great hurry. Her mother's fur coat billowed out slapping her arms and chest as they ran. She had been able to see her mother's face -- white, straining, with crimson lips parted, and eyes large with fear. Her mother's backward glance told of something horrible coming from behind. As she had been pulled up the metal stairs of the train, she had seen a crimson stain on the hand that held hers.

Now, Dick Morton stood with his back to her muttering in low tones and squeezing the muscles in his buttocks rhythmically. He tensed, walked back to her, knelt and ejaculated spermatic fluid over her face and breasts. Like a child playing in his own feces or an animal marking his territory, he carefully began to smear the fluid over her entire body.

When the sticky mess would go no further, he released the tension on her neck, laid on her again and fell into a deep childlike sleep.

CHAPTER FIFTEEN

The dogs yipped with excitement when they found Duke. The poor animal was almost gone, but licked the hand of Sheriff Swenson when he bent to examine the shirt and bra that had been used to staunch the flow of blood. "Better get this animal to the vet," he called to Larry. "Get him loaded into the cruiser. I want the rest of you to pair up."

"We'll comb the brush, dog handlers in first, officers next and finally volunteers. I want no one to take chances. The man is armed and dangerous. Use your radios to report any suspicious finds, any trails that look fresh. Does everyone understand what we're dealing with here?"

A general murmur of agreement ran through the group, but Swenson wasn't sure they realized the danger they faced. Dick Morton's trail was hours old. Dick Morton was not going to lie down and play dead at this point in his game. More than likely he would hole up somewhere and ambush the lot of them or play guerilla and pick them off one at a time. No matter which method he chose, there would be bloodshed before this chase was done.

He tied his hooded poncho more tightly around his neck and again checked his revolver. If he came face to face with the dentist, he was as ready as he would ever be.

With a huge sigh, he stepped into the gathering dusk of the big woods.

The dogs howled and bayed as they ran back and forth between two trails. "We'll have to split up," he called to the group. "Half go up the creek, the rest of you head towards the old camp.

☙

"Over here!" The call rose from the woods beyond the creek bank and was carried man to man to the fork in the trail that led to the Sheriff. No one remembered to use the radios.

Swenson passed a vomiting man as he pulled himself up the muddy bank. "It's Parrish," someone said.

"You mean what's left of him," another voice added.

He broke into the clearing and through the small crowd of men that surrounded the slashed and broken body of Roger Parrish.

"I want everyone back to the Creek," he shouted. "Everyone. And I want the area taped off in a quarter mile circumference. Call back the dogs."

"What will you do?" someone asked.

"We'll cordon off the area, regroup, call in the swat team from the city. We're dealing with a maniac here. I'm not going to be responsible for anyone else getting killed."

The men did not protest his orders, but huddled together in the small depression along the banks of Clear Creek like soldiers in a losing battle awaiting news of their buddies.

৵

"Dick?" Her voice startled her.

He was moving about in the silent space, dressed in blue surgical scrubs and booties, collecting things and depositing them on the surgical stand.

"Dick?"

He turned and smiled down on her. "Yes, sweetheart?"

"I have to go to the bathroom."

"You'll have to wait."

"I have to go bad."

"Damn it, Clover! I was just thinking that I'd forgotten to try your navel. You have a beautiful navel, but it's too shallow. I was going to make it big enough for me."

He raised the steel sponge-tipped instrument and a scalpel for her to see.

"I have to go to the bathroom," she cried.

"Well, I won't have you soiling my bed," he said peevishly. "You'll have to go outside."

"Help me."

"Damn it, Clover, you're making me angry!"

"I have to pee."

He loosened the ropes on her ankles and wrists. She slipped her limbs free and turned onto her belly. He tightened his grip on the rope around her neck and untied the far end of her waist rope. With a tether in one hand, like a cowboy on his horse, he stood behind her and smacked her buttocks. "Go," he commanded.

Her stiffened limbs would not move. A sharp pain in her abdomen folded her over at the waist.

He pulled on the ropes to drag her to a sitting position, covered himself with a forest-green slicker, and shoved a small revolver into his pocket.

Her head filled with a loud ringing. She shook herself and reached out for him.

"Don't touch me! You're unclean!" He shoved her towards the door.

She crawled on all fours up the three stairs and breathed deeply as cold air welcomed her. She moved a few feet into the rain.

"Here!" he said. "Right here."

She raised herself to a squat and tried to release her over-filled bladder. She pressed one hand into her lower abdomen, balanced on the other hand and half stood Her bladder muscles refused to cooperate.

"Piss!" he commanded.

"I can't. It hurts. I can't go."

"I'll drain you with my knife! Piss!"

She reached down to steady herself. Her hand touched rough wood. Something important here. Wood. Buried under the forest floor. A well. She was at one of the wells that she and K.C. had looked into.

He would kill her slowly and with more pain than he had inflicted up to now. He would open her bladder with the knife. She knew he would.

She could bear no more. She'd rather die in the well than by his hand.

Her movement was instinctive and quick. She threw her body onto the edge, careened on the brink, and flew through dank air. For a brief moment the ropes held her back. As she began sliding downward, she grabbed for handholds on the river rock that edged the pit.

Heavier Dick Morton crashed past her.

Her clutching fingers tangled in his hair. Within seconds both bodies jammed up in the narrowing opening. He was below her. She stepped on his head and, oblivious to the rocks and dirt that showered onto her face, scrambled back up the crumbling shaft.

There was no resistance. He had lost his hold on the ropes. On all fours she scampered away, the ropes tugging and catching as if the devil himself was holding her back.

She sat on the wet forest floor and pulled the chain from her neck. She could hear Dick thrashing about in the well. If she could climb out, so could he. She had to move.

The long length of rope around her waist caught on the edge of the well. It would not come undone.

She crouched and moved back, rolling the rope hand-over-hand and holding it to her like a baby to her breast. Her bladder burned, but she couldn't stop. Her stiffened joints resisted every movement she asked of them.

She reached the edge of the well and gave the rope some slack.

Dick's head bobbed just below the rim of the well.

She gave the rope more slack and tugged. It pulled free.

She rose to a slouch and hobbled into the darkness of the trees. Icy rain revived her and the fronds of ferns and evergreens offered cleansing relief to her dried and dirtied skin.

A sudden gush of warm fluid ran down her legs. Was she bleeding? She reached down and felt the liquid and laughed. Urine. Her bladder had let loose after all. She allowed the fluid to run freely.

She raised her face to the pouring rain and rubbed her soiled skin with her free hand as she ran. Blackberry vines tore at her naked flesh. Twigs and thorns penetrated her bare feet.

She began to move more quickly, felt warmth returning to her frozen joints and a pulse of hope awakening her senses. Fear spurred her on. He would not be far behind. He knew the pathways as well as any forest animal. She had to be quicker and smarter. Will was not enough.

She veered from the trail, rolled down a steep hillside, scrambled onto all fours and crawled through brush alder and Salal.

"Clo-o-o-ver."

Her name echoed from side to side of the small gully.

"Clo-o-o-ver."

She put her hands to her ears and ran on. Her feet gave way on a slippery edge. Clear Creek. She turned abruptly and began to climb along its course. If she could beat him to the survivalist's cabin, she might have a chance.

❧

The team leader had taken the time to paint his face and collect his night recognizance gear. He stepped from the trail with his group of armed men.

"That's where they found Parrish." Swenson pointed. "And up here, is where we found what looks to be Casey's bloody shirt and first aid stuff. The gun is a paint ball model. What the hell he was doing with that is beyond me, but there it is. The dogs want to go up the trail towards the old lumber camp, but all indications are that they went up the creek."

"We'll follow the dogs," the leader said. "And I'd appreciate it if you'd keep your men back. You can follow along if you'd like, Sheriff."

They left the group of men huddled in the safe depression between the banks of Clear Creek and began to make their way up the steep trail to the lumber camp. They moved without speaking and with precise cadence.

Swenson sweated with the effort of the climb. He stopped frequently to quell the shaking in his calves and thighs.

Flashlight beams muted into the mist.

The dogs yipped with excitement and moved noisily back and forth across the narrow path. Once, over the din of the dogs, he thought he heard a voice call 'Clover'. He stopped and listened, but the rising wind, sheets of heavy rain and the tramping footfalls of seven men erased any remnants of the call. The wind, he decided. The wind and wishful thinking, for, judging from the condition of the dog and Roger and Casey's bloody gear, he didn't believe for a minute that Clover Winters would be found alive.

As they neared the top of a rise, the commander called a halt and requested Swenson to come to the head of the group. "There's a small light up ahead. Can you see it?"

"Yes."

"Is there a house up there?"

"Shouldn't be anything lit up there. That's the old lumber camp. Been abandoned for thirty years. Is it a flashlight?"

"No. Seems to be electric. Doesn't move, too large to be anything hand-held."

"Campfire?"

"In this environment?"

"Guess not."

"We'll need to fan out, come up on all sides of the place."

"Can't."

"Why not?"

"Rocky cliff to the east. It would take climbing equipment in the daylight to get up on that side. There're some old wells on the upper end, rotted and dangerous. I wouldn't recommend trying to find your way through them in the dark. We'd best go straight on up."

"I'll send a man ahead to look it over."

"Suit yourself. We're wasting time. The guy doesn't know we're onto him. We'd have the element of surprise except for all these flashlights."

"If we've seen his light, he's seen ours. I stand by my decision. You want to volunteer?"

"Hey, fella, I'm no point man. With the dogs howling and all the lights I'd just be getting myself killed. You go ahead, send an expert up there." He moved off the trail and under the dripping limbs of a giant fir. " I'll wait here with you."

They lit cigarettes and shuffled about in the thick pine-scented needles of the hillside, alternately sitting on the damp ground or pacing up and down the narrow trail.

∽

Twenty minutes passed before the man returned. "It's clear, sir. But the strangest place. Looks like a den of some kind. Wired for electricity. Somebody's been there very recently. Place is still warm with a kerosene heater blowing about. The dogs are interested in one of the wells in the back."

"Let's go."

They crested the hill and headed directly to the open doorway.

"I'll be damned," the sheriff said. "Dick's made himself a little lair in the old root cellar. Now who woulda ever thought of that?" He stepped into the dim space. "Do you think he's got it booby trapped?"

"Looks like they left in a big hurry. Probably saw us coming."

"Woman's clothing and shoes. Could be Clover's. Hard to tell. Well looky here! Dental bags and instruments. He's our guy all right."

"Looks like a torture rack too. Not a pleasant place for a gal to visit."

"Jesus!"

One of the team stepped into the small space. "Sir. I think the dogs are onto something. Might be a body down the well."

"Get all the lights together and grab one of these ropes. Send somebody down."

Her limbs and brain had gone numb. She could process nothing more than the need to keep moving. Her breath caught in ragged gasps with each inspiration. Something hurt deep in her chest and her feet screamed with every strike of rock or stick on her bare soles. A square form took shape in the mist ahead. She ran straight out, her eyes on the cabin. An eerie silence surrounded her. She could no longer hear her own breathing.

Someone grabbed her ankle. She catapulted through the air. She beat at a large body with all her strength: kicked with her free foot and finally, unable to get free of the trap, fell upon him and began to beat him with her closed fists.

"Clover?"

"K.C.? Oh, God. Is it really you?"

"I'm hurt bad."

"Oh, God. Oh, God. He's coming after me."

He tried to raise himself, but fell back with a heavy grunt.

She straddled him, leveraged him up with a strength that surprised her.

He staggered and drifted backwards.

"K.C., he's coming. We've got to get to the cabin. He's crazier than anything. He'll kill us."

He stepped forward, his weight on her small shoulders. "You're naked, Clover."

"Yes. Come on."

"Did he hurt you?"

"Yes."

He moved ahead, reached out and touched the cabin wall. "The key," he said. "Under the white rock. Next to the shower."

She propped him in the doorway and ran for the key.

A bullet zinged past her head. She pushed over a white stone. Her hand fumbled as she felt for the key. There. Here. The key. She ran back to Casey and fitted the key into the lock. She pushed on the door. It wouldn't budge.

"Opens outward. In case a bear tries to beat it down." He rolled aside.

She pulled the door open and shoved him inside.

He sprawled on the floor, tried desperately to get back up.

"Stay there." She pulled the door closed and hooked the bar into place.

"Close the shutters," he mumbled.

She crawled to three small windows and locked the shutters.

A bullet shattered the glass of the last window. Another splintered the shutter as she pulled it closed.

She scrambled back to K.C. He was no longer moving. "Don't die on me," she ordered. "I can't stand anymore."

He opened his eyes. "My shoulder. The bleeding has to be stopped. A kit is in the cupboard next to the sink."

She crawled toward the sink on all fours. The rope around her waist slowed her progress. She tugged at the wet knots. They remained taut.

Another bullet ripped through the window. Her shoulder struck the table leg and reeled her about. For a moment she wanted to hunker down and hide. Someone would surely come soon.

Weapons. There had to be some weapons here. She moved forward again, stood and pulled the white first aide kit from the open shelf. Her eyes had become amazingly perceptive. She'd become an animal. Survival of the fittest. Is that how he feels too? She pulled the kitchen towel from a peg near the sink.

She ripped the shirt from K.C.'s shoulder without mercy. Black blood clots slithered out as she pulled off the matted cloth. Quickly she shoved the end of the towel deep into the gaping hole.

There was no response from K.C.

Another bullet came through the window. She pressed hard against the wound, pushing as much of the towel into it as she could.

"Clover!" Dick Morton screamed through the broken window.

"Go fuck yourself! It's the only way that's good for you!"

A bullet came close to her.

Shut up and move. She pulled a roll of bandage from the kit and began wrapping it tightly over the kitchen towel.

K.C. moaned and tried to move away. She smacked his face. "Stay still and shut up," she hissed.

She rolled another strip of gauze over his shoulder. The bandage seemed to be staying white.

He was shivering as much as she.

She pulled a wool blanket off the nearest cot and wrapped it close around him.

His arms and legs moved convulsively.

She pulled the blanket from the second cot, lay on top of K.C. and pulled the blanket over them both. If he had a pocket she would crawl into it. Afraid. She was so damned afraid. She had to get warm. She couldn't do another thing until she was warm.

∽

"I have a feeling," Sheriff Owen Swenson was saying to no one in particular, "that if we find Miss Winters at all, it will be in pieces like the others. I think he's trying to dispose of a body and if it's not in the well, he'll dig a hole and hide it."

"We've got him on the run," the swat team captain offered. "But he has the advantage of knowing this terrain and being able to navigate in darkness. I'm going to send my men back and have them drive out and cover the perimeters. We'll set up sniper posts at all strategic points. We'll get the bastard."

"I'll get the forensics in here to look for samples", the sheriff said. "Could you have your men back off and leave the place intact?"

"Hey, Captain, look what we've got here." The man held out an open metal case.

In the dim light Swenson made out several rows of white fingertips with brightly colored nails, lined up symmetrically on black velvet. "Jesus H. Christ! The kid wasn't lying. Close that up! My God! Put it back! Don't touch another thing!"

But another man was sorting through a neatly folded stack of clothing on a back shelf. The coveralls were wet on the legs and the socks and shoes were soaked. On a peg on the wall hung a very wet Gore-Tex jacket. "I think he may be out there naked," he said suddenly. "I think the guy booked out of here like a jaybird after a nut. Do you think she could have gotten away?"

"If she did, she's naked too," said another man who held up the pair of women's jogging pants and crimson panties. "She won't last long out there in the rain."

∽

As he began to stir, her instincts sharpened again. "K.C.?" she whispered.

"Yeah?"

"You feeling better?"

"Yeah. Where is he?"

"Outside. Close. Real close."

"We need a weapon."

"Are there any guns here?"

"No."

She rolled off him and pulled the blanket back over her shoulders, raised up on one elbow. "I need some clothes," she whispered. "Are there any here?"

"Camouflage stuff. Chest by the window."

She glanced at the shattered shutter. On the floor in front of it she could see the glistening remains of the glass window. She threw off her blanket and lofted it over her pathway to the chest.

A shot split the silence. Could he see her? Was he looking through that window even now? She took in a deep breath of air and scampered on all fours to the chest. If her heart continued to beat this fast, surely it would burst. She reached into the box, pulled a mass of clothing to her chest, and rolled back to Casey.

"I've got to get rid of this rope," she whispered. "Can you help me untie it?"

"There's a stiletto in my right boot."

She felt along his leg and located the handle of the blade. "Oh, God. Thank God!" She sawed off the longest length of rope near the knot.

She sorted through the armful of clothing she had found. A pair of huge thermal underwear felt warm in her arms. Quickly she pulled the legs over her bleeding feet and hitched the pants under the belt of rope. The elastic waist pulled tight above her breasts and the legs hung past the tips of her toes. She pulled the material taut and sliced off the bottom of each leg and inserted her arms into the remnants.

She pulled the blanket toward her and cut a wide swath; folded the piece in half and cut a hole for her head. The material yielded a few tinkles of glass when she shook it. She pulled the poncho over her head and secured it with a cut length of rope. She could barely breath, but the warmth was already staying in her bones.

She heard brush moving and twigs cracking outside the window. He would have difficulty seeing her now, she was sure of it. She cut several lengths of blanket and wrapped them around each foot.

"Thirsty." K.C. said.

She crept to the sink and tried to heft the washbasin from under the chronically dripping spout. It was too heavy. Carefully she lifted one edge and allowed most of the contents to flow slowly down the drain. She carried the pan to him and helped him place his face in the water and drink. When he had enough, she too drank doggy-style from the pan.

He seemed to gather strength.

"He doesn't know you're here," she whispered. "I don't think he can see you."

"I'm not much help. No gun. Too weak to fight."

"You give me strength. I was so afraid when I was alone. I didn't want to die alone."

"We may die here together if no one comes."

"Nobody knows we're here."

"Maggie knows. She was going to call the sheriff."

"He didn't believe her. If he had he would be here by now."

"I left a finger at Maggie's. It's proof that I'm telling the truth."

"How'd you find the fingers?"

"Just one. I cleaned out Dick's bathroom drain. It was lodged in the pipe. I told you all that on your machine."

And he listened in, she thought. That's why he came home for the gun. "He's sick, K.C. So God-damned sick!"

"Yeah. And he's been picking off women for years. He's probably the one who killed Maggie's granddaughter."

She nodded. "He admitted he did."

The butt end of a broken tree limb burst through the shutter.

"There's a cellar. And an exit from it."

"Where?"

"Under the window. It's not very deep."

"Can you move?"

"Yes."

She was already scrambling across the shards of glass, pulling on the trap door.

K.C. tried to crawl after her. He was too weak.

She placed the stiletto into her mouth commando-style, grabbed the remaining piece of blanket with both hands, and slowly dragged him toward the hole.

A hand reached through the opening in the shutter and began to manipulate the latch. She pulled the knife from her mouth; reached up, saw a glint of steel as the knife moved.

Dick Morton howled with pain. "You bitch! You fucking, slutty whore! I'll kill you for this!"

She smiled through the darkness, felt K.C. slide head first through the trapdoor. She dropped in after him.

∽

Swat team members had left for their assigned places around the perimeter when Swenson heard the first shots. He and the Captain hurried from the camp cellar and stood together in the cascading rain.

"Where'd it come from?" The Captain asked.

"I dunno. Someplace higher up on the creek. Only things up there are the Survivalist's cabin and Old Maggie's. Nobody home at Maggie's. I checked her place earlier."

"We'd better head on up and have a look."

"Go slow. He could be anywhere in here, behind any tree. He may be baiting us."

"Turn off your light. We'll stay together. You know the way, you lead."

◦◦

She tried to close the trap door, but the blanket wedged in the opening.

"K.C.?"

"Here. We'll have to crawl." His breathing was labored.

She moved toward his voice.

"I can't make it," he said.

She needed to crawl past him, but the tunnel was too narrow.

"The way widens up ahead. You'll need to go alone."

"I won't leave you. He'll get you."

"Give me the knife. I'll wait for him and cut him."

"He has a gun."

"He thinks you're alone. I'll stay to one side and ambush him."

They inched forward until the tunnel opened into the wider space. She passed him the knife. "I have to get to Maggie's."

"This tunnel exits by the creek. It was built for emergency water forays."

"For playing."

"Pretty stupid, huh?"

"Not now."

"Are you scared?"

"I don't think I can do it."

"You have to, Clover."

"My mother used to tell me I could do anything, then she left me in a tiny room and never came back."

"I'll be here when you come back."

"I'm afraid of him."

"You can do it."

"When I cried for my mother, the Billingsleys helped me. 'You can do it, Clover, you're a good strong girl,' they said."

"They were right. You made it."

"And I owe them so much."

"You found Jim's killer. You said you would and you did."

"And I won't owe them anymore?"

"Not really."

"I hate the way Jim died. And poor Roger. I caused both their deaths."

"No, Clover."

"I did. Dick said he killed Jim, did that awful thing to him, because Jim and Lisa were bad together. He said he watched them through their bedroom window."

"He's crazy."

"But I was bad. And I taught Lisa to be bad."

"You don't really believe that, do you?"

"I was a bad girl. I started doing bad things when I was thirteen. Everything I learned I told to Lisa. I taught her how to turn a man on, how to please him, how to stimulate him when he was too tired for more. That's how I repaid the Billingsleys for their kindness. I turned their daughter into a slut."

He pulled her head against his bandaged chest and stroked her hair with his good hand. "You can't teach people sex by talking, Clover. People learn it with each other. Even if you did tell Lisa about it, she and Jim would have learned it all anyway."

She was crying now, sniffling gently into his wet chest.

"And if telling makes you bad, then I'm guiltier than you. I taught everything to Jenny. Does that make me bad?"

"Of course not. You're her husband."

"And it was really Lisa's husband who taught her. The only bad person in this thing is Dick Morton. Blame him if you want to blame somebody. Hate him if you need to hate."

"I do hate him."

"Good."

"He did horrible things to me."

"I'm so sorry. I tried to help."

"He killed Roger like an animal."

"Where is Roger?"

"Back in the woods with his penis stuck in his mouth."

"Jesus, Clover. You poor baby."

"He's going to do the same to you if I leave."

"No. No, he won't. He's not going to get me."

"Promise?"

"Yes. Now go. Go to Maggie's and get the gun."

"I'll come back fast as I can."

"I'll be here."

She began to move away.

"Be careful. I left the dogs out, they'll come after you."

"I'm not afraid of dogs."

"You're a wonder, Clover."

She stopped suddenly. "That's what Dick Morton said."

"That's what everybody says. Hurry."

CHAPTER SIXTEEN

Moving quickly through complete darkness, she hit her head against a small door. She pushed her weight against it and found herself on the bank of Clear Creek. Somewhere downstream dogs howled. She crawled up the bank and looked back to the cabin.

Dick Morton's white legs dangled and kicked from the side window.

She ran helter-skelter up the ridge until she was forced to stop to catch her breath. She glanced back. The cabin had disappeared in the mist.

She turned fully, cupped her hands around her mouth and shouted, "Dick! You son of a bitch! I hate you."

She heard the steady drip of rain through the branches of the tall trees; the low rustle of the wind as it blew against the hillside. She waited, shivered in the cold darkness.

The bang of the cabin door told her he was coming. She listened to his footfalls as he began the steep ascent toward Maggie's. She turned and forced her aching feet to find purchase in the leaf strewn forest floor, willed her burning arm muscles to push against the rough barked trunks and propel herself forward.

Once again she had underestimated him; she could hear him closing the gap between them.

∽

Together they moved into the back area of the cabin. The door was ajar. "I'll check the perimeter," the captain whispered. "You clear the inside."

Owen kicked the door aside and flung himself into the building. Glass crunched beneath his feet. He stood quietly and listened before he turned on his light.

Debris littered the floor. No one. Under one splintered and hanging shutter, he could see the edges of a trapdoor held partially open with a blanket. With one foot he opened the door. His light cut a narrow line of clarity into the black space. He crouched and peered into the shaft. Could be another den. He turned off the light, took a deep breath and lowered himself through the opening. It was deeper than he expected. He landed with a dull thud.

∞

Clover could see the outline of Maggie's place against the clearing sky. It was very close. The muscles in her legs burned. The makeshift wrappings that bound her feet had unraveled. The thought of holding a gun in her shaking hands and turning it on Dick Morton propelled her forward.

There were no lights in the house. What if Maggie had begun to lock her doors? What if the dogs didn't recognize her in her rags? Her pace slowed. She was too tired.

She glanced back. He was close enough for her to see white wrappings on his left hand and a raised gun in the other. She dodged into the trees.

The gun fired. Not even close. As she cleared the ridge, her feet hit the welcome softness of manicured grass.

She sprinted awkwardly across the lawn and leaped onto the stairs. No dogs. Where were the dogs?

A bullet smashed against the porch floor as she felt the cold grasp of his hand on her ankle. She fell onto her stomach and tried frantically to catch a handhold as he pulled her backwards down the stairs.

The knot in the rope at her waist slowed her decline. She kicked hard. The makeshift cover on her foot gave way.

She was free.

She scrambled up the remaining stairs, straightened, crossed the small porch and pushed against the door. It gave way under her weight and sent her flying across the polished kitchen floor. A dim light showed through the pantry door.

He grabbed onto her makeshift trousers. She looked back. The rag on his hand was blood-soaked. He was having trouble targeting his pistol.

She kicked at him, pulled herself up and again crawled forward. Her elbows gained some purchase on the dining room rug. She was within yards of the back pantry and the gun locker.

∽

Owen Swenson crawled commando-style through the tunnel. He had lost his flashlight in the first few moments and could not find it in the darkness. He held his revolver in both hands and slithered forward on elbows and knees.

The tunnel walls rubbed against his portly torso. He was short of breath and nearly out of the adrenaline surge that had propelled him this far. Ahead he thought he could see a brighter area. He squinted and shook his head to try to clear some of the dirt from his eyes. Yes. It was an opening of some kind. With renewed vigor he stretched his legs and crawled forward.

In the darkness, he couldn't see what knocked the gun from his hands, but nearly lost control of his bowels when he felt an arm circle his neck and place the cold blade of a knife against his windpipe. One syllable escaped his lips. "Christ."

"Sheriff?"

"Casey?"

"Jesus, I almost killed you."

"Yes."

"I thought you were Dick."

"No."

"Do you know that it was him and not me that did the murders?"

"Yes. He has a record in Iowa. I believe you."

"If I let you go, you're not going to grab that gun and shoot me, are you?"

"No, Casey. No. Have you seen the Winters girl?"

"She's headed up to Maggie's to get herself a weapon. If she gets her hands on one, she'll shoot the bastard."

⟡

A nightlight glowed from Victor's room.

She cleared the door from the kitchen and held onto the jam so Morton couldn't pull her backwards. She raised her head. Something was out of place in the baby's room. Something was there that shouldn't be.

She blinked her eyes. The hated umbrella stroller. And, in it, Victor, his arms and legs folded neatly into the canvas and his large eyes gazing at her with love and the kind of innocence she might never believe in again.

She glanced toward the pantry door and caught a glimpse of blue-jean covered boots.

Maggie stepped into the room, out of Victor's line of sight.

The boy startled but did not cry out.

Clover let go of the door jam. She heard Morton's triumphal laugh as she stopped struggling and allowed her body to be pulled a few feet toward him.

The pistol Maggie aimed so steadily seemed overly large and heavy.

For a moment all was still.

Old Maggie's voice was barely a whisper. "I've been waiting a long time for you, Dick Morton."

The smile on his face became a mask of anger. He released Clover's ankle and lifted his gun.

Clover pressed her elbows against the flooring and pulled herself through the doorway.

A gun blasted.

She turned her head to watch as Dick Morton focused his eyes on Maggie. The gun fell from his hand. Fear filled his eyes.

Maggie's bulk came between them.

She wanted to kiss the woman's booted feet, but she could crawl no farther. She laid her cheek on the solid Maple floor and looked toward Victor.

His wide eyes were on her.

She smiled to reassure him. She wanted to tell him that Maggie had killed the bastard. Don't worry, Victor, Maggie is making all that noise for you and me.

She heard the dull thud of Maggie's boot against Morton's body.

"Still want to get her don't you, Dick?" Maggie murmured. "Still can't believe you're done?" Another thud. "Here you go, my boy. Try this one out for size."

One more gunshot echoed through the small rooms.

As if suddenly understanding, Victor clapped his hands with glee. A grin split his face and, with the determination only a two-year-old can muster, he turned in his canvas sling, pushed his rear into the air and shimmied out of his cage. With hands out and little feet pattering he ran toward Clover's gesturing arms.

"Victor," she cried. "Our little Victor."

Behind her she heard Maggie's joyful laugh.